A
French
Affair

BOOKS BY SUE ROBERTS

My Big Greek Summer
My Very Italian Holiday
You, Me and Italy

A Very French Affair

SUE ROBERTS

Bookouture

Published by Bookouture in 2019

An imprint of StoryFire Ltd.

Carmelite House
50 Victoria Embankment
London EC4Y 0DZ

www.bookouture.com

ISBN: 978-1-78681-497-5
eBook ISBN: 978-1-78681-362-6

For Derek Hudson.

Chapter One

'A toilet? You're quite sure about that?'

I'm sitting in my red tartan pyjamas chatting to a bloke about a cake for his father's retirement party. My curly brown hair is scrunched up into a messy ponytail and I've just noticed a blob of marmalade on my chest. It's a good job we're not speaking via video link.

'It's rather an unusual request. Are you sure that's what he'd like?'

'Positive. Dad was a plumber. He lived and breathed his job. In fact, I'm surprised he's even retiring. No, honestly, a toilet-shaped cake will be perfect.'

I suppose the customer is always right, but I tentatively offer a suggestion.

'Have you thought about a bath? It might be a bit of an easier shape to cut into.'

'Oh, I never thought of that. A bath? Mmm, possibly. My dad seems to spend half his life talking about ballcocks and flushes so a toilet was the first thing that came to mind.'

'It's up to you, of course, but I just think a bath might be a nicer cake. I could do a little model of your dad sat in it surrounded by bubbles, holding up a can of beer or something.'

'He doesn't drink beer.'

'Wine?'

'No, he doesn't really drink alcohol at all. And I don't think he's ever had a bubble bath in his life. He's got eczema, you see.'

This is proving trickier than I thought.

'OK, forget the beer. And the bubbles. In fact, why not just a nice rectangular cake decorated with a figure of your dad carrying a box of tools, and a white plumber's van, that sort of thing?'

'Brilliant. Let's go with that then. Will it be alright if I collect it on Friday afternoon?'

It's currently Wednesday morning.

'*This* Friday?'

'Err, yes.'

'That's a little short notice. I'd normally ask for at least a week's notice for something like this, and I've got a lot on at the moment.'

There's silence at the end of the phone.

'Oh bugger. My mum's going to kill me for this. She asked me to order this cake a month ago and I completely forgot about it. I'll have to buy one from a shop.'

I breathe out slowly. It's not the first time this has happened, but I would never turn a client away, as it could be professional suicide. I've stayed up half the night baking rather than let someone down.

'Right, OK, I'll do it. I hope jam sponge will be alright,' I say quickly, dispelling any notion of a fruit cake.

'Yeah, that's fine. Nice one, you've saved my life.'

'No problem. Could you just email me telling me exactly what you want? I.e. rectangular sponge cake with plumber figure for retirement party.'

'Yeah, sure, if you like. Thanks again.'

There's a good reason why I do this. In the early days, I would take phone orders without anything written down. I quickly learned that confirming an order by text or email eliminates the possibility of any sort of misunderstanding. Like the time I presented a customer with a cake of a goat (which made perfect sense, as it was a farmer's retirement party and, you know, I figured maybe goats were his favourite animal). Turns out his wife had asked for a cake of a *boat*, as they were selling up and buying a bungalow by the sea where they hoped to enjoy some sailing.

Ending the call, I realise that was the first request for a toilet cake that I've ever had. Don't get me wrong, I've been asked to bake some right corkers. I've done female torsos in basques, vampires and coffins. You name it and I've probably baked it. Even a penis. I don't like to imagine the afternoon tea party where someone was slicing a sharp knife into that particular part of the male anatomy.

I'm still smiling at the memory of the goat cake when Sam, my assistant, walks in to the kitchen.

'Morning, Liv,' she says, taking off her green felt beret and shaking loose her light red hair, which she likes to call strawberry blonde. Sam's never without a hat. Berets, woollen beanies and trilbies adorn her head throughout the year and she suits every single style. These are usually matched with a stylish coat and a slash of red lipstick that give her a type of Hollywood glamour at the tender age of twenty-six. Today she's wearing a mustard vintage dress, black tights and black suede court shoes. Her mum owns a vintage clothes shop in town, where a lot of her purchases come from.

'Morning, Sam. I've just taken a call for a last-minute sponge cake – for Friday afternoon, would you believe?' I brush toast crumbs and marmalade from my pyjama top.

'Do you want me to do it?'

'Would you? I wanted to get stuck in to icing that wedding cake tomorrow. And I've got to make a couple of birthday cakes, as well as some cupcakes for a local primary school for Friday.'

'No problem. Maybe you had better go and get dressed first though?' she laughs.

'Just let me finish my rocket fuel first.' I down the thick rich coffee that has just spluttered its way out of my ancient coffee machine. It was one of the first machines on the market and I'll never change it until it physically falls apart.

Baked to Perfection is the online cake shop I run from my kitchen, housed in the extension that was added to my two-bedroomed home just over two years ago. It was my thirty-sixth birthday, and my parents surprised me with a savings policy that matured on that date. Dad had set up a twenty-year savings plan when I was sixteen, even investing some of it wisely. That's Dad all over – and I'd never been so pleased to hear about his financial planning.

The monetary gift saw a kitchen extension with a huge oven and lots of shiny new bakeware ensconced in my home. I also have a tall larder cupboard, which I fill with boxed cakes ready to be despatched.

Everyone thought I was taking a massive risk going into the cake business; social media sites were flooded with them, prices were becoming more and more competitive. There was no money to be made. Friends thought I was crazy even considering packing in my primary-teaching job, and if I had a pound for every time someone said 'Fancy giving up all those school holidays', I'd be set up for life.

But even long school holidays couldn't ease the stress I was under working in an underfunded school with kids who displayed challenging behaviours. And it seemed that most of them were in my class. Add to that never-ending pupil assessments, paperwork, meetings and lesson planning and I became physically frazzled. The time I sat up all evening planning a particularly enriching lesson about fair trade (at least I thought so; we were going to design and make our own chocolate bars and everything), and then the kids just sighed in boredom, I realised that perhaps I was in the wrong job. Friends had suggested it may have just been the wrong school. Admittedly, it was a school in a deprived area with little parental support, but even so, wouldn't a gifted teacher have got through to the kids? I spent most of my evenings drinking wine and moaning to my friends that I didn't sign up for this, that I was a teacher and not a bloody social worker.

Baking had always been my antidote to stress, and whether I was up to my elbows in flour, tempering chocolate or gently folding meringue, it all had a relaxing effect on me. I'd always been good at baking. My mother, whose cakes always fell flat, told me that I must have picked up some skills from Aunt Genevieve, who runs a small bakery in the glorious Côte d'Azur in France, where I spent many summers. Although English, her French name lured her to France, where she met and married my Uncle Enzo at the age of twenty-five and has lived there ever since.

Largely self-taught, although no doubt learning a lot from my aunt, I experimented with recipes and bought every single cookbook until I had perfected the sponge cake. The fruit cake took a while longer to master, but ultimately became the cake most people rave about. When I enrolled on a cake decorating course things really took off. A close friend asked me to make her wedding cake and soon the orders started flooding in. I took a leap of faith and quit my teaching job after a particularly stressful term and thankfully I've never looked back. I even had to take on an assistant in the form of Sam who was a catering student at the local college. It was tricky when I first started up and we had to tighten our belts a little, but thankfully we were never short of orders. And right from the off I made sure I saved a little each month.

I've always been good at squirreling money away and saved quite a bit when I was teaching. I'm not sure my son Jake has the same sensible approach to money. He's away at university now and does a little casual work here and there, but he spends his wages as soon as he receives them. I brought Jake up alone, with the help of my parents, who live a short drive away here in Southport. It wasn't always the easiest, being a young single mother, but I wouldn't change a single day for anything. I managed to raise him without a man and I'm rather proud of how he's turned out. He's a kind, considerate son who doesn't return from uni with a pile of dirty washing, but rather (on Mother's Day at least) a large bunch of flowers and a kiss on the cheek. He'll be home again soon for the summer holidays and I can't wait to see him.

Chapter Two

It's Friday afternoon and I've called into my parents' house for a brew after I've been shopping on Lord Street, a glorious tree-lined boulevard in town, with metal facades overhanging the shops.

Mum and Dad live in a pretty whitewashed mews house in a small courtyard behind one of the main shopping streets. It has a glossy, newly painted blue front door, which Dad has finally got around to doing now that he's retired. Saying that, though, Mum has complained that it's the only DIY he's done since he finished work, despite years of promising her that he would 'spruce the place up' once he'd retired.

Which is exactly what you would expect from Eddie David Dunne. 'Steady Eddie'. Hard-working, loyal and proud of the fact that he hadn't taken a sick day in over twenty years. He drove the same car for twelve years, despite Mum's pleas for a new one, as there was 'nothing wrong with it'. He only ever drank beer at the weekends and bought new jumpers when the old ones had worn out.

Everything changed when he retired, though. Steady Eddie all but disappeared as Daring Dave took over. He came home from his retirement party at the printer's, where he worked as General Manager, clutching a garden centre gift voucher and the remains of his retirement cake wrapped in foil. 'That's that then,' he said. Mum had retired five years earlier from her job at Southport Theatre, where she worked in hospitality, organising big events. A rather glamourous blonde of sixty-six, she had confided in me that she was worried about Dad when he retired and wasn't sure what he would do to fill his time. Mum's always been a social butterfly and is a member of a gym, a choir and a book club. Dad has no friends and likes it that way. So when Dad arrived home one Friday afternoon with a shiny new campervan, Mum almost fainted.

'Right then, Gloria. I think it's about time we had some fun,' he announced, flicking open a map of the British Isles in their neat lounge. 'After we've toured Britain, we'll go wherever you fancy. The world's our oyster.'

And that's exactly what they've been doing for the past six months. They've been from Land's End to John O'Groats and everywhere in between, and they both look ten years younger. They're home for a couple of weeks before they set off for Barcelona. I'm thrilled that they are enjoying new adventures.

'Have you brought any cake to go with this tea?' Dad asks now.

'Sorry, Dad, I've just dashed here straight from the shops. I've been buying a new top. I'll bring your favourite next time; Bakewell tart, is it?' As if I don't know it's his ultimate weakness.

'Ooh, you really shouldn't, love,' says Mum as she enters the lounge. 'A moment on the lips, a lifetime on the hips.' She's managed to retain her trim figure with a love of dancing, walking and occasional treats.

'Bugger that. A lifetime in the factory means I've earned as many treats as I like.'

Mum tuts but she has a smile on her face. 'Anyway, you should be out on a nice date, not baking for us. Let's have a look at this top, is it for something special?'

Mum would like nothing more than for me to meet a nice man and settle down. I pull the red top from my bag and Mum runs her hand over the soft chiffon fabric. 'Oh, very nice. And I love that colour.'

'It's just a dinner with the girls. Really, Mum, who said I'm looking for the man of my dreams? Or even my nightmares? I'm happily single.'

Mum raises her eyebrows and gives me a look that says *How can you possibly be happy being single?* But the truth is, I am. I'm very busy with the cake business and I have a small bunch of friends who I meet up with regularly. And of course I have Jake. I don't need any complications in my life right now. My last break-up was just over four years ago. I'd been dating Simon, a teacher at the school where I worked, for six months when he moved into my place. And that's when I discovered we were completely incompatible and the only thing we had in common was work, which we talked about incessantly. After a year of quiet nights in with takeaways and bottles of wine, I ended things. I wanted more from life and felt we were going nowhere. Simon took the break-up far harder than I expected him to, as I never thought he considered me the love of his life. I certainly never considered him mine – that particular train left my station a long time ago.

'I just think you need looking after once in a while,' Mum says, coming over and giving me a kiss on the cheek. She smells of the Estée Lauder Youth Dew that she's worn forever. 'Especially with me and Dad off on our travels. Pity you can't come with us some time.'

I can't think of anything worse than being scrunched up in a caravan with my parents, spending sleepless nights on a pull-down bed and showering in draughty communal shower blocks. But I give a regretful nod in any case.

'Don't you worry about me, I'm doing great, really I am. It's time you both went off and had some fun together. Isn't that what retirement's all about?'

'Well, it might be nice if you came next time we call on Aunt Gen. How long is it since you've been to France?'

I realise with a shock that it's been five years since I last visited my aunt, and that was for my Uncle Enzo's funeral. Despite the circumstances, each time I ventured out I found myself gazing at every man I walked past, seeking a resemblance to my first love, André, who I'd spent the summer with when I was eighteen. People can change a lot over the years, though, and he might not have even been living in the South of France at the time. After all, the last time I saw him he was leaving for New Zealand and planning to travel the world.

That was just one of many summers at Aunt Gen's. As a child I would swim in the sparkling turquoise sea and run along the soft white sand at Antibes. I remember the first time I saw a giant orca at the water park and my dad told me it was the whale from the movie *Free Willy*. I never understood why he winked at my mother.

Having an aunt with a bakery was a lot of fun, especially as she would let me try out any new cake creations. I can recall the first time I sank my teeth into one of her light-as-a-feather meringues and savoured the soft chewy centre. My chin would dribble with the glossy red sauce from a juicy strawberry sitting on a bed of smooth crème pâtissière encased in melt-in-the-mouth pastry. I would perch on the end of a wooden stool in her kitchen and watch in wonder as she stretched and plaited puff pastry, dotted with chunks of chocolate for the pain au chocolat. She would wipe her brow and high cheekbones with the back of her hand as she placed the croissants into the hot oven. Her deep auburn hair was always swept up in an elegant chignon, her lips painted a soft peach shade. And I can so easily recall her smell: a mixture of soft vanilla and violets. I feel a stab of guilt that it's been so long since I've seen her, but thoughts of cakes remind me that I have a delivery to make.

'Right, I'd better be off now,' I say, draining my tea.

'Don't forget my Bakewell tart next time,' Dad says as I give them both a kiss on the cheek before heading off to the school where my friend Faye works. I'm glad I managed to get a top for tomorrow night. Sometimes it takes me hours to find something. Another thing ticked off my seemingly never-ending to-do list.

I cross the playground, passing a colourful wooden climbing frame, before ringing the bell at St Thomas Primary School: a grey stone Victorian building on the other side of town where I'm about to deliver some cupcakes. Within a few minutes, Faye appears at reception and buzzes me in.

'Cakes for your soirée,' I say, handing over an assortment of cupcakes with pastel-coloured icing.

Faye's dressed in a black knee-length skirt and pink shirt, giving no clue to her inner rock chick, apart possibly from her short spiky aubergine hair, which frames her large blue eyes and pretty, heart-shaped face. The eagle tattoo on her back is never revealed in school. Faye and

I have been friends since high school, and though we've got different tastes in a lot of things, some memories just bind you together forever.

'Who's leaving?' I ask as I follow her to the staff room down a magnolia-painted corridor, dotted with children's paintings of Van Gogh's sunflowers.

'Mike from Year Six. He's got a job in a school a bit closer to his home in Wigan. He's been commuting for over an hour every morning to get here, so I can't blame him. He's a great teacher though. The kids are going to miss him. We all will.'

I set the cakes on a dessert table alongside a selection of petit fours and a large rectangular cake iced with the message 'Good Luck Mike'.

'Who made the cake?' I ask – you have to check out the local competition.

'Costco's finest. Apparently, they are his absolute favourite. You know I would have recommended you for a home-made one.'

'Just checking,' I say, smiling.

If I'm honest, I'm grateful I was only called upon to do a batch of cupcakes. I can whip them up in no time at all. I've been really busy with wedding cakes lately, as it's summer and wedding season. I felt relieved that Sam took on the plumber's retirement cake. I'm not complaining, though; you never know when things can go a little quiet.

'Would it be OK if I have a quick drink? There's a funny taste in my mouth from Mum's tea. I don't think it's her usual brand.'

'There's only that cheap wine,' says Faye, pointing to a box each of red and white. 'That's about all the PTA can stretch to. I'm dying to get over to the White Lion and have a pint of real ale later. There's an Iron Maiden tribute band, if you fancy it?'

Faye likes a beer and can drink any bloke I know under the table.

'I meant a soft drink. I'm driving, remember.'

Faye pours some pink lemonade into a paper cup and hands it to me. She pours herself a cup of white wine and glugs it down in one.

'Thanks. I think I'll pass on tonight, actually. You know I'm more Whitney than Whitesnake. Plus, Jake's home later from university for the start of his summer holidays. I don't like the thought of him walking into an empty house. You enjoy yourself, though.'

'He's twenty years old, Liv. Anyway, bring him along if you like.'

'I don't think he wants to be hanging out with his mum and her mates somehow,' I laugh. 'No, really. I'm shattered. It's an early night for me.'

'It's a shame you're not into proper music – the music and the beer are the only things that interest me at the pub these days. There's been no new faces – i.e. fit blokes – in for a while. I might need to widen my net, so if you fancy a weekend away anytime soon, I'm your gal.'

'We'll see. Right, well, I'd better get on, so see you tomorrow. I'm really looking forward to a girls' night out.'

'Me too.' She kisses me on the cheek as I depart. 'It's been a stressful week. I'm hoping I'll be soothed by beer and handsome French waiters.'

As I head off towards the car park a text pings through from another friend, Jo, who works as a dog walker.

Are we still on for tomorrow? x

  Yep. Meet at the Grapes for a pre-dinner cocktail at seven.

  Can't wait. See you then. x

Jo is someone else who walked out of her ridiculously stressful job. Hers being in the mental health sector of the NHS. She could no longer take phone calls from people desperate to find relatives a room when they were having a breakdown, only to have to tell them there were no beds and redirect them somewhere miles away. Returning from a two-day break and finding her in-tray overflowing and her email inbox bursting was the final straw. She picked up her coat, walked out of the office, caught a bus home and sat in her flat for two days with the phone unplugged. She binged on a Netflix series before she pulled herself together and started up her dog-walking business.

I pull up outside my neat two-bedroomed terrace and notice a light on. Jake lifts the blind when he sees me and waves. When I open the front door the smell of brewing coffee drifts towards me. It's always good to have him home.

Chapter Three

Jake passes me a latte and we sit down on the sofa in the front room. As always when he's back from uni, I take in my son's appearance, wanting to be sure he still looks healthy and happy. Tall, dark and handsome just about covers it. He has a slight curl in his thick, dark-brown hair, large blue eyes and quite a full mouth, which he gets from me. He is currently sporting a neatly trimmed beard, which I think makes him look a little older than his twenty years.

'I found these in the tin. I hope they're still OK to eat,' he says, taking a huge bite from a Florentine without waiting for me to answer.

'Oh no, were they still there? I must have forgotten to bin them.'

Jake stops mid chew with a grimace.

'Only joking. I made them two days ago.'

He stuffs the rest of the Florentine into his mouth.

'Mmm, that tasted too good to be past its sell-by date. Florentines and macarons are easily my favourite things you bake.'

Jake's always had a preference for French fancies. I guess it must be in his genes.

'So, how are things going at uni? That last exam go OK?' I ask, wrapping my hands tightly around the delicious cinnamon latte.

'It went alright. It's all alright I suppose.' He shrugs his shoulders.

He seems distracted, and I immediately worry that he might be feeling a little stressed about something. Jake's face usually lights up when I ask him about university life. He's always ready to regale me with interesting and funny stories about what he's been up to, so his blasé comment surprises me somewhat.

'Just alright?'

'Yeah, nothing new. Everyone's gone home for the holidays. My friend Connor is going climbing in Scotland with his dad, which must be nice.'

Am I imagining a tone of bitterness in his voice when he talks about his friend's relationship with his father? There's just something about Jake today that is making me uneasy.

'Are you hungry?' I ask, glancing at my watch, which tells me it's almost five o'clock. 'I imagine those Florentines will keep you going for a bit until dinner.'

'You know me, Mum, I'm always starving. I grabbed some cheese on toast this morning before I set off but I've had nothing since. And the sandwiches on the train looked rough. Actually, I was going to make us some pasta. Got any bacon? And chilli?' He jumps up and heads for the kitchen.

'I always have bacon in the fridge when I know you're coming home.'

I can't help wondering how long this place will actually *be* his home. When he gets his degree, he could be off anywhere in the world. I suppress a little feeling of sadness when I think about it, wondering how often he would be in touch. I can't imagine how I'd feel if Jake went weeks on end without any sort of signal in a remote and unreachable destination. Or without contacting me, at any rate.

I follow Jake into the kitchen and pour us each a glass of red wine, still unable to shake a feeling that there is something on his mind. He's busy pulling ingredients out of the fridge, so I can't see his face properly. Taking a seat on a barstool at the chunky island, I watch him chop some peppers, onion and bacon. The kitchen is a mix of traditional and modern, combining the reclaimed-wood island and cupboards with modern wall prints, copper lighting and an exposed brick wall.

'I'm afraid I don't have any fresh chilli, it will have to be dried,' I say, pointing to the kitchen cupboard.

'Just as good. In fact, better. Nothing worse than chilli willy.'

I almost spit my drink out.

'What?'

'You know – if you don't wash your hands properly and touch your eyes… or somewhere else.'

I laugh loudly, then settle in and wait for the delicious spicy tomato sauce to be ready, realising I've barely eaten a thing since breakfast too. Jake doesn't say much as he finishes cooking, seemingly still a little preoccupied. Once again, I can't shake a feeling that something is bothering him.

'This is really good,' I say, forking the pasta into my mouth. 'I think you've missed your true vocation.'

Jake remains silent before finally turning to face me.

'It's funny you should say that, actually.'

Do I sense a little nervousness in his voice?

'Really, why?'

Jake exhales deeply. 'The thing is, I'm not really enjoying the course as much as I thought I would. I've been thinking about taking a gap year.' He grabs some utensils from a drawer, avoiding eye contact with me.

'A gap year?' I am completely astonished. 'Where has this idea come from? Has something happened?' I feel my heart sink. What has made him change his mind about university like this? Jake has gushed with enthusiasm for it for almost two years now.

'No, Mum, really. I'm just not fired up, that's all. I guess I've been feeling a bit lost lately, and Connor going off climbing with his dad kind of got me thinking about my own father.' His words come out in a rush, and he picks his wine up then heads to the kitchen window to peer out at the small back garden.

My own father. I guess I knew this day would come, but I'm not prepared. I try to breathe evenly and collect my thoughts before I reply.

'You're bound to think about him. And I understand it must be hard seeing other young men going off on holidays with their dad. But I've always tried to be honest with you about André. I wouldn't have known where to start looking for him and you never seemed bothered whenever I asked.'

'I was a child,' he snaps. 'Did you hope I would just forget about him?'

I try to compose myself before I answer, my whole body shaking with emotion.

He turns to face me and there's a look of sadness behind his pale-blue eyes.

'No, of course I didn't! Do you really think I would want that?'

'Who knows. Maybe it would have been easier for you.' He huffs, and turns back to the window.

My heart is beating fast. There's a resentment in Jake's tone that I have never heard before.

'Easier? You think being a single parent was easy?' It's impossible for me to keep the anger out of my voice now. 'I've always been honest with you about your father; I didn't know where to find him. It was over twenty years ago and he could have been anywhere in the world.'

'But did you even bother trying to look for him?' There's an accusing tone in his voice, and he winds me with his question.

'I wouldn't have known where to start. He sent me one letter in France after he left, telling me he was moving on within a week, travelling from place to place. I never heard from him again. What could I have done?'

My heart is breaking at how upset Jake is and I suddenly realise how naive I have been. Did I really think that Jake would never ask questions about his father? Have I been misguided in thinking that a cocoon of love from myself and his grandparents could be enough?

'Look, I don't want to talk about this any more. Thinking about my father isn't the reason I'm thinking about quitting uni. I want to explore cooking professionally. And I think it's time I started making my own decisions. I'm going to go up and watch a film – night, Mum.'

He sprints upstairs as the tears that have been building in me threaten to spill over. Have I subconsciously controlled him? It was my suggestion that he studied psychology in the first place but maybe that was because I had always been interested in it myself. Or is he just lashing out because he doesn't think I'll approve of this huge change? Jake says he hasn't made his mind up about his future yet. But I've made my mind up about one thing that I should have sorted out sooner. I'm going to look for Jake's father.

Chapter Four

The Grapes bar is fairly busy for seven o'clock on a Saturday evening.
I've had an awful day and I've only come out now because I hate to
let my friends down. Jake has been buried in his room most of the
day and I'm going to give him a little more space before we continue
our conversation. He's barely said anything to me all day, other than
a good morning when he filled a water bottle before heading out
for a run. I think this is the first time we've properly fought and I
feel drained. Everything that Jake said has been going round and
round in my head since last night. I'm haunted by the look on his
face when he confronted me. It was full of accusation and regret.
Even baking today (a dinosaur cake for a four-year-old and two
ruby wedding anniversary cakes), has done nothing to soothe me
and I can feel the tension in my shoulders still.

Despite everything that's been on my mind today, I'm determined to try and enjoy my night out with the girls. Groups of
young men are assembled around the polished wooden bar area
drinking bottled beers, and they cast a glance in our direction as I
enter the Grapes with Faye and Jo. One fair-haired bloke wearing
tight black jeans and a pale denim shirt catches my eye and smiles.
He looks about the same age as Jake and I suddenly feel ancient.

Faye nudges her way to the bar and a few minutes later we slide into an empty cubicle with a tray of drinks. Jo and I have opted for a pre-dinner margarita whilst Faye has her usual pint of real ale. She takes a long swig.

'Ah, I needed that. It's been a busy week. Roll on the school holidays, not long to go now.'

'You deserve them. Not everyone in that school works as hard as you,' I say, before taking a sip of my zesty cocktail.

I know this to be true. Faye doesn't leave the building until six o'clock most evenings, staying behind to mark books and plan exciting lessons for the following day. Her classroom is like a wonderland of creativity, displaying children's topic work on every available space. The kids adore her.

'So, any school gossip then?' asks Jo, a petite bundle of energy with long, glossy brown hair that she wears up in a bun when she's walking the dogs.

'Not really. Oh, apart from Mr Long and Miss Summer having an affair.'

'So together they make a long summer?' I grin. 'Hang on though, it's hardly an affair if they are both single, is it? They are, aren't they?'

'That's true, but they seem to like to sneak around in school cupboards. Maybe they like the excitement of getting caught. Either that or they just can't keep their hands off each other until home time.'

Ah, that first rush of love. I think of France in the summer of 1998 and how André and I felt exactly the same way. I recall that urgent need to kiss each other, to touch or hold hands. We would cast glances at each other across crowded rooms, desperately needing to be alone together. A passion like no other, that you are certain will last forever.

'I was doing an after-school tennis club when I went in search of some more tennis equipment,' continues Faye. 'Walking into the PE store, I wasn't expecting to be confronted with a totally different set of balls.' She roars with laughter before taking another long sip of her beer.

We have a catch-up about our week, Jo making us smile with a story of one of her dogs straining on the lead and defecating on someone's front door step, just as the resident was stepping outside.

'With me furiously pulling the lead. It would have to be the biggest bloody dog of the lot, too. Harold the Great Dane, which means it also had the biggest turd. The guy coming out of the house was really cute too.'

I can hardly breathe for laughing. This is why I needed to come out tonight. I tell my friends about the week's cake orders, including the toilet cake, which doesn't sound half as entertaining as the things they've told me. I've decided to hold off from telling them about Jake, as I need to think things through. Tonight, I just want a distraction.

'Right, girls, are we ready?' asks Faye as she drains her pint glass.

The young fair-haired guy at the bar turns and smiles at me again as we leave. Maybe I remind him of his mother.

☙

Le Boulevard restaurant has vivid red walls adorned with posters of the Moulin Rouge and other Parisian landmarks. The stripped wooden tables are set with chunky red candles and cast-iron wall sconces emit a gentle glow.

The first thing that hits my nostrils when entering is a waft of garlic.

Eric, a handsome waiter with olive skin and piercing green eyes, greets us. 'Bonjour ladies, ça va?

'Ça va bien, merci, et tu?'

'Très bien. Please, follow me.' Eric shows us to our table, which looks out onto the busy pavement of Lord Street. Groups of friends are excitedly heading off for their evenings out and loved-up couples with huge smiles on their faces link arms as they walk along.

'So, what's Jake up to tonight then?' asks Jo as she peruses the menu.

'If it's the same plan he mentioned last week, he's meeting up with a couple of old mates. I think they're going to watch a film and grab something to eat later.'

'Has he brought anyone home to meet you yet?'

'No, I know there's a group he hangs about with at university but he hasn't mentioned anybody special. I've given up asking about a girlfriend as he just tells me I'll be the first to know if there's anyone serious.'

Eric returns with drinks. Faye is slightly disappointed that they don't have any hand-pulled real ales and has settled for a bottle of French beer. Jo and I share a bottle of Chardonnay and place our food order. 'Oh, and I'll have a large brandy with that,' says Faye, snapping closed the drinks menu.

'Actually, Jake asked about his father last night,' I find myself saying, despite thinking I wouldn't mention it. I take a sip of the crisp, cold wine.

'Oh, wow. Well, it was going to happen one day I suppose,' says Jo gently. 'You knew that.'

'I know. I just don't think I was prepared for it. Stupid really, considering I've had twenty years to think about it. Time just seems to have raced along.' I take another long glug of wine.

Faye looks a bit shocked. 'Really? What, he just asked you out of the blue?'

'Yep, although he's obviously been thinking about it for a while. I'm surprised it hasn't happened before now. Maybe I've buried my head in the sand for too long. We had a row about it.'

'What did he say?' asks Faye, a concerned look crossing her face.

'Basically that I should have done more. He more or less accused me of wanting him all to myself and hoping he would forget any notion of ever wanting to find his dad.'

'Ooh, that's harsh. Are you sure you're alright?' asks Faye.

'Yes. I will be. I'll think about it more tomorrow. I just want to try and enjoy this evening. If that's OK.'

'Fine by me. How are your mum and dad?' asks Jo. 'Are they still busy navigating the globe?'

'They certainly are. It's given them a whole new lease of life. Turns out Dad's quite an adventurer deep down. They're setting off for Spain shortly.'

'Maybe he was just waiting for a chance to do it all when he'd finished work. Some people like to compartmentalise their lives, don't they.'

'Maybe. But sometimes the time has to be now. Make use of weekends. Old age isn't guaranteed to everyone.'

'I suppose,' says Jo. 'The woman in the flat below me, who worked as a civil servant, took up salsa dancing and joined a local rambler's group when she retired. She met her future husband there; I think they've just bought a holiday home in France.'

'Doesn't your aunt still live in France?' asks Faye.

'Yes, Aunt Gen. I really should go over and see her, and Sam's ready for more responsibility at work. Maybe I could do some digging as to André's whereabouts while I'm over there. Actually, as it's the school holidays soon, fancy coming with me, Faye? You too, obviously, Jo, if you can get the time off.'

'I'd love too, but I'm looking at booking some holidays in September to Greece. Cheaper flights then. Plus, I can't go letting my pooches down too often.' Jo smiles warmly.

'Are you kidding! I'd love to!' says Faye. 'I remember going there as a teenager with you. As I recall, I kind of set you up with André.' Faye is fired up with excitement. 'When do we go? This calls for a celebration!' She beckons our waiter again and orders another drink.

Thoughts of France disappear as a text message pings through on my phone. It's Sam telling me that we have an LMO, which is code for a last-minute order. Finishing my starter, I excuse myself and give her a quick ring in the ladies' room.

'Hi, Liv. Sorry to disturb your evening. I know you hate turning down business. I'll do the cake tonight if you like. I'm at a loose end.'

Sam is currently single after ending a two-year relationship that was going nowhere.

'Could you? What are they asking for?'

'A replica of the Houses of Parliament. Don't worry, I'll work through the night.'

'You're joking!'

'Of course I am. They want a jam sponge with "Happy Birthday Mum". Apparently, the customer had a go at baking it herself and burnt it to a crisp – she was engrossed in an episode of *Game of Thrones*. She'll probably try to pass the cake off as her own.' I can almost see the huge smile on Sam's face on the other end of the phone.

'OK. Well, you know where the spare key is. Just so you know, Jake is home for the summer now. He's out with friends tonight and may come home a little inebriated later. And don't you worry, I'll definitely compensate you properly for this. Weekend pay rates for starters.'

'Thanks, Liv. And thanks for the heads up about Jake. Enjoy the rest of your evening!'

꙳

We dine on the most fabulous food. Faye and I choose French onion soup for our starter, whilst Jo opts for pâté. For the main course, Jo and Faye choose moules marinière, which emanates the heady scent of garlic and parsley as the waiter places it on the table. I have a classic sirloin steak in a béarnaise sauce.

'This is just divine,' says Faye, wiping her mouth with a napkin. 'I hope the food as is as good as this in actual France. Ooh, I can't believe we're going!'

'Do you mind, you're making me jealous?' says Jo, rolling her eyes but smiling.

'Sorry. I just didn't expect to be getting away this summer.'

The news has completely made Faye's evening, which is also making me feel better about it. Everything seems possible when you've got a friend on your side.

I'm virtually silent as I devour my food. The steak is so tender and perfectly complemented by the creamy tarragon sauce. I'm so full at the end of the meal I wonder whether I can even manage a dessert.

'How can you not have a dessert in a French restaurant?' asks Faye, aghast. 'It's the best part of the meal.' She catches the attention of a passing waiter and orders another bottle of lager and a large Napoleon brandy.

I have a ten-minute break before ordering a café liégeois – coffee ice cream and Chantilly cream in a sundae glass. Faye and Jo order tarte tatin with vanilla ice cream and drool in ecstasy when it arrives.

All too soon, our evening has come to an end and we manage to hail a taxi outside on the busy road.

'I've got a bottle of Jack Daniel's back at the flat if anyone fancies a nightcap?' says Faye hopefully.

'Sorry, Faye, I've got an early start tomorrow,' I say.

'Me too. My first dog walk is at seven. It's a husky that basically rips the house apart if it's not taken out first thing.'

We all embrace and agree to meet for coffee later in the week.

'I'll have more details about France then,' I tell Faye.

I'm the first to be dropped off at home and, as I climb out of the taxi, I'm hoping Jake is still up so that we can have a chat. I hate any feeling of unease between us. I wave my friends off and have no doubt in my mind that Faye will have no trouble polishing most of that bottle of Jack Daniel's off all by herself. I don't want to be judgemental about Faye's drinking, but I do find myself worrying about her. Especially when she drinks alone.

Chapter Five

It's just after 12.30 a.m. when I let myself in, so I'm surprised to find Jake and Sam curled up on the grey fabric sofa in the lounge. Sam is wearing a black shirt adorned with colourful parrots and an orange mini skirt over black tights. Jake is wearing his usual attire of lounge pants and a black T-shirt.

'Hi, guys. Have you finished the Houses of Parliament then?' I ask Sam as I untwine my scarf and throw it on a chair with my black leather jacket.

Jake casts a quizzical glance at me but doesn't say anything. I think again that we need to clear the air when Sam has left.

'Changed my mind about that. I went for a ten-inch sponge instead. You look really pretty by the way, did you have a good night?'

'Thank you. Yes, it was great actually, we had a real laugh and the food was amazing. I would eat there every night if I could afford to.'

'Where did you go?' asks Sam.

'Le Boulevard, in town.'

'Ooh, yes. I love it there. You feel as if you're really in France,' Sam says dreamily.

Jake has still barely made eye contact with me and I think Sam picks up on this, her eyes darting between us. She drains her coffee and picks up her coat, ready to leave.

'Right, I should be off. The cake's all done. Thanks for the coffee and the company, Jake.'

'Anytime.' He smiles.

'You're an angel, thanks, Sam,' I say, crossing the room to hug her.

She follows me into the kitchen briefly, where the most charming cake is sitting on the kitchen counter. 'Happy Birthday Mum' is laced across pink icing in beautiful, feathery navy strokes. It's adorned with pink and white paper roses. It's absolutely perfect.

'Oh, Sam, it's gorgeous. Any mum would be over the moon to receive a cake like this on their birthday. And I know it will taste every bit as good as it looks.'

I see her out, and wave as she turns the corner in her red Fiat. Jake makes the effort as well.

'Did you have a nice evening with Sam?' I ask him when we head back inside.

'Yeah, I'd forgotten what fun Sam is.' He flops down on the sofa again. 'Actually, remember what we were talking about yesterday? Well, she might be able to help me out.'

'In what way?' I ask warily, as if I could forget yesterday's conversation.

'Well, it turns out her uncle runs a pub called the Bottle and Glass a few miles away. Apparently they're always looking for kitchen staff. There's a job there if I want it.'

'And do you?'

'Why not?' he answers, slightly defensively. 'I had a look at it online,' continues Jake. 'The reviews are really brilliant. Sam said I'd fit right in.'

It's true; the Bottle and Glass is a huge gastropub on the outskirts of town with a great reputation for food. But I find myself suppressing a slight feeling of annoyance towards Sam for clearly encouraging Jake's thoughts of quitting university. Despite his determination to leave, I just think he will have more opportunities in life if he finishes his education. Although it's becoming perfectly obvious that my opinion doesn't count.

'Are you absolutely sure about this, Jake? It's a big decision to make.' I walk into the kitchen to fill a glass with water. I can't risk a headache in the morning. 'Maybe you could work there for the summer, then finish your degree?'

'It's hardly a snap decision. I've thought of nothing else these past few months,' he says, lacing his hands behind his head and exhaling deeply. 'Cooking is just the only thing I feel passionate about lately.'

'But even if you don't love psychology, once you've got a degree you could always take a postgraduate certificate in education and give teaching a go.'

I realise I'm clutching at straws now. Teaching drained me, and it's his life. He's a grown man. I just don't want him to drop out. 'Yeah, right. Isn't that the profession you ducked out of because of the stress? No thanks.' There's an uncharacteristic note of defiance in his tone.

'I know, Jake. I'm just being a mum. I want what's best for you. Are you sure nothing else is prompting this?'

'I know you do. And no, there hasn't been any major thing that's happened. Although studying psychology has been a bit of an eye opener, so at least I've learned something.'

'What do you mean, an eye opener?'

'Learning about the effect on a child's development without a father and stuff like that. I'm not saying I was ever unhappy, but it got me thinking, that's all. Maybe it's never too late to have a father in your life.'

A feeling of guilt surges through my body.

'Anyway, we'll see. I haven't completely made my mind up. But if I don't feel differently by the end of the summer holidays I think this is what I'm going to do.'

I can only hope.

It's true enough what Jake has said, and I've always believed you should follow your dreams. I've met too many people in life who stay in torturous jobs, counting down the days to their retirement. But I'm practical about life too. I mean, my dream was to live in the South of France with the love of my life in a little house by the sea, and look how that turned out…

Chapter Six

It's Sunday morning and I'm going to see my parents later before they set off for Spain.

I grab two cake orders from the larder cupboard to deliver en route, and a Bakewell tart for Dad, as requested. My first delivery will need to be the kids' party cake – that's needed earlier. Parties seem to have reached a whole new level, with a three-tier unicorn cake baked by yours truly taking centre stage at a five-year-old's party recently. It was the centrepiece of a table groaning with an explosion of sugary treats, in a hired hall, complete with entertainment. I almost passed out when an actual unicorn arrived to give children rides outside. (OK, it was a pony with an artificial rainbow-coloured horn, but even so.) Whatever happened to jelly and ice cream and musical chairs in someone's cramped living room, leaving with a piece of cake wrapped in a paper serviette?

There's a flower shop next door to one of the customers where I'm dropping off so I'll nip in and buy Mum a bouquet. I've missed them both a little bit recently, as I've been rushed off my feet. It feels strange not being able to pop in when I'm in the area. Dad would be good to chat to about Jake. He would get to the heart of the matter in an honest, no-nonsense way.

It's a beautiful day, so I decide to have a little drive along the seafront after I've dropped off the cakes and purchased some freesias. It's a bit of a joke locally that people don't go swimming in Southport as the sea is always so far out. Right now the tide's in, gently lapping the sands as the sun dances on the water. I park up and stroll towards the long white wooden pier, which was completely renovated several years ago. A blue train is rattling along towards the beginning of the pier, ready to collect parents with children, who are giggling and waving excitedly at the driver. The train will take them to a café and an arcade at the end of the pier, passing a few stalls selling hot doughnuts and candyfloss on the way. A machine inside the café dispenses old-fashioned pennies to use in the Victorian games machines. There are floor-to-ceiling windows that give a glorious view of the shimmering sea. It's one of the nicest places to nurse a latte and contemplate life, as you stare out across the water towards North Wales.

I pass a colourful carousel that I used to bring Jake to as a child and watch smiling children clinging on to the colourful horses, their little arms wrapped around the necks of the brightly painted animals. I can recall Jake's smiling face as he bobbed up and down on them as if it were yesterday. I wonder where the years have gone. In a few years' time he may even bring his own children here. That's if he sticks around, which I guess might be more likely if he's so determined to leave his uni course.

I decide to stop and have a coffee. Taking my drink to a bench that overlooks the sea, it isn't long before a cheeky seagull perches itself on the end of the table, hoping for some food. It hangs around for a minute or two before realising nothing is forthcoming and squawking off into the distance. I never expected to be still be living here in my late thirties, although I suppose it's a decent enough town to live in. I have a job that I love, good friends and I'm lucky enough to still have both of my parents nearby. Well, most of the time anyway. But somehow, I expected my life to have taken a different path. But maybe lots of people feel that way. Years have rolled by so quickly and as I stare out to sea I wonder, not for the first time, if I should have tried harder to track down Jake's father. But there was no one to ask. He'd never taken me to his family home and I knew little of his friends. We spent every second together when he wasn't working, having eyes only for each other. Maybe I was a little half-hearted about tracing André on my last visit. But since Jake has spoken of his desire to meet his father, it's all I can think about doing. I just need to work out how to do it.

I'm pulled out of my thoughts by the sound of someone shouting, 'Slow down. Heel,' and then 'Oh bugger!', followed by the sound of barking dogs. A cocker spaniel and two golden retrievers are bounding along, followed by a small woman desperately holding on to a colourful woollen hat as she is dragged along. It's Jo.

The dogs are chasing a ginger cat, which leaps to safety onto a high railing that overlooks the sea.

'What the bloody hell is a cat doing near the water?' asks Jo breathlessly when she spots me. 'Where has it come from?

The immediate area is all confectionery shops, ice cream kiosks and arcades, with not a single house in sight.

'I'm not sure,' I laugh. 'Maybe one of the flats above the shops? Wherever it's come from I think it's had a lucky escape.'

Jo exhales deeply and takes a seat on the wooden bench.

'I'd stay and have a coffee with you but I'm already late heading over to my parents',' I say, glancing at my watch.

'No problem. I'm not stopping for a drink. Just getting my breath back. I've got two shih-tzus to walk in just over an hour.'

She's strolling along with me to my car, the dogs obediently walking beside her now that the cat has disappeared, when we glimpse Faye coming out of the pub across the road. Her vibrant hair makes her instantly recognisable. She looks a little unsteady on her feet as she stumbles, giggling, into a taxi with a male companion. We both raise our arms and give a wave but she doesn't notice us. I can't help feeling slightly concerned and vow to give her a ring later. I also take the number of the taxi firm. Just in case.

❧

I let myself into my parent's house and find them both sat at the pine table in the dining room, which has recently been painted in a shade of apple white.

'Hi, Mum, hi, Dad,' I say, waving the Bakewell tart at Dad.

'Ooh, very nice,' he says, folding his newspaper.

'Sorry, Mum, what was I thinking?' You're going away and I bring you flowers.'

'Ah thank you, I love freesias. And they last for ages. I'll pop a penny in the vase of water. An old trick, but it seems to work. I'll pop the kettle on to go with that cake.'

I follow Mum into the spacious country-style kitchen. She flicks on the kettle and spoons some loose-leaf tea into a glass teapot. As the kettle comes to the boil, the telephone rings and Mum nips off to answer it. I finish making the tea and carry it through to the lounge on a tray with the Bakewell tart. When Mum wraps up the call, she tells me it was my Aunt Gen.

'How is she? I was thinking about going to visit her soon.'

'Well, your timing couldn't be better,' says Mum as she pours the tea and cuts Dad a generous slice of cake. 'She's finally having surgery on that knee that's been playing up for years. Knee replacement is scheduled for next week.'

'Oh, well, she'll definitely need some help then, I guess.'

I have a vision of my Aunt Gen surrounded by baking utensils, flour scattered over the huge wooden island in her kitchen. A broad smile on her perfectly made-up face. Groomed to perfection, even when she baked.

'I know you're busy, but if you're serious, it would be good of you to go over and see her. You never know what might happen, she's not getting any younger; none of us are.' Mum's eyes mist over as she thinks of her older sister, who will be sixty-eight this year. 'I think if you can get out there soon, then we can change our plans a bit to see Gen after she's had her operation. We're staying close to Barcelona, so it's not too far. Really, she should have been taking it easy years ago but she never could stop. Valerie is perfectly capable of starting the baking in the morning but she's always there at the crack of dawn. I said to her, "What's the point in being the boss if you can't let someone else take the reins and take things easy every now and then?"'

'It's hard to do that when you have something running through your veins,' Dad chimes in. 'And when it's your own business you never really trust anyone else to run it in your absence, no matter how good they are.'

It's just as well I really trust Sam. I have no problem letting her look after things if I went away. I'm glad I've decided to go over with Faye now; as well as looking for André, I need to make sure my aunt is OK. The thought of this trip is filling me with excitement and apprehension in equal measure. It's time to face my past.

July 1998

'Bonjour and welcome to Marineland, the most exciting marine park in Europe. Are you ready to enjoy our show?'

The crowd, especially the young children, whoop and scream in delight. They stomp their feet in anticipation on the wooden floor and the sound echoes around the auditorium.

The young man continues to work the crowd. He has dark hair tied back in a ponytail, ice-blue eyes and the cheekiest smile you have ever seen. He's wearing black shorts, and the name André is written on a bronze badge attached to his red polo shirt. Faye and I are seated in the second row of slatted wooden benches. There's a smell of fish wafting from chrome buckets on the stage, ready to feed the seals and dolphins. I watch the young man in admiration as his entertaining manner effortlessly draws the crowd in. At one point, he makes eye contact with me for a few seconds and smiles broadly. I look away and hope I haven't gone bright red.

'He fancies you,' says Faye, nudging me. 'He hasn't stopped staring at you since the minute we arrived.'

'I don't think that's true. Besides, I bet he has his eye on at least one girl in every show,' I say, although I feel secretly flattered that he chose to single me out. He really is the most gorgeous man I have ever seen.

'And now, I wonder if I could have a volunteer from the audience to step right up and give our star attraction a kiss.'

Right on cue, a huge, glistening orca emerges from the pool, spouting water and drenching everyone in the front row, who squeal excitedly.

'Go on, now's your chance to get up close and personal,' says Faye, grabbing my hand and raising it up into the air.

'To a killer whale? I can't think of anything nicer.'

'I was thinking more of the trainer. I can tell by the way you've been staring at him that you fancy him as much as he fancies you. Go on,' she says, practically pushing me towards the stage.

'Ah, we have our volunteer.' The crowd clap as he helps me up the wooden steps and onto a platform overlooking the water. I tiptoe carefully onto the wet terrace, as I'm wearing vertiginous cork wedges.

'And what, may I ask, is your name?'

'Olivia, but my friends call me Liv.' I'm blushing furiously and can't believe my friend has actually encouraged me to do this.

'Then Liv it is,' he says, fixing me with those eyes. I seem to be falling right into them. And that accent!

André is even more handsome close up. His pale-blue eyes are framed by dark lashes that would be the envy of any woman. His skin is lightly tanned, and his teeth are the colour of snow. He reminds me of the footballer David Ginola. Looking at me, he'll be seeing someone tall and slim, with a mass of dark-brown curls, round green eyes and a full mouth. I've had no shortage of young men wanting to take me out but I've never really been serious about anyone. I'm only too aware of the college types who wanted to be your boyfriend over the summer holidays before dumping you at the beginning of the new term. Perhaps a cynical viewpoint for one so young. Maybe I've watched *Grease* too many times.

'So, Liv,' he says in his silky French accent. 'Walter, our killer whale, is very friendly. Would you like to shake his hand?' Right on cue, Walter extends a flipper and I take it uncertainly. The audience applauds enthusiastically.

'And now. How about a little kiss?'

André encourages me to step forward and lean in. Walter slowly edges towards me and opens his mouth slightly, revealing a set of razor-sharp teeth. I can't believe I am really about to kiss a killer whale. I lean forward and snatch a kiss before quickly backing away as the crowd erupts into more noisy applause.

'Thank you, Liv. Ladies and gentlemen, a round of applause for our beautiful volunteer.' The crowd duly oblige.

I return to my seat and Faye and I watch the rest of the show, which includes dolphins jumping through hoops and sea lions juggling balls and waving at the crowds. Young children are bobbing up and down in their seats with excitement.

When the crowds filter out at the end of the show, I'm not really surprised when André casually saunters over to me, his hands in his pockets.

'I'll meet you outside,' says Faye, winking at me and joining the throngs heading for the exit.

'So, did you enjoy the show?' He smiles.

'Very impressive. How long have you worked here?'

My heart is pounding in my chest, and I'm sure I must be blushing, but somehow I'm able to conquer it and talk to him. We fall into step, walking towards the exit, and he tells me he's worked at Marineland for just over a year and lives several miles away in a small village.

'I've been saving up,' he tells me. I could listen to that delicious accent all day long. 'At the end of the summer I am going to stay with a friend who lives in New Zealand. After that, who knows? It has been my dream to travel for as long as I can remember.'

I tell him about staying at my aunt's bakery for the summer, and a flicker of recognition passes across his face.

'Pâtisserie Genevieve? I know it. Do they still serve the cream bun glazed with honey and violets? C'est magnifique!

'I'll tell my aunt she has a fan. And yes, they do. It's called a bee sting. That's my favourite too.'

As we reach the exit, he fixes me with those eyes and asks me if I will be returning to watch the show again.

'Is there any point in seeing it twice?' I tease.

He cocks his head to one side and studies me.

'Maybe. Although in truth no, it will probably be the same. The point would be so I can see you again.' He laughs.

He's so ridiculously handsome I imagine he's accustomed to girls hanging on to his every word, and nodding eagerly when asked if they would return to the show. I can't help wondering how many have previously fallen under his spell.

'If you don't come for tomorrow's show, can I at least meet you for coffee? Or maybe an ice cream? Danielle's ice cream parlour on the seafront. I have two hours between shows. Shall we say one o'clock tomorrow afternoon? I must see you again. You have hypnotised me with those big green eyes.'

It's a cheesy line, although my eyes are the thing that everyone comments on. They *are* large, and a very distinctive pale green framed with thick dark lashes. My great-grandmother was Irish, and I seem to be the only one in the family to have inherited her colouring.

I'm determined not to fall for his charms, but with every second I spend with him I can feel my resolve weakening.

Sure enough, the next day I found myself at the little ice cream parlour overlooking the sparkling sea, and as we ate our sundaes, I could feel myself quickly falling under his spell. I met with him the next day and the day after that. Faye went home after spending a week with me and although we had fun together, even then, André was constantly on my mind.

We spent the summer swimming in the glorious warm sea and going for walks along the moonlit beach. When the morning rush was over at the bakery, André would call in before he started his shift at Marineland. He would lean over the glass counter and steal a kiss when my aunt wasn't looking. So quickly, we became one of those loved-up couples that stroll past families having picnics on the beach, me dreaming that one day *we* would be one of those families, playing with our own young children. We would make the most beautiful children – they'd have André's olive skin and my green eyes.

The first time he kissed me, in the dark shadows beneath the pier, I thought I was going to faint. I'd never been kissed like that before. He was only two years older than me but he seemed so self-assured, so worldly wise. We held hands as we strolled along the open-air market in Antibes, past the colourful flower and fruit stalls. André bought some strawberries and popped one into my mouth before dragging me down a side street and kissing me passionately. We were drunk on love.

By the end of the summer, I was certain he would abandon all thoughts of travelling to New Zealand now that he had met his one true love. I wasn't sure what my parents would say about me living in France, but at least I would have my aunt. I went shopping one day and bought a silver split-heart necklace; André wore the half that said 'eternal' and my half said 'love'.

My heart soared when he asked me to a 'special' candlelit dinner at a smart restaurant – La Terrace – the evening before he was due to fly off to the other side of the world. I felt so grown up, and I was so sure I was about to hear that he had changed his mind about going. It took me ages deciding what to wear that evening but, in the end, I chose a knee-length, slightly low-cut red dress. André told me I looked beautiful. We shared a plate of profiteroles for dessert, and when the meal was over, we wandered to the outside decking area of the restaurant, which was strung with lights, and gazed out across the sea.

'I will never forget this summer,' said André, pulling me towards him and gazing into my eyes. 'But we are so young, Olivia.' It was the first time he had used my full name.

The word 'but' gave me a pang in my heart. Suddenly, the pretty water features and plants of flowers bursting with colour dotted about the terrace seemed to fade to grey.

'We have our whole lives to live. We must follow our dreams,' André continued, as my heavy heart sank down to my pretty cork wedges. He continued to glance out to sea with a faraway look in his eyes.

'What *is* your dream André?' I asked, fearing the answer with every fibre of my being.

'I want to see the world,' he said. 'Swim with the dolphins in Florida, watch the killer whales in the Arctic. See the magnificent creatures I see at the water park in their natural habitat.' He spoke with a passion I had never heard in his voice before.

I felt such a fool as I realised that *my* dream was to live right here in Antibes in a little cottage near the sea, where one day I might have even opened a little patisserie with the love of my life.

I felt sick to my stomach. André didn't want to settle down. And who could blame him? He was twenty years old and I was only eighteen. But it was the same age my parents had been when they met, and they were still happy together. The following day he stepped on to a plane to New Zealand, with a promise to write, and I thought my heart would crack in two.

I received a postcard and a letter from André a few weeks later. He said that he missed me, but also he seemed so excited about his plans to go travelling with his friend around New Zealand, before heading to Australia. He didn't know what his next address would be but he would try to write again. If he did, I never received a letter and soon enough it was time to head back to England.

Aunt Gen had tried to cheer me up with specially baked cakes and drives along the coast to Nice, but nothing could lift my spirits. Everywhere I looked was a reminder of André: the beach, the little ice cream parlour and all the pretty street cafés where we'd held hands and laughed without a care in the world. And of course, the huge looming frontage of Marineland. In some ways, I wished I'd never set foot in the place. It had all been Faye's fault. If she had never raised my hand and volunteered me to go up on that stage. But well, we can't rewrite history, I suppose. And there is definitely a huge part of it I wouldn't want to erase.

I'd been feeling a little unwell anyway, and was rather looking forward to sleeping in my own bed and seeing my parents again. My aunt told me I was lovesick and pining and that 'the first cut is the deepest', which I've come to realise is true. The strange thing was, although my heart ached in Antibes, I was worried my memories would fade as soon as I returned to my life in the north of England. Little did I know that I would have an enduring reminder of that summer of 1998.

Chapter Seven

I ring Faye early on Monday morning to see if she's free for a coffee after school to discuss our trip to France, having already emailed Aunt Gen to check we could both come. I also want to check that's Faye's alright, after spotting her getting into a taxi with the bloke outside the pub. The call goes to voicemail and I feel ever-so-slightly anxious. It's a little before eight o'clock so she should be up and about. Maybe she's driving to work and can't answer the phone. I'll try her again later. To distract myself, I fire up my laptop up to check incoming orders, before contacting Sam to see if she is able to take charge of the business for a few weeks. Thankfully, she's fine with it, and has said she will draft her student baker friend Nic in, if things get really busy.

I pop some bread into the toaster and switch on the coffee machine as Jake strolls down the stairs. He's wearing jeans and a T-shirt.

'Shouldn't you be in running gear?' He goes for a run most mornings. A habit I should probably try to copy if I want to keep in shape and avoid my own knee surgery when I'm older.

'I think I'll give that a miss. I fancy doing bit of baking, actually. Fancy a lemon drizzle cake for later, Mum?' Jake picks up three lemons from a wire basket and begins to juggle them.

'Lemon drizzle, hey? You are full of surprises.' My toast pops out of the toaster and I spread it thickly with butter. I have decided to be as open-minded as I can about Jake's plans for his future. 'Well, I love lemon drizzle, and I'm willing to be a fair judge on whether catering is going to be a good path for you, so go ahead. I'm going to answer these emails and Sam will be around shortly to make a start on a football-pitch cake.' I pour us each a steaming mug of coffee.

'Cool. Maybe I can help her.' Jake grins.

'Not a chance until I've judged your lemon drizzle; you're still an amateur. I have my reputation to think of,' I say, as I jokingly wave a jam-covered knife at him.

'At the moment I am.' Jake cheekily pinches my buttered toast and drops two more slices of bread into the toaster.

It's harder than I thought to be relaxed about Jake leaving uni. I don't want to pressure him by talking about his university course, and the more I've thought about it I know he's right to be uncertain about finding gainful employment with a degree in psychology. I just wish he could at least finish his education. Jobs are hard enough to come by these days. I also need to find the right time to tell him about me going to France.

First things first, though. I settle down with my delicious coffee and jam on toast and set about answering my emails when a new message catches my eye. It's from Aunt Genevieve.

Hello Liv,

It was so lovely to get your message and I'm absolutely thrilled that you will soon be coming over with Faye. I know how much fun you two have together. Your mum has told me how busy you are with the cake business. I'm so glad it's going well! There's something truly satisfying about creating something for someone's special occasion, isn't there?

As you know, I have taken a little bit of a back seat here these last few weeks as my knee has been really bothersome. But don't worry. I'm sure my forthcoming surgery will sort me right out. Luckily, Olivier offered to come over and help out as soon as I told him about my operation. He says he will always be grateful to me for teaching him to bake. I think he likes to indulge his passion now and again.

Lilian Beaumont still comes into the shop every morning and gives the loaves a little squeeze. You'll see when you're here, some things never change.

Anyway, I'll let you get on. Let me know as soon as you and Faye have flights booked.

Speak soon, love always,

Gen xx

I close the email and feel a longing to see my aunt as soon as I can. And seeing Olivier again is no bad thing. Although a seasoned playboy, he has a heart of gold and an irrepressible humour. My aunt told me that he was always in and out of her shop as a child, peering at the cakes and inhaling the aroma of the bread. When he was barely a teenager, she offered him a weekend job and taught him to bake bread, for which he displayed a real talent. He comes from a family of wealthy business owners, who own a large yacht and want for nothing, yet he loves to call in to the bakery and help out whenever he has the chance. And I smile as I think of Lilian Beaumont. She's Gen's best friend in France. Outwardly fearsome but as soft as a fluffy meringue underneath. When I was a child, she would teach me French words and told me that good manners would take you anywhere in the world. She had the air of a film star, her soft black curls framing her pretty face. Her complexion was pale and alluring and she was a thin as a reed. She always left a cloud of Chanel No. 5 in her wake.

Finishing up with my emails, I give Faye another quick call and she answers on the second ring.

'Hi, mate, what's up?'

'Hi, Faye. You're not driving, are you?'

'Wouldn't have answered the phone if I was,' she laughs. 'I've just pulled into the school car park; last week of term, I can't wait for the holidays. Are you OK?'

'Yeah, I'm fine. I'm just checking that you are, actually.'

'Oh, why wouldn't I be?'

I'm not sure I should even be saying anything about seeing her and suddenly feel a bit awkward. She's an adult with her own life. Maybe I should have just arranged to meet up for coffee.

'Oh, nothing. I just saw you in town yesterday, that's all. Me and Jo gave you a wave but you never noticed us. You were getting into a taxi with some bloke.'

She is quiet for a second or two.

'Is there a law against that?' she says finally.

'Of course not! It's just… Oh, never mind.'

'No, go on, it's just what?'

'Well, you looked a bit unsteady on your feet. As your friend, I was just a bit concerned that you were getting into a taxi with a bloke, that's all. You hear all sorts these days.'

'You worry too much. And for your information, I vaguely knew him. He did a bit of supply teaching at the school a couple of years ago. Do you think I'd be so daft as to get into a taxi with a complete stranger?'

'Sorry, Faye, no, of course not.'

'Thanks for caring though,' she laughs. 'Although if I was in any danger, it would have been in danger of being bored to death – he went on and on about his job on a farm. It seems teaching wasn't really his thing either. I know everything there is to know about arable farming and crop rotation. Not to mention topsoil and manure. Then he banged on for an hour about the organic coffee we were drinking, envying the farmers of the Ethiopian forests: "I bet you wouldn't need to wear your thermal vest over there." He was actually leafing through *National Geographic* magazine! When he said come up for coffee, I didn't think he actually meant it! I called a cab an hour later and got the same driver home and we got chatting. We're going to watch Disciples of Doom together next week at the pub. Anyway, gotta dash. Just time for a quick brew before I bring the kids in from the yard. But it is almost the last day of term. Woo hoo! Coffee tomorrow at the pier café? Shall we say five o'clock?'

'OK, I'll message Jo, see if she's free. See you tomorrow.' As I ring off, I wonder when Faye will meet the man of her dreams. Although I suppose my mum wonders exactly the same thing about me. The difference is, I'm not even looking.

☙

I have a few cake deliveries to make in the afternoon, and arrive home to find Jake in the kitchen stirring a pot on the stove.

'Something smells good,' I say, shrugging off my coat.

'It's a new pasta sauce. I created it myself,' says Jake proudly. 'Sit down. Do you want some wine?'

'Go on then, just a small glass.'

Jake pours me a glass of Merlot and I notice a cake on the kitchen counter.

'Lemon drizzle for dessert, as promised,' he says proudly.

'I'm impressed. Maybe you have picked up something from watching me bake all these years.'

Jake serves up a beef tagliatelle dish, the smell of the herbs making my stomach rumble. I wrap some of the pasta in the creamy tomato sauce and take a bite. It's absolutely delicious.

'Oh wow, Jake, I can see how good you are at this cooking lark.' I'm thinking that maybe he is right in toying with the idea of pursuing a career in catering. 'So, what else have you been up to today then?'

'Apart from creating culinary masterpieces? Not a lot really. Sam called around earlier. We chatted while she was icing that football pitch cake.'

'You like Sam, don't you?' I say, taking a sip of Merlot before devouring the rest of the tasty pasta dish. At twenty-six, she's a bit older than Jake, but they do seem to get along well.

'Yeah, she's cool. I've never really met anyone like her. She's not like the girls I've met at university. Maybe it's because she's a bit older. She's different, so down to earth considering her parents have got a few quid.'

Sam's lucky enough to be able to take her time deciding what she wants in life, although she's made no secret of the fact that, one day, she would like her own cake business.

'I know, I've been to her family home in Churchtown. It's one of those huge Victorian houses with a garden that goes on forever. Her mum runs a fancy-dress hire shop as well as the vintage place and her dad's a scriptwriter for screen and stage. He's had stuff on the telly, apparently.'

I think of the other evening, when I returned home and found them curled up together on the sofa, and wonder whether there might be something between them. But I don't want to get distracted with those thoughts; I've got to talk to Jake about André.

'So, Jake, I've been thinking of visiting your great-aunt in France for a while. You know she's about to have knee surgery, and I've decided to go over and help her out a little.'

'OK, cool. Well, you know this place will be in safe hands with Sam. And I can help out with deliveries and stuff. I'll be around during the day. I've manged to get a few shifts doing bar work at the Victoria.'

The Victoria is the local pub around the corner.

'What about kitchen work at the Bottle and Glass?'

'It's a bit of trek out of town. I might look at a place more local. The Vic will do for now though, I could use the extra cash.'

I dare to hope that Jake might drop all notion of working in a kitchen and go back to university after the holidays.

'It would be great if you could help Sam with deliveries, thanks. Actually, Jake, I've been doing some thinking. Maybe I could make some enquiries about your father when I'm out there.'

Jake turns to face me.

'Really? Oh, Mum, do you think you'll be able to find anyone that knows him?' Jake's face looks so eager, I can tell how much this means to him.

'It's a long shot,' I sigh, not wanting to get his hopes up too much. 'But worth a try, hey? If that's still what you want.'

'It is. Thanks, Mum. Will you let me know as soon as you find anything out? Wow, I can't believe it.'

We chat about this and that before Jake jumps up and retrieves two small plates from a kitchen cupboard. I feel tremendous relief that we're on speaking terms again. I'm still a little anxious about his uncertainty over university, but have parked that particular worry for the time being. I don't want to harp on about it and risk alienating him further.

'And now,' he says, cutting two generous slices of lemon drizzle. 'The pièce de résistance.'

I sink my teeth into a slice of the cake. *Damn.* It's possibly the best lemon cake I have ever tasted. It's as light as a feather with a buttery, zesty tang that tickles the tastebuds.

'Oh my word. Jake – this is exceptional. It's probably better than mine.' I could greedily eat another huge slice.

'High praise indeed, but you *are* my mum. I'll take it anyway.' He beams.

'Trust me, I'm telling the truth.' I lick my lips, not wanting to waste a morsel of the sticky lemon glaze.

'Thanks, Mum. I told you I enjoy baking. I might have a go at making meringues tomorrow. Oh, I'm out tonight. There's a few of us meeting up in town for drinks then going back to Matt's. I'll probably end up crashing there.'

I have a check of my emails before heading upstairs for a long soak in the bath. Jake heads off out, grabbing another piece of lemon drizzle and stuffing it in his mouth before he leaves. I try to switch my mind off, but can't now that I've told Jake I will try and trace his father. Downstairs, I flick the television on and the movie *Chocolat* with Johnny Depp is about to start. I'm not sure I can face it, so settle on watching one of those real-life programmes about the emergency services.

I suppose it was inevitable that the time would come to track down Jake's father. I'm not sure what will happen if I do find him, or how I will tell him that he has a son.

Chapter Eight

I can't believe I'll be back in France in a few days' time, in my aunt's three-bedroomed flat above the bakery. As a child, I was fascinated by all the things in my aunt's place. I thought it was like a film set: the French doors leading on to a large balcony where you could glimpse the sparkling sea across the rooftops. The whole place was stylishly furnished, with huge cream sofas and plants in large brass pots dotted around. Heavy lamps sat on polished onyx tables.

The walls were adorned with photographs of Gen and Uncle Enzo, smiling on deck as they sailed the turquoise waters of the Côte d'Azur. They had a small boat and would often sail around the coast, taking me for days out when I visited. I recall stopping at secluded coves to swim and snorkel in the crystal-clear waters, before having a BBQ on the boat.

I woke up in the early hours this morning, and as I passed Jake's room I noticed the door was open and he wasn't there. I had a moment of panic until I remembered he was staying at a friend's. I wonder if we ever stop worrying about our children? Jake recently turned twenty but I still worry about him as if he were a young child. Maybe it's because I've always been the one to look after him.

I'm just retrieving today's deliveries from the larder when the phone rings.

'Hi, Liv, just a quickie. I'm free to meet you and Faye at the pier café at five. I might ask them if they've got any jobs,' Jo sighs.

'Are you having a bad morning, Jo?

'You could say that. I stupidly let a Labrador off the lead in Hesketh Park when I thought there was no one about, but around the next corner a group of lads were playing football. The daft mutt peed on someone's rucksack before stealing a meat pie out of someone else's bag. Not content with that, after wolfing the pie down it bounded onto the pitch, stole the football and raced off with it. I've never been so embarrassed in my whole life.'

'Oh, Jo,' I say, laughing loudly. 'At least your job is never boring. How long do you think you would last serving coffee at the end of the pier?'

'That's true I suppose. And I do love the dogs. I couldn't do it if I didn't. Anyway, catch you later.'

Carefully loading my cars with the cakes, I drive off, still smiling at Jo's dog story. I've got a few local deliveries around town, including a cake for a gothic wedding. The cake is decorated with black icing laced with red spiderwebs. The ceremony is being conducted in the grounds of a hotel, beside an ancient tree that is believed to be a fertility symbol.

As I walk up the path of a smart semi-detached house to deliver a mermaid birthday cake, I spy a small girl looking out the front window. She pokes her tongue out at me and I resist the urge to give her a rude hand gesture in return. Mum gushes over the cake and admires the iridescent hues of the glittery icing around the fishtail.

'Ooh, look, Chantilly, isn't this beautiful?'

The little girl looks over the lid and blows a raspberry. 'It's not very big. I wanted one this big,' she says, spreading out her slightly chubby arms.

'Oh baby. Never mind, you can have a much bigger one next time,' says Mum, looking slightly crestfallen even though the cake is a good size and beautifully detailed.

I tuck the payment for the cake into my purse with a wide smile and tell Chantilly I hope she enjoys it. She looks at me without expression, arms folded. I'm not sure a life-size fairy princess castle cake could satisfy this child.

As I make my way down the path, I wonder whether her mother realises she has named her child after a French vanilla cream.

&

I jump on the blue train for the café at the end of the pier, as it's a bit of a blustery day and I don't really fancy the half-mile walk. Just as I'm nearing the end, I spot Faye and Jo walking along, huddled into their coats.

'You lazy article,' says Jo as I disembark. 'I've been walking dogs all day. I should be the one getting the train.'

'I know. I think maybe I am getting a bit lazy.'

'I needed that walk to blow the cobwebs away,' says Faye. 'The last week of school is always so manic. Yesterday a kid only blinking well climbed over a fence into the street going after a football he'd kicked over. The head was having palpitations.'

'Kids never behave the way they're supposed to, do they?' I say, thinking back to my teaching days.

'You can say that again. Come on, let's get inside. I need a drink,' laughs Faye.

Jo and I order a latte and a panini whilst Faye opts for a large glass of white wine.

'You're starting early,' I remark as we take our seats overlooking the sea.

'Too right. I am officially on holiday and I need this.'

We find a table overlooking the water and I wrap my hands around the tall glass coffee cup. Even on a mild day in July, the wind at the pier is bracing.

'Just think, in a few days' time, you two will be looking at the turquoise waters of the Mediterranean,' says Jo, glancing out across the slightly wild Irish Sea, the waves crashing against the pier.

'I must admit I'm looking forward to a nice warm walk along the beach. I bet the rest of the summer here will be the usual washout,' I say, as a huddle of dark grey clouds drifts by.

We refresh our drinks then chat for another hour before Jo suggests we change some money into old pennies and have a go on the machines in the penny arcade.

The Victorian room always transports me back to when Jake was a child and I would bring him here after a ride on the carousel. There's a tarot gypsy head in a glass case that spits out your fortune on a little white card when you insert a penny. There's roll-a-penny machines, a haunted mansion game and a variety of other nostalgic pieces.

'I'll drop you off if you like,' Jo says to Faye, who came by bus, as we step outside onto the bracing pier a little after seven thirty. The blue train is rattling towards us and this time we all step on for the return journey.

'I'm in the mood for another drink; the night is young. Anyone fancy joining me?' asks Faye as we disembark.

'No thanks,' I say. 'I've got another early start tomorrow. I couldn't have a drink every night.'

'I was only thinking of a pint or two. I don't feel like going home yet, that's all. I hope you're not judging me?' she says, a slight sharpness in her tone.

'Of course not! I just know that I couldn't get up for work in the morning if I had more than a couple.' I try to laugh it off but I can see I have offended Faye.

We hug each other tightly before saying goodnight, and Jo asks me to pass her good wishes on to my Aunt Gen.

'See you on Friday,' says Faye. 'I've dusted off my old French phrasebook. I can't wait!'

As we head off, I hope Faye has the holiday she deserves. And despite the circumstances of my visit, I'm hoping I can have a good time too.

Chapter Nine

'Right. Now there's six cake deliveries for tomorrow. Nic has promised to do the pier café blueberry scones and a large Victoria sponge and carrot cake for Tuesday. The wedding cakes aren't ready for icing until next week.'

I'm going through everything with Sam in the kitchen on Friday morning, sticking Post-it notes on the boxes in the larder.

'Everything is super organised,' Sam says with a smile on her face. 'Stop worrying.'

'I know, sorry, I can't help it. I've been to the wholesaler too and stocked up on just about every food colour and flavour you can think of, so you should be OK. I know I'm leaving everything in safe hands,' I say. Although I know I'll still be checking the emails every morning and fretting over whether the orders will be delivered on time. Sam's friend Nic has agreed to help with deliveries and even do a little baking. She recently knocked up a couple of batches of blueberry scones for a local teashop I supply and the owner declared them the best yet. It's good to have someone you can call upon when things get busy. There's no time for ego in business.

Jake's hovering in the background.

'Don't worry, Mum, I'll ice those wedding cakes if you like,' he teases.

'Right, that's it. I'm not going.' I sit down on a chair in the kitchen.

'I've told you, Mum. I'll do deliveries. Any cakes I bake can be purely to satisfy my own gluttony.'

I go over everything for the umpteenth time before finally setting off.

'Right. Ring me if there's any sort of emergency.'

I hug them both and plant a kiss on Jake's cheek before glancing around the kitchen, wondering if I've forgotten something.

'Mum, just go,' says Jake, picking up my case to carry to the car and practically shoving me out of the front door.

I exhale deeply as I start the car and head towards Faye's flat.

❧

After an uneventful flight, we arrive in France to a glorious eighty-degree heat and not a cloud in the pale blue sky.

'I'll grab us a nice cold drink,' says Faye as we trundle our cases along the polished tiled floor of Nice airport, passing the throngs of holidaymakers wearing hats and sunglasses as we head to the car hire counters. I'm dismayed to find a queue at our car rental stand, as the ones either side have no one waiting. Typical. The line is moving at a snail's pace, as there is only one sullen-looking moustachioed bloke at the counter.

'Unbelievable,' moans an elderly English bloke behind me. 'It's not like Tesco, is it? *They* open another checkout when there's a queue.'

Faye returns with two bottles of ice-cold Orangina. I unscrew the cap and take a long, thirsty gulp. The airport is stifling. After fifteen minutes I'm losing the will to live, when suddenly another assistant appears behind the counter and gestures the customer at the front of the line towards her. Thank goodness for that. It isn't long before we are despatched with our paperwork and directed to the car park across the road to take delivery of our vehicle.

As we head outside into the bright sunshine and the sultry summer heat massages my bare arms, I feel a thrill of excitement. I put my sunglasses on and turn to Faye, who is exhaling deeply.

'Don't you just love that holiday smell you get when you get off a plane?' she gushes.

'Yep.' I inhale the humid, unfamiliar air and watch some palm trees gently swaying. 'Are you ready to hit the road?

She places her own sunglasses on her face. 'Ready.'

Travelling along the coast to Antibes, the familiar sights and sounds of the beach road fill me with nostalgia. We drive through Nice and the palm-lined promenade of Cannes, glimpsing the yachts in the harbour. We stop at a zebra crossing to allow glamourous, stick-thin women wearing wide-brimmed hats and designer sunglasses to cross the road.

'Is it film festival week?' says Faye, as she cranes her head to look out of the rear window. 'I'm sure that was Tom Hanks.'

The sun roof of the Renault is open, allowing the smells of the coast to permeate the car. It's a mixture of pine, salty sea and that undefinable scent that stirs the senses. I find myself once more thinking of André as I drive along. The sun dancing on the water stirs up memories in my soul. Twenty-one years ago. I can hardly believe it. I remember that last evening together with André and the sick feeling in my stomach as if it were yesterday. I wonder where he is now. And how on earth I'm going to track him down.

My shoulders begin to relax again. As we drive along the undulating roads of the Côte d'Azur, a slight breeze from the sunroof blows my hair gently and I exhale deeply.

There is a day that I will never forget, when André and I hired bikes and cycled from Antibes to Saint Raphael along a bike path. We passed the yachts lazily bobbing in the Mediterranean Sea before heading on through Juan-Les-Pins. I remember stopping and taking a long glug of lukewarm water and André teasing me for being unfit. I was relieved when we rode through the wide, open and flat roads of Cannes, palm trees towering over the boulevard. Cycling on, we passed the seafront shops – the big names in fashion all jostling for position. I told André that one day I would return and buy myself a dress from Gucci. We stopped for a delicious pizza in Théoule-sur-Mer, where the views over the azure blue of the water took my breath away. After that, we spent an hour on the sun-kissed beach eating ice cream and stealing kisses. When we finally reached our destination of Saint Raphael, we changed into our swimming costumes and cooled down in the sparkling turquoise sea. As the sun began to descend lower in the sky, we boarded the train back to Antibes, happy and exhausted. It's still one of the most memorable days of my life.

After half an hour of driving, the medieval walls of Antibes loom into view, and the rough ancient stone of the Chateau Grimaldi, that now houses the Picasso museum. We pass slowly through the port before entering the old town of Antibes. It's bustling with tourists, meandering through the streets lined with cafes and shops, soaking up the atmosphere. We snake through the town, and soon enough we are parking up in the private car park at the rear of the bakery and stepping out into the warm sunshine.

As we enter the white-walled shop with terracotta floor tiles, the scent of bread wraps me in a hug. I immediately see my aunt behind the counter, along with Olivier and a dark-haired assistant in her early thirties. Three customers are gazing into a glass counter filled with tempting pastries. Olivier's face breaks into a huge smile when he sees me and as my aunt follows his gaze her eyes light up.

'Ma famille!' she calls out, walking around the counter and crushing Faye and I in an embrace.

'Olivia, bonjour, comment ça va?' Olivier asks, his face breaking into a broad smile.

'Bien merci, et tu?

'I am OK,' he says. I'm pleased he remembers that my French conversation skills don't go much beyond introductions. He greets us both with a kiss on both cheeks and introduces us to Valerie, the dark-haired assistant.

I look over at Faye to see her mouth 'He's gorgeous' behind his back.

'You look well,' Olivier tells me.

'So do you,' I reply. Nothing about him has changed, and I eye his face suspiciously for signs of Botox. He is still muscled, brown-eyed and drop-dead gorgeous. 'And I hope this doesn't get confusing; Olivier and Olivia working side by side. You must remember to call me Liv.'

'But of course, Liv.' He smiles.

'Aunt Genevieve, what are you doing down here? Shouldn't you be resting?' I ask, crushing her in a hug.

My aunt looks as glamourous as ever in a yellow cotton dress with a white pinny over it. Her hair is pinned up as usual. She looks wonderful, a slight limp being the only clue to her forthcoming surgery.

'I was getting bored resting upstairs,' she laughs, before nipping behind the counter and serving a customer with two baguettes, which she places into a brown paper bag.

'Well, you shouldn't be overdoing things.'

'Huh. Don't you think I'll have plenty of time to rest when I'm recovering?' She places some money into a till and snaps it shut. 'I'm dosed up on anti-inflammatories, but hopefully this operation will sort my knee right out. But I will allow myself a break for tea –' she turns to Olivier – 'if you can manage for a short while. But only because you've come all this way to see me,' she says with a wink.

We take tea on the balcony upstairs. Gen brought some baguettes up from downstairs, which she filled with egg mayonnaise and smoked salmon and cream cheese, batting me away in the kitchen as I tried to help. 'I've told you. There will be plenty of time for you to look after me when I'm convalescing.'

Faye, Gen and I drink tea from floral china cups and long glasses of iced water as we bask in the afternoon sunshine. The balcony gives a glimpse of the glorious yachts in the harbour and I exhale deeply, thinking how nice it must be to wake up to this view every single morning.

'Liv, you look very well,' says my aunt. 'Very healthy.' She gently pinches my cheek.

'Do you mean I've put on weight?'

Faye smiles uncertainly. She knows I hate the fact that I've put on a few pounds.

'As if I would say such a thing! But maybe a little rounder in the face. It suits you. Although maybe you should cut down on the sugar as you get older'.

'I know, and don't worry. I've decided to cut back anyway. I've had to buy a few new clothes recently, which is annoying, as I've got some lovely summer outfits in my wardrobe back home that are just the teeniest bit tight around the middle. I probably could have got away with them if I abstained from food and drink for the whole of my stay here, but that could never happen in France.'

'Right, talking of food, tonight I recommend dinner at the Bistro Lemaire near the port. They do the best lobster you will ever taste.'

'Lobster, hey? Pushing the boat out tonight then, Gen?' asks Faye, as she eyes a selection of petit fours. Faye can annoyingly eat whatever she wants without gaining a single ounce.

'You bet I am. I'm having everything on the menu, with a good bottle of Beaujolais,' she laughs. 'Tomorrow I will be nil by mouth.'

Chapter Ten

I text Jake and tell him that we've all arrived safely and he tells me to give his love to Gen. He sends me a photograph of a huge, fluffy-looking Victoria sponge that he has baked this afternoon. It looks amazing.

I hang my clothes in the wardrobe of my elegant twin guest room, which has green walls and white antique French furniture. After a long shower, I slip into a pair of white linen trousers and a blue floral-patterned vest before nipping downstairs to the bakery, whilst Faye enjoys a gin and tonic on the balcony with Gen. I remember that she got on really well with Gen the summer that we were out here together; I guess they both have a similar zest for life. When I go down, it's almost three o'clock and the shop is empty.

'Do you have time for a latte?' I gesture Olivier to the back of the shop as Valerie serves at the front.

'Yes.' He smiles. 'That sounds nice.'

'So, how's life treating you then?' I ask.

'Well, I can't complain. I'm still footloose and fancy-free, if you're interested.' He beams. I had forgotten what a flirt he is.

'Not really looking,' I laugh.

'What about your beautiful friend?'

He's leaning on his hand and staring at me with his exquisite brown eyes. It's easy to see why women are so drawn to him.

'Behave yourself, we've only been here five minutes.'

The resort is no doubt full of beautiful women, yet here he is checking out the new arrivals in town. We chat for a few more minutes and Olivier asks me what time I'll be starting work in the mornings.

'Well, I'll be looking after Gen post-op, but a few hours here and there was all I was expecting to do down here. Aren't you here for the early starts?'

'No, I thought you were baking all the bread in the morning so I could concentrate on some new cakes,' he says, a serious look on his face.

'Really?' I say, suddenly panicked. 'Gen never said anything about me baking bread. I thought I was here to rustle up some tarts and Florentines. Croissants and baguettes aren't really my thing. Although, of course, I will if you need me to.'

'I'm joking,' says Olivier, a grin spreading across his face. 'Although I have been reliably informed that your baking is excellent, so we should definitely have one or two of your signature bakes.'

'Early starts and French tarts. What have I let myself in for? Anyway, I'd better get off and find something to wear for this evening. See you later.'

Bistro Lemaire has a prime location on the harbour, overlooking the yachts. We're dining outside, watching an impossibly glamourous family walking down the gangplank of a chrome and white yacht called *Marinella* before getting into a waiting chauffeur-driven car. The blonde mother and daughter are sporting glorious tans and designer clothes and sunglasses, the mother carrying an oversized handbag, whilst the daughter has headphones plugged into a bejewelled phone. The handsome, dark-haired men, presumably father and son, follow behind in their effortlessly chic smart shorts and short-sleeved shirts. I wonder where they're going. Perhaps they are heading into St Tropez. There are so many playgrounds to choose from on the Côte d'Azur.

'They're not short of a bob or two,' says Faye as she sips a cold French beer and peruses the menu.

'Which have only been recently acquired,' says Gen as she sips a large glass of Beaujolais from the bottle we're sharing.

'How do you mean?' I ask.

'Lottery winners from the UK, apparently. They spend their money like there's no tomorrow. It won't last long if they carry on the way they do. The local restaurateurs aren't complaining though. Apparently, they are huge tippers.'

'What would you do if you won the lottery?' I ask Gen.

'That's easy – I'd buy one of those.' She points to a cruiser in the water. 'Not a huge one, but big enough to have a decent outside area for drinks.'

'Right, well, I'm having the lobster, since you recommended it, Gen,' says Faye, snapping her menu closed. 'I am on holiday after all.'

'It might even be the last supper for me,' Gen says, somewhat theatrically.

'Don't talk like that. You're fitter than women half your age,' I say. Which is actually true apart from the worn-out knee. 'I'm having a rump steak with chips and onion rings.'

'Do you mean pommes frites?' asks Faye.

'If you say so.' I close my menu and take a sip of the smooth red wine.

I'm keen to compare my steak dinner to the one I had at Le Boulevard restaurant back home in Southport. I wonder whether you can ever truly emulate the food from another country. Will the customers at the bakery know I've baked some of the things at Gen's shop? I wonder if my bakes will taste different to those made with French fingertips.

After dining on our utterly delicious food (it blew Le Boulevard out of the water), including a sharing croquembouche for dessert, we are seated in a lounge area on some comfy bamboo chairs with lime-green padding, drinking Napoleon brandy as a nightcap. We watch the world go by as an orange sun gently sets on the horizon. A young couple walk past. The man is wearing an earring and has his long dark hair tied back in a ponytail. He bends to kiss his curly-haired date and a torrent of memories come flooding back. Where will I even start to look for André? The sights and smells of the harbour front catapult my thoughts right back to 1998, and even now my heart lurches. I'm relieved when we finally pay the bill and head back to the apartment.

Chapter Eleven

The next day I grip Aunt Gen's hand tightly as the porter arrives to take her down to the operating theatre.

I give her a hug, gently pat her arm and say 'see you on the other side', which thinking about it probably wasn't the best thing to say.

'Would it be too much to ask for some champagne when I wake up?' asks Gen drowsily.

'You can have whatever you want. Although maybe the champagne mixed with the pain meds might not be such a good thing. We'll have some champagne when you're home and well, I promise.'

Gen closes her eyes and gives a half smile.

❧

The waiting is the worst part. Around two hours, the surgeon said. I down endless cups of coffee while Faye reassures me that everything will be alright. I decide to use the time to nip outside and check that everything is OK back home. Jake answers on the second ring.

'Hi, Mum. Is everything OK?' he asks breezily. He's munching on something, as usual.

'Hi, love, yeah, Gen's in surgery as we speak. I'm sure she'll be fine. At least I hope so. It's the waiting around that I can't stand.'

'I can imagine. She'll be alright, Mum. I might pop over and see her myself when you get back.'

'Good idea. I'm sure she'd love that. Is Sam around? Just want a quick rundown of how things are.'

Sam comes on the line. 'Hi, Liv. That was perfect timing. I've just this second finished the icing on an anniversary cake. How's your aunt?'

'In surgery. She should be up soon. How's everything there?'

'Fine. We've done today's baking. A couple more orders came in earlier, birthday sponges and cupcakes for a baby shower. Nic's been around and baked for the café at the pier. Her blueberry scones really are a big hit with the customers. So much so that they've doubled the order for next week.'

'Really? That's great news.'

'I know. It's been great having Jake around to help with the deliveries too. It means I can really concentrate on the cakes. I suppose he does have his uses.'

I can picture her glancing at him as she says this.

I finish the call by talking to Jake, telling him how lucky I am to be leaving things in such capable hands. He laughs and tells me, 'Flippin' heck, Mum, you've only just gone. Chill out. Oh, and try to grab a couple of days for yourself to relax.'

The captivating surroundings could relax even the most stressed-out person, so I must learn to unwind. Or at least try to.

I'm just about to put my phone away when a text comes through from Jo.

Hi how's things?
Has your aunt had the op yet?
Jo xx

As I have some time on my hands waiting around, I decide to give her a quick call.

'Hi, Jo. Is this a good time to talk?'

'Hi, Liv. It is, actually; I'm just home having a coffee between walking the pooches. You won't believe the morning I've had.'

'Try me.' I love hearing Jo's stories about her dog-walking escapades.

'Well, remember when Harold the Great Dane took a dump outside hunky bloke's house?'

'Yeah. How could I forget?'

'Well, this morning as we walked past, hunky bloke was just leaving his house, looking hot in a sharp navy suit. Anyway, for some reason Harold decided to leap on him and almost pin him to the front door, licking his face. *Mortifying.* I grabbed at Harold, he clumsily pawed at my skirt, and I lost my balance. I bloody ended up on the floor, didn't I? And it *would* be the day when, instead of wearing my usual jeans, I was wearing a knee-length skirt that ties at the side.'

'Any particular reason for dressing up all girly?' I ask, with a smile on my face.

'Whatever makes you ask that?' she replies in mock indignation. 'Anyway, not realising the skirt was loose, I stood up and the whole thing began to slide down my legs. It was as if it was all happening in slow motion. The next thing, the skirt was around my ankles. I WANTED TO DIE.'

'Oh, Jo!' I'm laughing hysterically and cringing with embarrassment at the same time.

'In the meantime, Harold had put muddy paw prints all over hunky guy's suit, so he had to go inside to change. Not before asking me, "What time will the circus show up next week?" He was *fuming*. Slammed the front door and everything.'

'I'm guessing that wasn't the impression you wanted to make?'

'You're not kidding. I was wearing knee-length boots, chic leather jacket, the lot. I even wore make-up, which I don't normally bother with on the walks.' She sighs.

'Oh well, at least you've made a lasting memory,' I say, laughing.

'Oh yeah. Of me in my tights – which bloody had a huge ladder on the thigh after Harold had pawed me. We are NEVER walking past that house again. EVER.'

I'm heading back towards the ward, inwardly smiling, when a trolley is wheeled up by a porter in a green uniform. A drowsy-looking Gen is lying on the bed, covered in a pale-blue cellular blanket. She catches my eye and smiles. She's back in the land of the living. I breathe a huge sigh of relief and follow them into the ward.

A nurse appears and adjusts some settings on a machine that Gen is hooked up to.

'Did everything go OK?' I ask the nurse.

'Yes. The operation went very well. But she will be on high doses of painkillers today which will make her very drowsy. Perhaps you should go home and get some rest yourself. Tomorrow she will be a little more alert.'

I glance at my watch.

'Maybe I should head off then.' I realise I'm feeling exhausted.

I give Gen a kiss on the cheek and tell her I'll be back tomorrow. She takes my hand and gently squeezes it before drifting off again.

I head out of the ward and breathe a huge sigh of relief – the surgery appears to have gone well.

Chapter Twelve

The next morning, I open my bedroom window as bright sunlight filters into the glorious bedroom and caresses the huge mirror on the facing wall. Faye is snoozing in the adjacent room, making the most of a holiday lie-in.

It's almost seven thirty – I slept like a baby after dinner and a few glasses of wine at a local bar. That was after I had nipped into the shop and prepared some cinnamon rolls, leaving Olivier a note to pop them in the oven as soon as he arrived in the morning. I quickly shower and dress, before heading downstairs to find Olivier in the kitchen area, taking some bread out of the large oven. Valerie is serving a queue of customers at the front of the shop. On a metal tray, I spot the freshly baked cinnamon rolls – the smell is divine. I thank Olivier and carry them to the display case in the shop, placing them alongside coconut madeleines, macarons and crème-pâtissière filled fruit tarts. I also spot several honey-glazed buns, or 'bee stings', and recall how André had said they were the nicest cake he had ever tasted.

'I didn't expect things to be so busy,' I say to Olivier, noting that it's only ten minutes past eight.

'We open at eight o'clock. People like to get their bread early,' he says. 'Valerie and I both arrive at five a.m. I have normally gone by lunchtime.'

I think of how he hung around yesterday when we all arrived. He must be exhausted.

'Well, make sure you do go at lunchtime today. I can take over here for a few hours. Especially while my aunt is still in hospital. I should have come down even earlier. Knocked up a few dozen cupcakes.'

'Tomorrow,' he says, as he places another tray of bread in the oven, 'you can do just that.'

I serve some customers at the counter and when there's a lull in service a while later, Olivier wipes his floury hands on a tea towel and gestures to the coffee machine.

'Would you like one?'

'I'll do that. You carry on,' I say.

'That's the last of the bread for now. It should keep us going throughout the day.'

'Do you have much left over at the end of the day? It must be difficult to know exactly how many to make.'

'You get to know roughly the amount you need, as the locals buy most of the bread. It's the cakes that can be a little unpredictable, as holidaymakers often pop in for a sweet treat,' Olivier tells me.

'Are you two slacking again?' I turn around to find Faye standing behind me, looking striking in a black cotton jumpsuit and perfectly applied make-up.

Olivier is on his feet. 'Please join us.'

'I'll help at the counter.' I vacate my seat for Faye.

There are six people in the queue but I recognise her immediately. Madame Beaumont is wearing a white cotton dress covered with pale-blue flowers and matching blue sling-backs with kitten heels She looks a little older, but as beautiful as ever, with her carefully applied make-up and wavy dark hair framing her pretty face.

I dash around the counter and her eyes light up when she sees me.

'Ah, bonjour, Olivia, how are you?' She greets me with a kiss on both cheeks.

'Bien merci. Et tu?'

'Très bien, merci. Jusqu'à quand restez-vous ici?'

She has just asked me how long I will be staying here, and my mind races to recall the correct reply in French. Suddenly I'm back at high school, fearing ridicule and admonishment from my French teacher if I get it wrong. Madame Beaumont is smiling and nodding her head encouragingly, but my brain remains empty.

'Pendant deux semaines,' I say triumphantly. It's almost two and a half weeks really, but I don't know how to say that in French.

'Bien joué!' she says, clapping her hands together. 'You see, you can do it. The trick is to speak a little French every day or you will forget everything you have learned. Use it or lose it.' She winks.

I see she has no problem in still using 'it' to attract admiring glances from the local men. She returns them with a sidelong grin, only too aware of her timeless beauty. In her early sixties now, she looks at least a decade younger. Her usual Chanel No. 5 scent lingers in the bakery.

'Will you please take this to the hospital for your aunt?' she says, fishing a card in a lilac envelope from her handbag. 'I may go and see here in a few days' time, when she is more up to seeing people. Although I know I would hate to receive visitors lying in bed and not looking my best. Now then,' she calls to Olivier in the back as she takes her place at the front of the queue, still using English. 'I will have one of your loaves that have just come out of the oven, please.'

'Of course.' Olivier jumps from his stool and retrieves a freshly baked loaf from a cooling tray.

'Be careful, it's still very hot,' he says, placing it into a paper bag.

'Well, I was not planning to take a mouthful of it right here. But at least I know it as fresh as it can be.'

'It is all freshly baked—'

'Yes, I know,' she cuts in. 'All freshly baked this morning.' She lifts her head and flashes a wide red-lipped smile as she departs.

'It is so good to see you, Olivia. Look after yourself.' She looks me up and down. 'You look very well. Just remember, cakes should be an occasional treat. Au revoir.'

It's official. Madame Beaumont has spoken. I really need to start resisting those cakes...

❧

'What time are you going to see your aunt?' asks Olivier as we finish up in the kitchen.

'In a couple of hours, why?'

'I was wondering if you would like to go for a walk, as it's such a beautiful day. It's my lunch hour soon.'

'Yes, OK, that would be nice.'

Faye has headed upstairs do some sunbathing on the balcony, as she isn't really one for walking in this heat. No doubt topping up her tan ready for the date Olivier has persuaded her to go on with him tonight, although I'm not sure she took much persuading.

We stroll down towards the harbour in the glorious sunshine, chatting easily. As we pass a crêperie, I inhale the smell of sugar and vanilla, swiftly followed by the scent of summer blooms from a flower shop next door. They're displaying huge sunflowers, lilies and irises in steel buckets. The roads are as busy as ever, cars crawling along, hoping to be lucky enough to stumble upon a parking space, pedestrians zig-zagging their way across gaps in traffic. I soak up the atmosphere of this wonderful town, and after a while we stop for an ice cream, taking a seat on a bench overlooking the water.

'So, tell me about your cake business back home.'

'It's going really well. I have an assistant and when it's really busy, or when I'm away, we draft in an extra pair of hands. My son seems to be showing a bit of a flair for baking too, which has surprised me no end.'

'You are lucky to be making a good living from it. It can be a very competitive business.'

'I know. I must admit it was rather a gamble giving up a steady income, but thankfully I've never looked back. Orders flood in each day and we supply a few local cafés on a regular basis.'

As I work my way through the delicious vanilla ice cream and waffle cone, I tell Olivier more about Jake and his thoughts of leaving university.

'It's always hard for a parent to hear that their child doesn't want a profession. I think my father was disappointed when I showed no interest in working in the family business. The idea bored me. I prefer running my tourist boat – it is better to be happy in life.'

'Remind me, what business is your father in?' I ask.

'Beauty. He made a fortune in cosmetics. He had several large manufacturing sites that he sold when he retired.'

I think of Jake and hope he couldn't see the disappointment in my face when he broached the subject of going into catering. And I know Olivier is right to remind me that being happy really is the most important thing in life.

We finish our ice creams and walk along the harbour, continuing slightly out of town until, half an hour later, a familiar building looms into view. The modern plastic frontage is an update on the wooden, slightly faded sign with peeling paint from all those years ago. Marineland. Even now, the sight of it gives me butterflies in my stomach. If I close my eyes, I can hear the cheers of the crowd, smell the pungent fish buckets, and feel the tingle of excitement as André made eye contact with me.

I'm quiet as I stand and stare at the grey building, lost in my memories, and after a few minutes Olivier asks me if everything is OK.

'It just feels strange seeing this place, that's all. And it's changed so much. I met my first love here.' I'm surprised at how I'm opening up to Olivier, but he's just so easy to talk to.

'Ah, the days of misspent youth,' he says with a smile. 'And it has changed a lot. It had a refurbishment in 2016. There are shark tunnels and all sorts now. Even a crazy golf course, would you believe.'

'Actually, I'm just going to pop inside and ask if anyone has worked there for a long time. They might have some memory of my old friend.'

Olivier waits for me outside in the sunshine and I join him a short while later.

'Any luck?' Oliver is standing against a railing overlooking the sea, attracting admiring glances from every female who walks past.

'No, not really. There was someone there called Patrice who worked there that summer and vaguely remembered someone with a ponytail, but that's it. They weren't exactly friends so never kept in touch. He suggested I look in the local phone directory. I wouldn't have even thought of that.'

Five years ago, when I visited my aunt, I mentioned André's name and asked Olivier if he knew him, but back then he shrugged his shoulders and said he had never heard of him. I suppose it was unlikely anyway, as André lived in a village on the outskirts of town and would cycle to work each day. He could be anywhere…

Heading back into town from Marineland, my mind full of memories, I stop and stare at the small boats bobbing in the crystal waters of the harbour.

'Don't you just love living here?' I ask Olivier as I take a lungful of sea air and admire the stunning surroundings.

'Of course, but the scenery today is better than ever,' he says with a cheeky wink.

'I'm not sure I could ever tire of this place.' I sigh, thinking about how I once longed to live here with André.

'If you grew tired of living here you would be tired of life.' Olivier lowers his sunglasses and gazes after a particularly stunning woman who has just sashayed past.

'I think Samuel Johnson said something similar about London,' I muse.

'Really? Then he clearly never came to the South of France.'

Chapter Thirteen

My aunt is sleeping when Faye and I visit the hospital, but the colour has returned to her cheeks a little.

We take our seats by the bed and, after a while, Gen's eyes open and she smiles at us in recognition.

'Wow. You look well,' I say, gently hugging her.

'Oh yes, marvellous. I bet I look like bed warmed up.'

'I think you mean death.'

'What?'

'You said "bed warmed up". I think you meant "death warmed up",' I say, then wonder why on earth I mentioned the word death.

She smiles. 'Oh yes, death. I think I'm a little fuzzy from the drugs. I'm alright though.'

She's definitely high.

A minute or two later she eases herself up and now appears fully awake.

'So, how are you?' she asks.

Typical of my aunt to ask how we are whilst she's recovering from surgery.

'Absolutely fine. Oh, and Lilian Beaumont sent this.' I fish the lilac envelope out of my bag.

'Thank you, how is she? I bet she's still quizzing everyone about the freshness of the bread.'

'She is. She said she'll visit you in a day or two if you're up to it.'

'She is a good friend.' Gen smiles. 'But you can tell her to wait until I'm home if you like, which won't be too far in the future.' Her eyelids are heavy.

'Have the doctors said how long you'll need to stay in hospital?' I ask as I place some magazines on to the bedside table.

'Not exactly. Perhaps a day or two. The physiotherapist will be around later to discuss my treatment. Apparently, I have to get moving rather quickly.'

I think of Lilian Beaumont and her reference to 'use it or lose it'.

We stay for around an hour, before my aunt yawns and lays her head back into the pillow.

'I'm sorry, it's just the drugs,' she says, her eyes already half closing.

We say our goodbyes and set off long the coast road towards Antibes. Palm trees gently sway as we drive along the beachfront of St Tropez, passing smart couples wearing sunhats and shades, one pair taking a photograph with a selfie stick in front of the sparkling sea. Other couples are strolling hand in hand along the wide boulevard, and parents are pushing children in buggies, the whole family licking cooling ice creams. We drive past miles of endless beach, with little huts at the roadside selling hot snacks and cold drinks.

'Oooh, can we stop for a crepe or a waffle?' asks Faye, spying a wooden stall up ahead.

'Go on then.' It sounds tempting. Despite the fact that I'm trying to avoid too many sweet treats.

We take a seat at a wooden bench and I stare out at the sea and close my eyes briefly as the sun gently massages my shoulders. Families are seated on blankets on the sand, having picnics. Two young girls in matching yellow swimsuits are running along squealing, one chasing the other with a bucket of water. A young couple are holding hands and running into the turquoise sea, reminding me that I did the very same thing with my first love all those years ago.

Sometimes I feel sick to the stomach when I think about Jake not knowing his father. But if I do manage to find him, what will he say knowing he has a son that he knew nothing about? And did I really think I could keep it a secret forever? They say the past has a habit of catching up with you, so I don't suppose you can avoid it forever. If only Facebook had been available to me back then. Social media makes it far easier to locate people these days.

I'm shaken out of my thoughts as a waitress brings a tray of desserts and places them in front of us. Rich red raspberries, juicy strawberries and blueberries sit atop the creamiest vanilla ice cream on a home-made waffle. It's finished with a dusting of icing sugar and a drizzle of maple syrup. I don't think I'm going to eat for the rest of the day after this.

'Bon appetit.' The pretty waitress smiles before disappearing back into the little wooden kiosk, where a small queue has formed.

I watch a black and white dog chase a ball along the golden beach and briefly think of Jo back home, wondering what antics have befallen her today as she walks the dogs. In the distance, I can see the pier at Antibes and recall the evening I had that first heart-stopping kiss with André beneath it. I remember his breathing becoming heavy as his hands roamed over my breasts, but I pushed him away. We'd only known each other a short while, and I wasn't going to be a holiday conquest. Yet, despite my initial resolve, as the weeks went by, I slowly surrendered to my own lust for him, feeling sure that he felt more than just a physical attraction.

'I'm not sure I should have eaten all that,' says Faye, pushing her plate away from her. 'Maybe I should have just had an ice cream.'

'Eyes bigger than belly,' I laugh. 'Maybe we should go for a jog later, when the weather cools a little. Or at least a long walk.'

'No chance, I've got a hot date, remember? Although I wouldn't mind going for a long stroll to somewhere secluded with Olivier,' she says dreamily.

'Right then, do you want to head back?' I ask.

'There's no rush, is there? Whilst Gen's in hospital we might as well relax a little. Fancy a paddle?'

She's already walking down the steps to the beach, having left a small tip on the table for the smiling waitress, who is collecting the dishes.

I'm about to say that we haven't got a towel when she shouts to me to grab her beach bag from the back seat of the car. The sun is strong in the sky and it's a little after three o'clock as we stride into the sparkling water. I splash Faye and she jumps away with a squeal. To anyone observing, we are two young women having fun on a girlie holiday. But the real reason I am here is never far from my mind…

When we arrive back at the bakery, a little after four, I head out to the market at Antibes. Many of the stalls have started to close up for the day, and are stacking their wares into cardboard boxes and loading them into vans. There's a jewellery stall selling silver and semi-precious stones and I promise myself I'll call over again another day. Another stall is selling olive oil and French delicacies, along with bottles of herbs and soaps. I'm happy to find that the fruit and vegetable stall, a kaleidoscope of colours, is still trading.

'Bonjour,' says the handsome trader. His hair is close-cropped, and he's probably in his mid-thirties. 'Are you looking for something special?'

'Basil.'

He points me to box containing bunches of fresh herbs.

I eye the neatly presented stall, displaying courgettes, waxy purple aubergines and huge red tomatoes. My eye scans tied bunches of tarragon, parsley and fragrant basil, and I select a huge bunch of the latter. I also buy a selection of vegetables to make a ratatouille.

'Merci,' says the stall holder as I hand over some money. 'I hope you enjoy the vegetables, which are all freshly picked. And the basil makes a wonderful addition to any sauce.'

'It's actually to put in some cakes.' I can see the look of surprise on his face.

'Really? That is surprising to hear.'

'Strawberry and basil. They really are quite delicious. Maybe I'll bring you one to try.'

'Merci,' he says with a broad smile.

It's a glorious day with the sun still bright in the sky, so I decide to go for a little walk before I head back to the flat. The market is a feast for the senses, the rainbow colours of fruits piled high on carts and the contrasting scent of sugary popcorn and pungent cheeses from adjacent stalls. Taking a right turn out of the market square, I head up an old cobbled road with a slight incline, passing bakeries and clothes shops. At the top, I stop and take a breather on a bench after buying an iced lemon tea from a street kiosk. The high position gives a glorious view of the castle walls and the harbour beyond. I complete a circular walk, and as I head back through the market square the veg man is piling the last of his boxes into the van. He smiles at me and says, 'Do not forget the cake sample.'

Later, having prepared some dough ready to pop in the oven first thing, I settle down with a book for the evening. Faye appears on the balcony and gives a little twirl. She looks fabulous in a short flowery summer dress. She has the type of smooth olive skin that is already sporting an attractive tan.

'Wow. Olivier's in for a treat. Have fun.'

'I'll try.' She laughs before kissing me on the cheek and departing.

A couple of hours later, I take my make-up off then climb between the cool sheets of the comfortable bed. I come out of my emails, switch onto Facebook and for the first time ever use the search function. Maybe it's something I should have done before now. Perhaps Jake was right; maybe I was too comfortable with my life at home. But now it's time, especially as Jake is curious about his father. I nervously type the name André Duvall into the search bar.

Chapter Fourteen

There was no one in the search results who even vaguely resembled André, and this morning I'm wondering where I should look next. With hindsight, I'm wondering what I would have said if I'd found him anyway. 'Oh hello, André. Remember me from the summer of 1998? Oh and by the way, you have a twenty-year-old son.'

I must have fallen asleep over my laptop, as when I woke this morning, I nudged it with my leg and almost sent it crashing to the floor. A glance at the bedside clock told me that it was only 5 a.m., but dawn was almost beginning to break. I have no hope of returning to sleep, as my mind is whirring, so I decide to pull on some jeans and a T-shirt and head down to the bakery. Olivier is just arriving as I'm unlocking the door.

'Mon dieu, you are up early. I thought you were an intruder. Good job I didn't bash you over the head.'

'An intruder with a key?'

Olivier laughs. 'I never thought of that. So, I take it you couldn't sleep?'

We head inside, me flicking the lights on before Olivier fires up the huge bread oven.

'I fell into a deep sleep, actually. I just woke early and once I'm awake I'm awake. I thought it might be a chance to rustle up some cupcakes. They take no time at all. How was your date? Faye was still dead to the world when I left her.'

'Amazing. Your friend is a lot of fun.'

No doubt Faye will fill me in on the details of their date later.

Olivier sets about moulding the dough into various shapes before placing them into the hot oven with a long wooden paddle. He sets some pain au chocolat into an adjacent oven, along with some brioche.

By six thirty, the loaves are ready and I'm icing some cupcakes whilst another batch is in the oven. My work is a good distraction this morning, as I try to push thoughts of André to the back of my mind.

'So, what do we have here then?' asks Olivier, eyeing the bowls of different icing.

'Salted caramel, orange and lemon and strawberry and basil,' I reply, piping a spiral of icing onto a cupcake.

'May I?' asks Olivier as he dips a spoon into the strawberry icing, infused with basil. He nods his head as he tastes it.

'I really like it, but are you sure the town of Antibes is ready for your strawberry and basil cakes? '

'It's not at all how you imagine, is it? Although I must admit it's a bit of a Marmite cake.'

'You put Marmite in it too? The yeast spread?' asks Olivier, looking aghast.

'No,' I laugh. 'I mean you either love it or hate it.'

'I happen to love it. Where did you get the fresh basil?'

'I called into the market yesterday on the way home from the hospital. I'd forgotten how lovely the market here is.'

By the time the door is open at eight, a bright sun is already shining and a small queue has formed outside. Lilian Beaumont is first in line.

'Bonjour.' I smile as the customers filter in towards the counter.

'You are up early,' I remark, as Lilian eyes the selection of cakes under the glass counter.

'I am doing my shopping early. I have a date later.' She winks. 'It's not with someone who really fires my libido, but I'll give him a chance,' she says matter-of-factly. 'Now then, what do we have here?' She scrutinises the cakes, even though I've written cards displaying the flavours.

'Just something a little different from the usual. Depending on what customers think, they may never be seen here again.'

'Hmm. Orange and lemon or St Clements, I quite like the sound of. But why anybody would put salt in caramel is beyond me. I often wonder if it wasn't discovered by accident when a baker mistook salt for sugar.' She sniffs. 'And basil and strawberry? How did you come up with that?'

I decide to take one of each cupcake and cut them into small pieces for the customers to try.

The salted caramel and orange and lemon are met with a huge thumbs up. As expected, the vote is fifty-fifty for the basil and strawberry cake.

'It is indeed interesting,' says Lilian, wiping her mouth with a paper napkin. 'Not unpleasant, but maybe an acquired taste. I do admire someone who pushes the boundaries though,' she says with a broad smile. 'Well done.' The orange and lemon cake she declares 'Quite delicious.'

I feel like the star baker in a certain cookery show and feel rather proud.

Madame Beaumont leaves with a loaf, two orange and lemon cupcakes and some pain au chocolat.

'Au revoir, I hope your date goes well.' Olivier smiles with a raised eyebrow.

'Merci. We're going to a concert together. A recital of Bach's *Toccata and Fugue* in D minor. I do admire a large organ,' she shouts over her shoulder to Olivier, whose mouth gapes open.

The morning passes as quickly as it did the day before, and soon it's time for Olivier to head off home. I walk him to the door during a lull in service.

'So, what are your plans for the rest of the day?' I ask.

'I will probably sleep for a while. Early mornings usually mean I have a bit of a snooze in the afternoon. I'm out tonight though. I'm going with a friend to watch a Black Sabbath tribute band in a bar just out of town.'

'Do you like rock music then?'

'I love it. One of my prized possessions is a T-shirt signed by Ozzy Osborne himself, from the Black Sabbath millennium tour.'

'I know someone who would love that.' I tell Olivier all about Faye's love of rock music and pub cover bands.

'Really? I do not meet many women who share my taste in music. Then she must come along too. And you of course, Liv.'

'Umm, thanks, but it's really not my thing.'

'So are there many rock venues in Southport? Maybe I should take a little trip over there some day.'

'Quite a few. Pubs usually. There's a band with a huge following called Toxic Voltage appearing at the Atkinson Theatre this summer.'

'Sounds shocking.'

*

Faye and I arrive at the hospital to be greeted by the sight of my aunt sitting up and sipping a bowl of vegetable soup that she declares pretty good for hospital food.

She tells me that the doctor thinks she will be well enough to go home in another day or two.

'I feel fine,' she tells us. 'The physio is coming around again tomorrow. She must be on loan from the army bootcamp.'

'It's for your own good,' I remind her.

'So how's everything going at the bakery?' she asks.

'Everything is going really well. The customers have all been asking after you.' I take out several get-well-soon cards from my handbag. 'And it goes without saying that Olivier is a huge hit with the customers. Not to mention a certain friend of mine.' I grin broadly at Faye.

'Olivier is a darling. I've known him since he was a young boy. But –' Gen fixes her gaze on Faye – 'he is a free spirit. Fine if you aren't looking for anything serious.'

'Lucky I'm not, then.'

When we say our goodbyes, I find myself wondering when Olivier will find the love of his life, if ever. Some people can go a whole lifetime without finding the one that really feels like their other half. I thought I had found that in André before we parted ways.

Arriving back at the bakery, I head upstairs and fling open the patio door – the rooms are stifling in the heat. I head to my bedroom overlooking the main street and fling the window open there too. Lilian Beaumont is walking past. I call down to her.

'Bonjour, madame. How was your date?'

'Bonjour, Olivia. Not bad. He was entertaining enough. In fact, I had a thoroughly pleasant afternoon. I'm not sure I will be seeing him again though.'

'So, you weren't overly impressed by his organ?'

She raises her perfectly arched eyebrows then bursts into laughter.

'Mademoiselle Olivia. A real lady never tells!'

Faye brings us a fresh orange juice each, which we take outside onto the balcony.

'I thought you might have preferred a glass of wine?' I glance at Faye, who is looking relaxed and tanned.

'Sorry, did you want one?' She stands up to head inside.

'No, not at all. Orange juice is fine.'

'You just think it's unusual for me to be drinking orange juice on holiday?' she says, but with warmth in her voice. 'It's OK, I know you think that I drink too much.'

'The question is, do you think you drink too much?' I ask her honestly.

'I have been lately, yes.' She twists her glass around and gazes out across the harbour.

'Is it the stress of work?'

'Not really. Don't get me wrong, there's a lot of pressure, but I love my job. Sometimes I just get a bit lonely in the evenings, so I end up going to the pub because I know everyone there. Or drinking alone in the flat, which is even worse. I woke up with a hangover a couple of weeks ago and was almost late for school. I swore that wouldn't happen again. It was a bit of a wake-up call. I'm not going down that road.'

I feel a little guilt at not realising Faye felt lonely in the evenings. We meet up at least a couple of nights a week, but it's clearly not enough. I'm quite happy with my own company in the evening after a busy day. I guess we're all different. Then again, it might not be the kind of company I offer that she's longing for.

'Don't ever feel lonely.' I place my hand over hers and squeeze it gently. 'I'm just in by myself most evenings too. Call over anytime you like. I mean that. And remember, there's always cake…'

'So my liver will be OK but I'll gain about three stone?'

'Oh of course – you drink that low-calorie real ale, don't you?' We both burst out laughing. 'We should go for walks in the evening when the weather's nice. There's no excuse with those lovely coastal walks on the doorstep.'

We chat a while longer, and I feel happy that Faye has recognised that she needs to moderate her drinking. My phone starts buzzing into life and it's Jo. She's video calling.

'Hi, Jo, how's things?' Faye and I are waving furiously as her face comes into focus.

'Good thanks. Missing you already though. Coffee at the pier café isn't quite the same without you two. What's the weather like there?'

I hold the phone to show her the brilliant blue sky.

'Right, that's enough of that then. It's windy and cold here today.'

Faye tells her all about her date with Olivier.

'Well, you never told me there would be a hot Frenchman working at the bakery. I might have come along after all.' She laughs.

'Who said he was hot?' says Faye.

'Well, is he?'

'Gorgeous,' says Faye. 'I'm glad you didn't give me any extra competition.' She laughs, although I think she half means it. 'It's nothing serious. He's never exclusive with anyone. He could have his own website called playboy.com'

'Oh dear, I've conjured up a completely different image.' Jo roars with laughter. 'Right, I'd better be off. I've got to pick a poodle up from a dog grooming parlour – it's had pink highlights put in.'

'You are joking!'

'I'm actually not. I swear they'll be painting their claws next. Maybe even a bit of intimate sparkle. Dog vajazzling could be the next big thing.'

'Oh good grief.' I'm laughing so hard my stomach aches.

'On a serious note, have you started asking around about André?'

'To be honest, I haven't, not yet. Gen's only just recovering from her operation.'

We chat for a while longer with a promise to talk again soon, waving furiously again as she hangs up.

August 1998

'A day at a casino?'

'Sure, why not?

André is filled with excitement and is almost bouncing around with pent-up energy.

'In Monte Carlo?'

'But of course, where else?' He grabs me by both hands with a huge grin on his face. His enthusiasm is infectious.

'I just kind of thought you would need a lot of money to go to those kinds of places, that's all,' I say, although I feel a tingle of excitement.

I imagine men in tuxedos and women in glamourous dresses sitting at poker tables drinking champagne, but André tells me that there are slot machines at the casino where anybody can try their hand without going anywhere near the gaming tables.

'And the machines can pay out big money. Last year a widow from St Raphael won the jackpot – 300,000 francs. Really, you will love it!'

His enthusiasm is infectious and I find myself imagining what it would really be like to go there.

'Monaco is not very far from here. It is a must-see place while you are in the South of France. When the Grand Prix is on, the roads are closed down and people watch from the top of the hill. Some residents in the tall apartments can even see the circuit from their bedroom window.'

'Sounds exciting.'

'Maybe you should come back and experience it sometime.'

'Do you think I would be able to get David Coulthard's autograph?'

'Who knows? But why would you be interested in Formula One drivers? They have quite a reputation as playboys.' He pulls me towards him protectively.

'Are you jealous?' I tease. 'Maybe if I scoop a big prize I can mingle in the same circles.'

André picks me up and throws me over his shoulder. 'Right, you are going nowhere near those gaming tables.'

We kiss passionately and I feel a flutter of excitement at the possibility of being able to return here during Grand Prix week.

❧

The next day we took a bus along the coast road as rain lashed down. I thought it looked miserable and that everything looks better in the sunshine. Then, just as our bus approached the sign for Monaco, the clouds parted and a bright sun beamed down from the sky, illuminating the yacht-lined harbour. Before long, the marble and gold casino looms into view. André tells me it is a lavish example of belle époque architecture, and I'm impressed by his knowledge.

I'd made a special effort to look smart, as I didn't want to risk being turned away for being too casual, despite André's reassurance that many day-trippers entered the casino to play the machines. As the doormen eyed us both up and down before allowing us entry, I felt like a schoolgirl who was completely out of her depth. We headed to the slot machines in the Amerique room, which opens to the general public. André held my hand tightly and told me that he felt lucky and maybe it was because he had the prettiest girl in the room by his side. I felt giddy with excitement when André slid the first coin into the machine, a feeling that was quickly replaced by anxiety as his money was frittered away. He held the last franc in his hand, kissed it and said, 'This is the one.' And as the coin noisily juddered into the bowels of the machine, unbelievably, it was.

My mouth gaped open and my heart raced as 6500 francs came cascading noisily out of the machine. André let out a cry before he lifted me off my feet and swirled me around, calling me his lucky charm. He kissed me on the lips in front of a crowd, who were clapping and cheering. My head was reeling. It was a small fortune to us.

We wandered the historic streets of Monte Carlo, dined on food in the smartest of cafés and drank champagne in chic bars. Some of the well-heeled diners gave us sidelong glances as we giggled and chattered away loudly, but we didn't care. André whispered to me that his money was as good as anyone's and we ate and drank with a feeling of defiance.

Passing a hotel as evening slowly began to draw in and the glamourous people from the yachts on the harbour came out to play, we passed a hotel and André took me by the hand and eyed me seriously.

'Let's stay here tonight,' he said, staring at me with his hypnotic eyes. 'Let's live a little. It's been such a wonderful day – I don't want it to end,' he breathed as he kissed my neck and drew me close to him. I telephoned my aunt from a phone booth and told her that we were heading to a nightclub with a group of André's friends and would be staying over at one of their apartments. I felt torn, half guilty about lying, half excited. Yet I would have been so embarrassed about her knowing I would be spending the night alone in a hotel with André.

Inside the smart hotel that overlooked the harbour, André and I slipped between the crisp cotton sheets of the bed and made love for the very first time. It was the evening that changed everything in more ways than I could ever have imagined. The type of memorable evening that is replayed in the memory over and over again as the years roll by. Shortly after midnight, I awoke to get a glass of water and watched a firework display over the harbour from the bedroom window. It captured the magical feeling of the evening just perfectly.

Chapter Fifteen

Three days later, Aunt Gen has been discharged from hospital and is making good headway, moving slowly around her apartment with the aid of crutches and reading on the sunny balcony. Mum and Dad have not long arrived from Spain, and are already fussing over Gen. They're staying in the third bedroom tonight, so Faye will move into the twin guest room with me.

'Make sure you keep moving,' Dad is instructing Gen in a tone that is kind but firm.

Mum is bustling about in the kitchen, making tea.

'I'll leave them to it.' Mum smiles as she fills a kettle. 'Your dad is the best person to get Gen up and about again. I'm afraid I'm far too soft.'

'She's determined, Mum. I'm sure she'll be up and about properly in no time.'

Mum places some tea and a bowl of chicken soup and bread onto a tray to carry into the lounge for Gen.

'Right, I'll see you shortly,' I say. 'I'm just heading downstairs for the last hour in the shop. How are you feeling?' I ask Gen.

'Fine,' says my aunt in a slightly exasperated tone. 'Your father is so bossy.' She shoots a sidelong glance at Dad but there is a smile on her face.

'It's the best way. The doctor said you have to get moving around quickly, not languish in your bed.'

'Languish?'

'Sorry, you know what I mean. Anyway, that's probably enough for one day. At least I know you can get yourself around now.'

'I can always help walk you to the toilet,' says Mum, patting Gen's arm affectionately.

'Gloria, you're not helping,' says Dad. 'We're supposed to be encouraging independence.'

Gen flops down on to the pillow. 'Maybe when the führer isn't looking,' she whispers to Mum.

My parents follow me down to the bakery to meet Olivier. There's a trio of young women at the counter when we enter the shop. They're in a huddle, eyeing what's left of the day's bakes as Olivier chats to them. They're hanging on to his every word and laughing.

His rippling arm muscles are on display today in a tight white T-shirt. He smiles a dazzling white smile and steps forward to kiss my mother on both cheeks.

Mum pats her hair coyly and looks a little flustered by the Olivier effect. Dad intercepts his embrace with a warm handshake.

'Bonjour, enchanted to meet you both. I can see where Olivia gets her good looks from.' He charms Mum as Dad feasts his eyes on a chocolate and vanilla brioche.

We chat for a while longer, Mum telling Olivier how wonderful my cakes are.

'I agree. I'm sure she was inspired by Gen, just as I was,' she tells him before heading back upstairs with dad.

It's a little after seven in the evening, and after making a light supper of smoked mackerel and salad, I leave my parents enjoying a glass of wine on the balcony whilst Gen is gently snoozing. As it's still warm outside, Faye and I decide to head down towards the beach for a stroll. Some families are only just packing up their things and heading off, no doubt grateful for the long, lazy days of summer. A young couple are still swimming in the sea as an orange sunset gently begins to set over the horizon. I exhale deeply and take in my surroundings. What would it have felt like to have settled in a place like this? Maybe even raised a family here? Those thoughts have flitted in and out of my mind over the years, but standing here I am filled with curiosity and what ifs. Tomorrow, without fail, I will ask around about André.

Sitting at a small café overlooking the beach and enjoying a frappé, I notice a couple coming out of the café opposite. A man is smiling at a brunette woman of a similar age and holding a young girl's hand. The child, about four years old, stretches her arms upwards and giggles loudly as the man hoists her up high on to his shoulders. They look like the perfect family. I feel a pang of regret that I never got to experience the same thing with Jake when he was a child. As the man turns, I catch a glimpse of his face. The smile looks so familiar. His demeanour, the way he walks. I am almost frozen to the spot. My heart quickens pace as I continue staring at him, barely able to move. As he turns in my direction, I cover my face with a menu. I'm pretty sure it's him. I've just seen André. He's with his family. I breathe deeply as I try to compose myself.

'What's up with you?' asks Faye. 'You look as though you've seen a ghost.'

'Maybe I have. I'm sure that was André.'

'What?! Where?'

She glances over in the direction in which I am pointing, as the family walk on.

'Quick. Let's follow them,' she says, throwing some money on the table and grabbing my hand.

'And then what?' I say, stumbling along as Faye leads the way.

We follow them for a short distance before I lose my nerve and duck into a nearby alleyway. Faye has put her sunglasses on and turned the collar up on her white shirt.

'This is madness,' I sigh. 'What am I supposed to say to him? He's clearly with his family. I think we need to leave. And look at you – all you need is a false nose and glasses. He doesn't even know you, Faye.'

'I haven't changed that much.' She pouts. 'He might recognise me as your friend. My hair is still the same.' She strokes her short, aubergine-coloured crop.

'Don't be ridiculous. It was twenty years ago.'

We peep out from the alleyway as the family take a seat on a low wall.

'Let's go back,' I say, as we scuttle along furtively in the direction we have just come from. I feel like I'm in a scene straight from the Pink Panther movie.

I steady my breathing as we head back through town towards the bakery, shocked at the effect seeing André has had on me. He was with his family. A family that knows nothing about the grown-up son he has in England. Christ, he doesn't even know that himself. But what the hell did I expect? Did I think time would somehow stand still for him? I may have thought about André many times over the years, but for him I may have been nothing more than a holiday romance. Twenty years have passed by. It was a lifetime ago when he was with me. I feel such an idiot.

Arriving back at the bakery, I feel the need to talk to my son. I'm about to call him when my phone rings. It's Jake.

'Hi, Mum, how's it going?'

It feels so wonderful to hear Jake's voice and I'm tempted to tell him everything, before calmness takes over. Besides, what would I tell him exactly?

'Pretty good thanks. Gen's on the mend and your grandparents have arrived. Dad is bossing her about and making sure she does her exercises correctly. How are things with you?'

'Good thanks. I created a new cake today. Sam said you should add it to your menu.'

'Really, what is it?'

'It's a lime and passionfruit cupcake with a coconut frosting.'

'Wow, that sounds amazing. If Sam thinks it should be included in the cake menu, then go for it.'

'Really? That's great. Anyway, I'd better go. I'm on a shift at the pub soon.'

It feels good to be talking about normal stuff after spotting the potential André. We chat for a little while longer, and soon I'm in bed trying to read a chapter of my book but feeling distracted, my mind racing. By the time I'm dozing off, I've accepted that it might not even have been André – we never got a clear look at the guy, it's been twenty years and I've been so preoccupied with what he might look like now. But even if it wasn't him, seeing someone so similar stirred up memories in me – and my panicked reaction hardly suggested I'm ready for a calm and rational meeting with the father of my son. I eventually drift into a fitful sleep, another early start just around the corner.

Chapter Sixteen

I arrive at exactly the same time as Olivier in the morning. He's dressed casually in jeans and a black T-shirt and quickly retrieves a white apron from the back of a door.

'Bonjour, Olivia. I hope you are well this morning.' He flashes a wide smile with impossibly perfect teeth and sweeps back his dark, thick hair.

'I'm fine, thanks. A little tired. I wake up much later back home.'

I tell him a little more about how I run my online cake business.

'Ah, one of the benefits of working from home.' Olivier sets about making some bread and I notice that he works quickly and efficiently. I find myself staring at him as he expertly stretches and kneads the dough, shaping it into loaves with his strong hands. Gathering everything I need, I set about making the cakes for the shop and we chat easily as we work alongside each other.

'Do you miss working on the boats when you're in here on a day like this?'

'Not really. It makes a refreshing change. A little of what you fancy does you good.' He winks.

'I suppose so. Messing about on boats sounds like a dream job, though.'

'I can't deny it's a lot of fun. Especially in the summer months. My father's yacht is the one to party on, though.'

Good looks and a family with money. Some people have all the luck.

'Who's been running the boat while you've been here this week?'

'My brother. He's happy to take to the open sea every now and then. He's a sculptor. He sells his work at a tiny studio near the harbour.'

'My aunt tells me you showed a real flair for baking from a young age.'

'Really? She told you that?'

He turns to face me with his incredible chocolate-brown eyes.

'She did.'

'I spent a lot of time in here when I was young, buying all sorts of things. I had a great teacher in Gen. I'm happy to indulge my passion for a week or so and I was happy to help out. I don't think I could do it every day of my life, though.'

'So you don't see yourself ever opening your own place?'

'I'm not sure I could give it the commitment.' He turns to face me, his eyes crinkling at the corners as he smiles.

I do get the impression commitment is something Olivier would have a problem with.

The morning passes in a blur, and the shop seems to be full of hungry young women lingering around the counter and flirting with our hunky guest baker. Olivier chats to them all, and they glance over their shoulders as they leave and say they will see him later down at the harbour. Faye pops her head in too – she's off clothes shopping further down the coast. As I'm replenishing some cupcakes under the glass counter a woman walks into the bakery and stops midway across the tiled floor and stares at me. As she walks closer, her face breaks into a smile.

'Excusez-moi, is your name Olivia?'

'Yes, it is.' I scan her face for some sort of clue to any past acquaintance.

'I worked at Marineland many years ago. You used to come often?'

The mention of Marineland makes my heart thump faster in my chest.

'Yes, I did, but it was over twenty years ago. How did you recognise me?'

'That fabulous hair.' She smiles. 'You haven't changed.'

I touch my brown curls; they really have changed little over the years. I have no recollection of the woman standing in front of me, although I suppose back then I only had eyes for André.

'My name is Françoise,' she says, extending her hand. 'I worked in the gift shop over the summer. I remember you being the envy of all the female staff – you were the one who dated André.'

'You remember André too?'

'Of course. Who would not? All the girls had a crush on André. I remember, you used to sit in the front row watching the show, or wait outside for him to finish.' She has a broad smile on her face.

'I think I was probably one of his many conquests.' I sigh.

Françoise frowns. 'No, I do not think so. He was never with any of the girls who worked there, despite their best efforts, of course. And I do not think he ever got involved with tourists. It would seem he made an exception for you, though. I think I have a photograph of you two somewhere.'

'A photo?' I say in surprise.

'Yes. There was a board in the staff room full of photographs taken in the show arena. There is a picture of you and André together, I am sure of it. When I stopped working there, I took a few of the photographs from the board as souvenirs.'

I'm speechless. The one thing I never had was a photo of André and me together. I had one of those disposable cameras at the time and did actually take some photos of us – not the close-up selfie style photos of today, but snaps that André had taken of me throwing my head back and laughing or swimming in the sea. I remember asking a stranger to take one of us together, leaning against a beach wall. When I arrived home, I was devastated to discover that I had somehow managed to lose the camera in transit, or forgotten to pack it. I never thought I would have a photo of that summer we spent together, and feel excited by the thought.

'Would you mind if I had a look at it? Do you live locally?'

'Not far away. I live in Juan-Les-Pins. Maybe we could meet somewhere for coffee sometime?'

We chat for a while longer before swapping numbers and vowing to meet up.

'Have you ever seen André around?' I ask, as I grab a brush and begin to sweep the shop floor – it's pointless this far from closing time, but I need to do something with my hands as nerves take over.

'Never, but as I say, I live in the next town. Although I may have passed him in the street without even realising it. Most people change a lot. Apart from you, that is.'

I've often thought about how I spent most of the summer with André, yet he never took me to his family home. In truth, I've spent the last twenty years thinking maybe that was a sign that he wasn't as serious about our relationship as I was, but Françoise's memories of us reminds me that what we felt was strong, and mutual.

I still can't believe I will soon be able to look at a picture of me and André together. A visible memory of my past. And perhaps more importantly, something to finally show Jake.

Later that evening, we take Gen for a gentle walk around the block as the sun begins to set, before returning to a supper of a pork and apple casserole that had been slowly simmering in the oven.

'I'm going to miss you when you go home. I've been thoroughly spoiled by your cooking,' says Gen, about to retire to her room with a cup of tea. 'My very first walk and I'm exhausted. Bonne nuit, everyone.'

'I'm heading to bed too. I've been up since five thirty this morning,' I say.

'I've told you. Take a little power nap in the afternoon, it works wonders,' says Gen.

'Maybe I should try it. Good night everyone.' It's a little after nine thirty as I head to my bedroom. My head is a jumble of thoughts. André could still be in France. Sometimes I think I have forgotten what his face looks like, but I will soon have a picture to remind me. I pick up my phone to find a text from Jo.

Hi Liv, Hope all is good with your family! Another funny story for you and Faye: I bumped (literally) into hunky guy in the pub today! Made him drop a whole tray of drinks and as I ran away heard him say something about me not being able to blame it on the dogs this time. Mortified! BUT, I think he had a smile on his face so maybe there's hope! Ring me when you've got time. xx

I snuggle under my sheets with a smile on my face and, feeling exhausted, soon drift off into a deep sleep.

Chapter Seventeen

The St Clements cakes have been such a big hit with the customers that the next day, around lunchtime, I nip to the market for some oranges and lemons to make some more. The guy on the fruit and veg stall places the fruit in a brown paper bag and tells me with a wink that he is still waiting for one of my strawberry and basil cakes.

'I'll have to make you one especially, then.' I smile. 'They haven't really been back on sale. A mixed reaction from customers, I'm afraid.'

'OK. Do not worry. A St Clements will do.'

'Probably a safer bet. They really are selling like hot cakes.'

'I will add a little extra for the trouble,' he says, popping an extra orange and lemon into the bag.

The market is flooded with sunlight as midday shoppers browse the variety of stalls on the cobbled street. A flower stand is displaying beautiful blooms in buckets alongside a bread stall selling fresh brioches and farmhouse loaves. A man on a fruit stall is calling out, telling people about a special offer on raspberries. I'm buying two large tubs, deciding raspberry buns will be on sale tomorrow at the bakery, when I spot a woman at the bread stall with a young child. The little girl is pointing to a stand next door that is cooking fresh crêpes and displaying jars of Nutella, but Mum shakes her head and says something in French. Mum is probably around the same age as me, and is slim and stylish with shoulder-length dark hair and huge designer sunglasses. As they pass alongside me, I catch my breath. It's the same woman and child who I spotted with André near the beach café two nights ago. The child glances up at me with her striking blue eyes and smiles. She has the same eyes as André. I'm about to speak to her, but she darts past before I get the chance. I try to hurry the fruit seller so I can follow them, but by the time he has laboriously sorted out the best raspberries for me, mother and daughter have disappeared into the busy crowd.

Back at the bakery, I put the raspberries away and make myself a coffee to gather my thoughts. I am certain now that André has a family of his own. Thinking logically, what exactly did I think he would be doing all this time? Nobody goes travelling forever. But I can't quite stop the disappointment I feel in my heart. I need to figure out what I do next though, as I need to keep my promise to Jake. I'm lost in my thoughts when I feel a gentle tap on my head with a tube from an empty kitchen roll.

'I think your lunch break is over,' says Olivier. 'We have run out of those orange and lemon cakes again and customers are asking for them.'

'No problem,' I say, slipping off my chair and gathering the ingredients to make another batch.

Glancing out towards the shop front, I notice the woman and child from the market enter the shop. The little girl points to some pains au chocolat and the mum purchases six. Olivier chats to them for a few minutes, and his eyes follow the mother as she leaves.

'Do you know that woman?' I demand from Olivier when they close the door behind them.

'No, I've never seen her before. I'm sure I would have remembered her.' He grins. 'She was just telling me that her daughter wanted to buy a crêpe from the market but she told her there was a shop nearby that sold the most delicious pastries.'

This is the moment. My heart racing, I decide to be brave and go haring out of the shop to speak to them, flour in my hair and apron on. But once again, they are nowhere to be seen.

'Are you OK?' Olivier asks when I return. 'What was that all about?'

'Oh, never mind. Just someone I thought I recognised. Anyway, it's just as well your pains au chocolat are up to the same standard as Gen's, or she might have been in for a disappointment.'

I'm keen to steer the conversation away from the woman and little girl. Olivier gives me a sceptical look but clearly decides not to push me.

'As good as? Not better?'

'They are both excellent,' I say, diplomatically.

꽃

The afternoon is pretty quiet in the shop and we have tidied up and cleaned the kitchen with an hour or so until closing time. Olivier left at two, so it's just Valerie and me in the shop.

'Why don't you get off early?' I suggest. 'I can manage here. It's a beautiful afternoon; go and enjoy some sun.'

'Are you sure? There is over an hour to go.'

'I insist. And don't worry, you won't be paid any less,' I tell her.

'Merci, Olivia. If you are sure. I will see you in the morning.'

While it's quiet in the shop I sit and think about tomorrow's cakes. As well as the raspberry buns, I decide on St Clements cakes, madeleines and chocolate éclairs. It's been a while since I've made choux pastry so I decide on a practice run. I'm just blending some butter into the flour with my fingertips when the bell on the shop door tinkles. It's Lilian Beaumont.

'Bonjour, Olivia. Do you have anything left?'

I nod to a few crusty loaves in a basket, three St Clements cakes and a large chocolate and vanilla brioche.

'Surely you are not buying bread at the end of the day?' I ask in surprise.

'Of course not. I'm having a friend staying with me for a short while. He's recuperating from a motorbike accident. It was probably the drugs that caused it,' she says matter-of-factly. 'I really can't be bothered making a dessert. Hmm, there doesn't seem to be much left here though.'

'Is it the man with the organ?'

'No. It's an old flame I met yesterday when I went for a day out to St Tropez. He bought me a cocktail in a bar then drove me home, as I'd taken the bus there. I was rather disappointed he didn't have his motorbike with him as I fancied a zip along the coast. He's still feeling a little fragile and has a bit of a bad leg following the accident. He lives alone so I said he could stay with me for a few days. I'll soon have him back to peak fitness. He was a superb lover, as I recall. I do not remember why I dumped him.'

'Lucky you,' I say, thinking that nothing Lilian Beaumont says ever surprises me.

'Excusez-moi? Don't you mean lucky him?' She raises a perfectly plucked eyebrow.

'Bien sur. Right, well, if you call back in an hour, you can have some fresh chocolate éclairs if you like. The front door will be locked, but I'll still be here, just knock on the side door.'

'Très bien, excellente! A chocolate éclair will be just perfect. You really are a good girl, Olivia.'

A good girl. A great friend. A wonderful mother. That's me. Only I've carried a hulking great secret around for over twenty years from Jake's father. Maybe I'm not as perfect as everyone seems to think I am.

Chapter Eighteen

A week after aunt Gen's operation she is steadily getting her strength back as she continues her short daily walks with my parents. She has been inundated with well-wishers, and has spent several afternoons sipping tea (or gin and tonic) with them on the sunny balcony of the apartment. I don't know what they talk about, but judging by their throaty laughter carrying through into the lounge, it must be something pretty entertaining.

I had a text from Françoise this morning, and I'm meeting her for coffee at three o'clock in a place called Café Flore on the seafront of Juan-les-Pins. I didn't manage to speak to André's wife the other day, but if I can get the photo from Françoise, it will be something for Jake, and she might know something else that could help me find André now. Olivier tells me the bus that stops across the road is a short ride to the café, which is handy as Faye is taking the car tomorrow for a drive into Cannes to do some shopping. I'm excited at the thought of looking at some photographs of Marineland all those years ago.

Finishing up in the shop, I pop two orange and lemon cakes into a bag with an unsold brioche. I make the short walk to the market in the hope that the fruit and veg man is still there. I find him packing away the last of his things, about to leave.

'You are here late today,' I remark, as he's usually gone by four.

'I know. Trade has been non-stop today. I have sold all of my salad and strawberries. This glorious weather is good for business.'

'Well, have a relaxing evening. Here's a little something for after your supper.'

'Ah, merci,' he says, peering into the bag. 'The smell of the vanilla in the brioche is making me hungry. But I must resist! My wife will not be happy if I don't eat her cassoulet. Have a good evening too. Au revoir.'

I enjoy the ride along the coast road on the bus, watching people strolling along the promenade and others on the beach beyond, lazing around on sun loungers as the sun continues to beat down. At traffic lights, I glance out of the window and meet the gaze of two young men in a red open-topped sports car. One of them raises his sunglasses and winks at me, which makes me smile. My white broderie anglaise dress is sleeveless, showing off my tan perfectly. Just under twenty minutes later, I disembark and walk along the beachfront in search of Café Flore, which I find on the left-hand side of the pier. Françoise isn't there when I arrive and, for a minute, I wonder whether she will even bother turning up.

The café has blue walls adorned with watercolours and floor-to-ceiling windows that overlook the sea, and I can't help thinking of the café at the end of the pier back home in Southport. I spy a blackboard displaying today's specials – chicken suprême, coq au vin, crème brûlée and plum tarte tatin – and realise I am rather hungry.

A few minutes later the door opens and in walks Françoise, her blonde hair scraped back in a ponytail. She's carrying a brown satchel over her shoulder.

'Bon soir, Olivia. How are you?'

'I'm OK, thanks. Are you hungry at all?'

'Yes, very.'

'That's good. I'm dying for a plate of coq au vin.'

'I'll have the same.'

We place our food order with a passing waitress, along with two mineral waters.

Françoise opens her bag and takes out a brown envelope that she slides towards me. I tentatively open it and take out a photograph, and find myself staring into the blue eyes of André. Even now my heart lurches. We made such a good-looking couple, if I do say so myself. André has his arm draped around my shoulders and we're both beaming for the camera. We both look so happy, and they do say the camera never lies.

'Thank you, Françoise,' I say quietly. There are six other photographs, including one of the killer whale, and I smile at the memory of me kissing him.

'Keep them all, I've made copies.' Françoise smiles.

I thank her and slip them into my bag. 'Sorry to ask, but do you know anything about André's family? Did they live locally?'

'I'm afraid I don't. As I say, I never really knew him that well.'

A few minutes later, a waft of something wonderful signals our food arriving and we hungrily tuck into the tasty, rich casserole. The chicken, which is falling off the bone, is nestled in a thick red wine and garlic sauce. It's heavenly.

'I'd better not kiss anyone this evening. All this garlic,' says Françoise.

'I know. I think I might have to sit at the back of the bus on the return journey, away from everyone.'

We sip our water and Françoise tells me that she is married with a ten-year-old daughter, and works part-time at a leisure centre as a receptionist.

Soon enough, it's time for us to go our separate ways.

'Well, bye, Françoise. Thank you so much for the photos. You have my number now, if you ever fancy another meet-up.' I realise I mean it, as Françoise and I seem to have really clicked. She may have been a friend to me all those years go if I hadn't been so wrapped up in André.

'For sure,' she says, stepping forward to give me a hug and a kiss on each cheek. 'Au revoir, Olivia. Take care.'

I take out the photo on the bus journey home and find that I can't stop staring at it. I'd forgotten how much Jake looks like his father. He has the same captivating eyes and the same strong, masculine jawline. Jakes's full mouth is the only thing he's inherited from me.

It's just before nine when I disembark the bus a few stops before my own one, as I feel like a little walk. Heading down towards the harbour, the twinkling lights of the boats come into view as dusk gently falls. Suddenly I hear someone call my name. Olivier is standing on the deck of a smart-looking yacht with his arms draped around two stunning bikini-clad women, one blonde, one brunette. Faye has texted me to say she has a bit of an upset tummy so will be staying in tonight and will see me back at the apartment. It doesn't look as though Olivier is losing any sleep over it, I can't help thinking. Although knowing Olivier as I'm beginning to, I think maybe a lot of it is just image.

'Olivia! Come and have a drink,' he says, raising a glass of champagne. He's looking gorgeous and every inch the playboy in a pink shirt, tight white jeans and designer shades.

I stroll over towards the yacht and can smell his expensive after-shave as I approach him. 'Sorry, Olivier, but I'm ready to go to bed.'

'Without me plying you with champagne first?' He wiggles his eyebrows up and down and the brunette pushes him on the arm playfully and tuts.

We chat for a short while before I head off, exhausted, feeling like I could sleep forever. Olivier looks as fresh as a daisy. I tell him I hope he won't be late for work in the morning but he shrugs and tells me his timing is perfect. Perhaps he takes afternoon power naps like Lilian Beaumont and Gen.

Back at the apartment, I say goodnight to my parents and Gen, who are in the lounge drinking tea and having a game of Scrabble, before heading into the bedroom. Faye is sat up reading a magazine, a bottle of water on her bedside table.

'How are you feeling?' I ask, flopping down on to the adjacent bed.

'A lot better thanks. I'm not sure if it's something I ate or a little bit too much sun.'

After changing into my pyjamas, I take the photograph out of my bag and glance at it once more before showing it to Faye. I barely recognise the young woman staring back at me, her eyes filled with love. My head was full of dreams at the time, believing anything was possible before the reality of returning home and raising a child alone became my life. Time has flown by so quickly. It's nice to have a piece of my past to look back on, however bittersweet some of those memories are.

'Oh my goodness, I had forgotten how gorgeous he was,' says Faye when I show her the photo. 'No wonder you were so smitten by him.'

I tell Faye all about Françoise and that she knew nothing about his family or where he may be living now.

'I'm sure everything will turn out exactly as it's meant to,' Faye tells me reassuringly.

'Not if I don't do a bit more asking around. Someone in this town must know what became of him and I owe it to Jake to at least try. It might be easier now that I have a photograph. I could ask people locally if they recognise him. I think I'll go back to Marineland too. The photograph might jog the memory of one or two workers there.'

'It's worth a try I suppose.' Faye shrugs.

We chat for a long while and I ask her how she feels about Olivier.

'I really like him. But I'm realistic. He's a player and I'm on holiday. I don't expect it to go anywhere.'

It's just as well, I think, as I get an image of the glamourous women draped all over him this evening.

If only I had her confidence.

I say goodnight to Faye and snuggle down into my quilt, leaving the photograph on my bedside table. Soon enough, I am out like a light.

❧

The next morning, my mother is tapping on my bedroom door and I wake with a start. I glance at my watch and to my horror it's 6.45.

'Oh no! I must have slept through my alarm. I wonder if Olivier's arrived?' I say, sitting up and rubbing my eyes.

'Olivier has been downstairs since before six. Valerie has been in for a while too, whipping up some cakes, so don't worry.'

She places a cup of tea on to the bedside table and I notice her cast a glance at the photograph before I quickly put it away. Faye is still flat out, despite us chatting.

'Thanks for the tea, Mum.' I gulp it down quickly before heading downstairs. Olivier is taking a tray of bread from the oven and smiles broadly when he sees me.

'Ah, good morning, Olivia.' He looks ridiculously fresh. 'Maybe it's just as well you didn't join me for a drink last night. You would have still been out for the count,' he teases.

Valerie casts a sideways glance at me and grins.

'Sorry about that. I think the early mornings caught up with me, that's all. And I do stay here until closing time,' I say in my defence.

'I know. I am teasing.' He smiles.

Valerie has whipped up some fruit tarts and cream horns and is currently putting the icing on some red velvet cupcakes.

'They look amazing, Valerie. I'll make some Florentines and raspberry buns.' I scrape my hair back with a band, hook an apron over my head and set to work.

The morning is busy as usual, the local women still making eyes at Olivier when they call in for their morning bread. Around lunchtime, I take a short break and nip upstairs. It's been over a week since Aunt Gen's operation and she's coming on leaps and bounds.

Mum follows me into the kitchen with some teacups as I pour myself a glass of orange juice.

'The man in the photograph I noticed on the bedside table,' she begins, turning to face me. 'He looks just like Jake. Is it his father?'

Mum does not believe in beating about the bush. I tell her all about Françoise calling in to the bakery and meeting with her. I don't know why, but I don't tell her that I think I've seen André in town with his wife and child. Although the more I think about it, I'm not even sure it was him.

'It must be difficult,' she says as she rinses the teacups in the sink. 'Jake has never known his father. I wonder if he still lives around here?'

'I don't know.' I shrug. 'He could be anywhere in the world. We were just kids when we got together.'

My mother pats me on the arm and smiles.

'I know. It's never too late to meet your biological family, though. I watch that long-lost family programme and some people haven't seen each other for over forty years. Jake's still a young man.'

I wonder if this is Mum's way of saying that I should track down André now that I'm over here. If she only knew that's just what I'm trying (and currently failing) to do.

There's a huge bowl of salad niçoise in the fridge and I take some out on to the huge balcony to eat, enjoying the feel of the sunshine on my arms. It's a very relaxing space, despite the faint noise of traffic coming from the street at the front.

Back in the shop, afternoon trade is slow and I'd be tempted to shut up early if there wasn't quite so much so much stock left. Maybe I'll reduce the price of the cakes in the hope that the news will quickly spread around the neighbourhood.

I discuss it with Valerie and she agrees it's worth a try, so she knocks up a poster and I pop it in the window. Within fifteen minutes there is a small queue as customers line up to buy some sweet treats for after dinner and we quickly sell out. One of the customers is the guy from the fruit and veg stall in the market.

'Bonjour. I heard there was a cake sale. News travels fast around here.' He smiles as he buys the last of the day's bakes. As he is about to leave, I grab the photo of André from my bag and walk around the counter.

'Can I ask you something? Have you lived in Antibes all your life?'

'My whole life, yes. Why do you ask?'

I show him the photo and ask if he recognises the man in the picture.

He studies it for a few seconds before answering.

'I cannot be sure, but he does look like a man who works in Café Rouge.' He directs me to the café which is a few streets away.

I decide to head there right away and my heart is thumping as I step inside. There's a man behind the counter with his back to me as he prepares a coffee from a machine. He is the same height and has the same build as Andre. His hair that touches his neck is brown with grey streaks. My mouth is dry as I wait for him to turn around.

It seems like an eternity before he turns and places the coffee on the counter for a customer.

'Bonjour, madame, what can I get you?'

I can hardly speak as I study his face. Those hypnotic eyes, the same strong jaw. He looks so familiar. But it's not him.

'Madame?'

'Yes. Oh, I'm so sorry for staring, I was just looking for a man.'

He chuckles as he flashes his wedding ring. 'I'm afraid I cannot help you.'

'No, I mean this man. Someone thought it might have been you.' I show him the photo and he studies it.

'It was taken a long time ago, but perhaps he hasn't changed much,' I tell him.

'I am very flattered. He is a handsome man. But sorry, I do not know who he is.'

I thank the café worker then head back to the bakery as I consider my next move.

'That cake sale was a good idea,' says Valerie as she wipes down the glass display fridge. 'Maybe it's something we should do every day. I hate to throw anything away.'

'Perhaps you're right. Although it's unusual to have so much left at the end of the day.'

Before long, Valerie is gathering her things and saying goodbye and I have one last tidy around before closing up for the day. Tomorrow there will be more buns, madeleines and cupcakes on sale that will keep fresher a little longer than the cream-filled cakes.

Heading towards the front door to close up, I notice a woman approach the shop. It was the woman I spotted with André. Today she's alone.

'I'm sorry, but we've sold out of everything.' I force a smile. I'm determined to speak about André, but my heart is beating fast, and my mouth suddenly feels dry.

'Don't worry, I haven't come to buy any bread. I have come to talk to you. That is, if your name is Olivia?'

Chapter Nineteen

The woman, who introduces herself as Angela, suggests we go for a coffee at a nearby café so I grab my bag and lock the shop door behind me, wondering where on earth this meeting is going to lead. Maybe I was staring at her in the market. I haven't seen André in twenty years, yet I feel an irrational sense of jealousy towards this woman. It's ridiculous. What right do I have to feel like that?

We order two coffees and take a seat on at a table outside.

'So, how do you know my name?' I ask, eager to get to the point, intrigue running through my body.

'From conversations with my brother. I called in at the shop with my daughter yesterday,' she says, fixing me with her striking blue eyes.

'Yes, I remember. Sorry, do I know you from somewhere?'

'You don't know me and, in truth, I don't really know you. But I know of you.'

'I'm not sure I understand.'

I'm pretty sure I'm not notorious, unless I've suddenly become known as Antibes' best baker, or the idiot relative ruining Genevieve's shop.

'Well, the thing is,' she says, taking a sip of her coffee, 'I am André's sister.'

I sink back into my chair as I process what she has just told me. So she isn't his wife! Maybe he doesn't even have a wife. But that little girl – she reminded me so much of André. She has his eyes. I was sure she must be Jake's half-sister.

'I saw you with André near the market square,' I finally manage to say. 'I thought you were his wife – that your daughter was his daughter.'

'No.' She smiles. 'We all look very similar. We have strong family genes, I guess.'

'You certainly do,' I say, recalling the blue eyes of the little girl.

'So, what brings you here?' I ask, my heart thumping in my chest.

'I quite often call in at the bakery when I have been to the market. Just recently I have been around a little more, as I'm doing a dress fitting locally. When I saw you there, I knew you had to be Olivia. From the way André talked of you it couldn't be anyone else.'

'André spoke about me?' I ask in surprise.

'Bien sur. Admittedly not lately, but I remember him talking of a girl he dated many years ago. A girl with curly brown hair. He told me your aunt owned Pâtisserie Genevieve. He also told me that he never forgot you. When I called in two days ago, I knew it had to be you. Are you here on holiday?'

'Kind of. I'm helping my aunt out after a recent operation.'

I find myself telling Angela all about Gen's knee surgery, and even about my cake business back home.

'So you were inspired by your aunt?'

I think back to my childhood, spending summers here and watching my aunt work her magic in the kitchen. 'Yes,' I eventually reply. 'I was.'

'My grandmother inspired me. I'm a dressmaker, and as child I used to sit beneath the table when she worked and press the foot pedal on her sewing machine.' She has a fond smile on her face at the memory. 'I was more of a hindrance than a help, really. I hope your aunt is soon recovered.'

I'm finding this all pretty convivial, but I'm desperate to hear more about André. As if reading my thoughts, she looks me directly in the eye.

'Anyway, this isn't why I came to find you. I wanted to ask, how would you feel about seeing André again?'

I'm quiet for a few seconds as I digest what she has just asked me. I remember the young man and the long heady summer of 1998, but he must have changed so much since then. I know I have. I'm not sure I even truly knew him back then. Not really. He did tell me about his brothers and sisters, but I never got to meet them or visit his family home. Maybe I should have read something into that. But I was young, foolish and infatuated. It's almost surreal to think I'm sitting here having a coffee with his sister, all these years later. Not for the first time, I'm wondering whether or not I should have left well alone. Yet I owe it to Jake to carry on.

'How do you know he would want to meet me?' My eyes meet hers. 'Surely his life must have moved on?'

'André went to live abroad for a while. I think you know that he went travelling. Anyway, he ended up in Canada, working in a wildlife colony, and that's where he got married.'

'He's married?'

'Was. He was with Jenny for six years before the marriage broke down and he came back home. He's been back in France for almost ten years now. He's had one or two girlfriends since, but he's been single for a few years.'

'Where does he live?' I can feel butterflies in my stomach at the thought of actually meeting André again, and staring into his mesmerising blue eyes. And he's single. I imagine his easy smile and ready wit.

'Several miles away, in the house we grew up in. My parents died within one year of each other three years ago.'

'I'm sorry to hear that.'

'Thanks.' Her smile is bittersweet. 'They were always going to be that couple who died within a short time of each other, as they were so much in love. I'm surprised my father lasted a whole year after my mother died.'

Angela shows me a photograph of her with her siblings on the beach when they were children. They all look so similar, with shining blue eyes and silky-smooth olive skin. A very good-looking family. They look just like the children I imagined I would have had with André.

'Do you see the little bistro in the background?' She points to a white-fronted café towards the end of the harbour in the photo. 'Our father told us that one day he would buy that place and turn it into the best seafood restaurant in town. He'd been a successful fisherman with his own boat and saved hard over the years. When the bistro came up for sale when the previous owner retired, he finally bought it. He hired a talented young chef and it became a huge success. André had a challenge when he took over the place after my father's death, as everyone adored our father. Plus, he knew nothing about the business. He was working for an animal charity at the time, but the staff supported him totally. He made the restaurant more modern, chic, and it's better than ever. I am very proud of my brother.' She puts the photograph away and smiles fondly, then glances at her watch and tells me she has to leave.

'I'm seeing a bride for a dress fitting. I should not keep her waiting. Nerves can fray during wedding planning. She might be a – what do you say? – bridezilla.' She drains her coffee than stands up to leave.

She hands me a card with André's phone number on it. 'In case you want to give him a call.' She kisses me lightly on both cheeks and walks away.

'Wait,' I call after her. 'Are you absolutely sure André would like to meet with me?'

'Trust me,' Angela says, walking back over and placing her hand lightly on my arm. 'He definitely thinks you were the one that got away.'

I walk back to my aunt's in a haze, turning over the business card in my hands. André is here in Antibes, running a restaurant at the far end of the harbour. To think it was only a matter of time before I would have walked along that far. I might have bumped into him, taken completely unawares. I might have sat in the bistro and ordered food from him. This is going to be monumental news for Jake.

Angela telling me that André never really got over me has put my mind into a complete spin. I wonder if André told her that himself? I try to gather my thoughts, because when I do finally get to meet him again, I'm going to have to tell him all about his son.

Chapter Twenty

It's barely a week and a half since her operation, but this morning, just after ten, Gen makes an appearance in the bakery.

'Bonjour, Madame Genevieve. Are you here to keep an eye on us?' Olivier beams.

'I'm sure there's no need for that. I have every faith that you and my niece would maintain my standards.'

Olivier lifts his strong tanned hands. 'Completely. I've always been good with my hands.' He casts a sideways grin at me and Valerie rolls her eyes.

'How are you feeling?' I ask.

'Bored,' says Gen. 'I've read two novels and dozens of magazines. I have a view of the harbour every day from the balcony and I'm itching to get down there.'

'But you must be patient. You've had surgery, remember,' I say.

'How could I forget. But really, I'm fine. My knee is still a little sore but I can barely wait to get back behind this counter. Lilian is taking me out for a drive later. There's a little clothes boutique along the coast road with a café next door. A bit of retail therapy might do me the world of good. Besides, I think your parents might appreciate a bit of time to themselves.'

'If you're sure it won't be too much for you,' I say anxiously.

'Well, if you want me back in hospital with mental health problems after sitting upstairs all day long going crazy then I won't bother. But really –' she smiles – 'I will be fine. Just a little gentle browsing and a leisurely lunch overlooking the sea. I'm sure it will do me the world of good.'

'OK. But make sure you take your phone and ring me if you have to.'

Maybe I'm worrying too much. Gen does seem a little more sprightly when she spends time around other people.

'Of course. Right, I'll be off. I'd better go and find something decent to wear. I don't want Lilian showing me up.'

I barely slept a wink last night. I tossed and turned and imagined the meeting with André. I'm fearing the worst over having to tell him about Jake. Every year as he grew older, I had conflicting feelings of thinking Jake was doing just fine and guilt over his father not knowing of his existence. And, of course, the years rolled by so quickly. It seems that one day I was waving him off for his first day at school and in no time, he was finishing his A levels and looking at university courses. The longer something goes on, the harder it is to change things.

'You are distracted today,' notes Olivier as I forget to put sugar in a cake mix, thankfully remembering before it goes in the oven. 'Are you OK?'

'I'm fine, I just didn't sleep too well last night, that's all.' I stifle a yawn.

'You should definitely take an afternoon nap today. It's what keeps me going. A couple of hours in the afternoon and I'm ready to go all night.'

That conjures up quite an image.

'Maybe you're right. I'll head off around four, if you're OK for the last hour or two?' I say, turning to Valerie.

'Bien sur. You have let me finish early before. I owe you.'

The next couple of hours pass quickly, and just after two I spot Lilian Beaumont's red sports car pull up outside the shop. She steps out wearing a lemon shift dress and a wide-brimmed straw hat. A few seconds later my aunt appears, looking equally elegant in white linen trousers, green silk vest and matching scarf. They both pop their heads into the shop.

'Au revoir, ladies. Please be sure to look after my aunt.'

'But of course.' Lilian smiles. 'We shan't be going man-hunting until she is fully back on her feet.' Gen pushes Lilian gently on the arm and laughs.

'Talking of men, how was your date the other night. Did he enjoy the éclairs?'

'He never ate any. He does not eat gluten or dairy, which he completely forgot to mention. And I'd made an utterly delicious beef a la crème. Most inconsiderate of him.'

'What, being gluten and dairy free?'

'I mean not telling me about it. It would never work between us. I do not have the time to be cooking for someone special meals. I shan't be seeing him again. Genevieve – la voiture, vite vite.'

Before Lilian departs, she decides, once again, to test my French.

'Qu'as-tu mangé au petit déjeuner?'

'Café au lait, et croissant avec confiture de framboise.'

'Très bien. Speak a little French each day. À plus tard.'

❧

Soon enough, it's late afternoon and I'm ready to go upstairs and grab a couple of hours' sleep. I check in with Jake on the phone and, as usual, everything seems to be running smoothly. As I plug my phone to charge another text comes through from Jo.

Hi Liv, hope all is OK. I went for a walk past hunky guy's house today (despite me saying I wouldn't) with two shih-tzus, who I figured wouldn't cause me any trouble. It may also have been about the same time I saw him leave before, and there he was again! Who'd have thought? We actually got chatting and guess what? His name is Guy! I laughed when he told me! He's asked me out for a drink tonight at a wine bar. I'll let you know how it goes. Lots of love xx

Another text follows straight after.

P.S. What do you call a magician's dog? A Labracadabrador.

I quickly reply, telling her that I hope her date goes well and that I'll get all the details when we're home. I really do hope she has a good time with the hunky guy. If he's dating Jo, I think he's one lucky Guy.

❧

I wake a little after six to find my aunt sitting on the sofa with Mum, surrounded by shopping bags.

'Hi, Gen, did you have a nice day?'

'I did, thank you, Olivia, it was just the tonic.'

'I hope you haven't overdone things.'

'If I'm honest, I was worried it might be a bit ambitious, despite my desire to leave the apartment. But typical Lilian, she had phoned ahead and arranged a wheelchair at the boutique. She pushed me around as I browsed the store and bought some lovely things. We ate at a smart little fish restaurant overlooking the sea. I've had a perfectly lovely day. Here, I have a little something for you.'

She hands me the most beautiful pink silk purse, studded with Swarovski crystals, and I let out a gasp. 'Gen, thank you! It's absolutely stunning. Now I just need somewhere smart to go to use it.' She has also bought a pretty silk scarf for Mum and a brown butter-soft leather wallet for my father.

'Just little gifts to thank you all. I'm so lucky to have such a wonderful family.'

Mum collects the teacups and takes them into the kitchen, and I follow her through.

'Do you think Gen's alright? She looks exhausted,' says Mum as she places the cups into the dishwasher.

'It sounds like she was pretty well looked after by Lilian, Mum, so don't worry. She was beginning to get a little depressed up here so it's probably done her the world of good.'

'I suppose so. I think she should definitely spend the next day or two taking it easy though.'

I shower then pour myself a glass of Chardonnay before flicking the balcony light on and heading outside with a book. It's a balmy evening and the lights from the harbour twinkle in the distance. I must get out on to the water one day. Maybe I'll take one of Olivier's water taxis over to Cannes and spend the day there.

Faye and I are heading to an open-air cinema tonight, near the beach, to watch *Dirty Dancing* under the stars (thankfully it's in English with French subtitles). The story of a young woman's summer romance with the man of her dreams. As if I hadn't been thinking about André enough today already. Tomorrow I will make that phone call.

Chapter Twenty-One

The next morning Faye and both I have another text from Jo, who is clearly missing our regular group catch-ups.

Hi girls. Just had to let you know that my date with Guy went really well last night. Give us a ring if you get a minute and I'll fill you in. xx

I ring her at once, and put her on speaker so Faye can listen in too.

'Hi, Jo, are you OK to talk?'

'Hiya, Liv, yeah, not long woken up.'

'So how was the date?' asks Faye.

'It was amazing. Guy's really nice, I felt so relaxed with him. After the wine bar we ended up having a curry at a place down a side street called A Passage to India. I never even knew it existed, so maybe it's new. We should try it on our next night out; the food was to die for.'

'Sounds good, we definitely should.'

We chat for a while longer and Jo's dog stories make me smile, as usual. But soon enough my thoughts turn to meeting André. Maybe it's time to make that call.

I held the phone in my hand for so long before I contacted André but in the end I couldn't even phone him, as my voice was shaking at the very thought of it. I sent him a text message and he rang me almost at once. His delicious French accent, tinged with emotion and shock, made my heart thump faster as I tried to keep my tone even. We didn't say much, just arranged to meet up this evening. My palms were sweating by the time we had finished speaking. I'm finally going to see him again after all these years.

I've arranged to meet André at six at a bar in Port Vauban. I've barely eaten a thing all day as my stomach has been doing somersaults, and I've constantly questioned myself as to whether I'm doing the right thing. But the thought of André's arms around my waist still sends my heart into a flutter. I must see him. And even if things aren't the same between us any more, he has a right to know about his son.

I change about three times before I finally decide on an outfit. How do I want to look? Fresh and casual? Sexy and alluring? I realise that it's been quite a while since I've been on a date. In the end, it's Faye who helps me choose.

I eventually slip into a white linen shirt-dress with lots of silver jewellery, before carefully applying some make-up. My hair needs little attention other than some mousse scrunched through it. I feel good, and dare to think that I look pretty good too.

'Perfect.' Faye smiles.

'You look lovely, are you going somewhere special?' remarks Mum as I pass her on the stairs. I consider not telling her, but I feel too guilty, especially as I've told Faye already. I sigh. 'I've managed to find André. I'm sorry I didn't tell you, Mum. I'm just trying to figure things out in my own head first. I'm going to meet him now.'

She has a look of surprise on her face. 'When did this happen? How did you know where he was?'

I tell her all about his sister coming into the bakery and telling me that André is single again and living back here on the Côte d'Azur.

'Don't say anything to Dad just yet, Mum. I want to see how this meeting goes first. It's taken me completely by surprise, my head's all over the place.'

'You know I can't have secrets from your father,' she says loyally. 'And he only ever has your best interests at heart. Maybe you ought to tell him yourself.'

'Tell him what?' Dad emerges from the kitchen with a plate of cheese and biscuits.

I glance at my watch. If I'm going to be there on time, I'd better get a move on.

'I'm going to meet someone. Sorry, Dad, will it be OK if Mum fills you in? I don't want to be late.'

I head downstairs feeling like a coward for leaving Mum to chat to Dad, but there really wasn't time to explain things a second time over. Heading down towards the harbour, there's an excitement in the pit of my stomach that I haven't felt in a long time. I wonder if he's changed much? His sister certainly looked good for her age.

Taking deep breaths to try and steady my nerves, I decide to walk the long way to the port along the cobbled side streets of the old

town. As I pass through narrow alleyways with street artists painting
in the late afternoon sun, their exhibits spread along the pavement,
I try to relax. A portrait artist is sketching a young girl with long
dark hair as her parents watch and sip frappés at an adjacent café.
The smell of vanilla hits my nostrils as I pass a bakery and I can't
resist taking a peek at the window display of charming cakes. A
charcuterie next door emits the smell of salty hams and herby
salamis. Cutting down a side street towards the port, the cafés are
full of people. Groups of young women weighed down with bags
from boutiques chat and laugh, seemingly without a care in the
world. I wish I could feel that way right now.

As I approach the harbour, my nerves almost get the better of
me and I think about turning around and heading back. Is this all
a huge mistake? How do I deliver the news that he has a son? Yet
I know I must. I'm doing it for Jake. He has a right to find out
about his father.

The map on my phone tells me to turn right as I approach the
port and that my destination is getting close. As I walk towards
the bar, I notice several couples seated outside on blue metal chairs
drinking bottles of beer and glasses of wine. There's a handsome
man with swept-back dark hair faintly streaked with grey, and
faint designer stubble on his chin. He's sitting alone with a bottle
of wine in an ice bucket and two glasses on the table, glancing at
his watch. It's André.

He stands up as soon as he sees me and I feel like I'm walking
towards him in slow motion.

'Olivia. Is it really you? You look beautiful.' He takes in my appearance for a few seconds, before kissing me lightly on both cheeks.

I stare at the attractive man stood before me. He has kept himself in really good shape and is dressed in smart jeans and a light blue shirt that brings out the blue of his eyes. The ponytail has gone but his face has barely changed. He still looks like David Ginola to me. It's as if the years have melted away and I'm that eighteen-year-old girl again.

'Hi, André. How are you? You look well.'

We both take a seat at the small table and face each other, our eyes locking. I feel a charge of electricity that I'm sure André must be feeling too.

'I'm good, thanks. Is wine OK?'

I nod and he reaches for the bottle from the ice bucket and pours us each a glass of Sauvignon Blanc, barely taking his startling blue eyes off me the whole time.

'I can hardly believe it's you. You've barely changed.' His sexy French accent is as enchanting as ever.

André drinks in my appearance and I self-consciously push a beer mat around the table.

'I was shocked when my sister said she saw you behind the counter at the shop. She wasn't sure it was you, of course, but from the way I had described you she was pretty certain of it.'

'I guess it's my trademark hair.' I give my thick curls a shake.

André is smiling and shaking his head. 'I can't stop looking at you.'

I'm finding it pretty hard to peel my eyes away from him too. He's still gorgeous. I take a sip of the refreshing ice-cold wine.

'How is your aunt?'

I tell him all about her operation and how I've come over here with my friend Faye to give a hand.

'Faye came here with me years ago. It's her fault I met you, actually.'

André looks puzzled.

'She volunteered me to be your assistant.'

'Ah, so I have her to thank.' He takes a sip of his wine and smiles.

'Angela tells me you run a fish restaurant at the far end of the harbour. I was sorry to hear about your parents. That must have been hard, losing them so close together.'

I can't imagine life without my own parents and realise how lucky I am. They've had such a happy life together that I feel sad André and I never experienced that. But maybe there is a reason we have been given this chance to get to know each other again.

'It was, but it was merciful. Neither one of them could have survived without the other. In truth, I wasn't really interested in running the restaurant when my father died. It can be quite demanding and I'd never really been interested in the industry. But, you know, I really enjoy it now. I get to meet some wonderful people.'

'Life never quite works out how we expect it to, does it?'

'C'est vrai.' André takes a long sip of his wine.

He tells me a little about his travels and some of the places he has worked over the years and listens with interest as I tell him about my cake business.

'So, a talent for baking runs in the family.' He smiles and I can't help thinking about Jake's newly discovered love for it too. 'Would you like something to eat? I can get us a menu,' asks André, standing up to head inside.

I realise I am hungry, as I haven't felt able to stomach anything all day. Feeling a little more relaxed after the wine, I nod.

'Yes, OK. That would be nice.'

André returns with a menu and I order a seafood risotto whilst he opts for a boeuf bourguignon.

'I hope the risotto is as good as the one we serve at the restaurant.' André smiles when our food arrives. 'You must come down and judge for yourself.'

'Yes, I'd like that.'

We chat easily despite my underlying nerves, knowing I have a secret I must soon impart to him. André tells me about his sister and reveals that he is closer to her than he is to his brother.

'You never intend to drift apart but I suppose it just happens.' He shrugs. 'My brother moved thirty miles away along the coast, near Monaco, so I don't see him too often. We get together at Christmas and on special occasions. I saw him recently when he called in at the restaurant. He's an architect and had been in the area working.'

The mention of Monaco makes me think of the night we spent together at the hotel there. The night Jake was conceived. I wonder if André thought of that evening as often as I did. Looking at the present-day André, with the designer stubble and piercing eyes, he's probably even sexier than he was as a young man.

The risotto when it arrives is creamy and delicious, with a good amount of seafood nestled amongst it and topped with generous shavings of parmesan. André closes his eyes and savours the first mouthful of bourguignon, which he declares 'excellente'. The smell of red wine and herbs fills the air as he digs his fork into it.

We order a second bottle of wine and, as the night draws in, I feel so relaxed sitting under the stars on this quaint cobbled street that I wish I could stay here forever. Laughter is ringing around from couples and groups of friends enjoying the evening together.

I feel slightly tipsy as André walks me home and as we stroll along the harbour, he wordlessly takes my hand in his. The strains of music from nearby bars fill the air and couples sit on the decks of yachts, drinking and laughing. Gentle ripples on the moonlit water give everything a romantic feel. We pass Olivier's father's yacht, but it's in darkness tonight, so perhaps they have gone out for the evening. I realise with a guilty pang that I still haven't spoken of Jake yet. It is, after all, one of the reasons I came here.

'Can I meet you for lunch on Friday?' asks André, which is the day after tomorrow. 'I just need to organise someone to take my place at the restaurant for a few hours. Have you ever been to the Picasso museum at Chateau Grimaldi?'

'No, I haven't, but I'd like that. Maybe I wasn't interested in such things when I was a young girl.'

'I had a little interest in art when I was younger because I enjoyed drawing,' André tells me. 'A pastel drawing of Monet's waterlilies was given pride of place on a wall in my classroom.' There's a hint of pride in his voice.

André looks at me and suddenly cups my face and gently turns it to one side.

'You have such a beautiful profile. I would paint your picture if I was talented enough.'

My skin is burning at his touch and I hope I haven't gone bright red. I feel a frisson of excitement as I walk alongside André and those teenage feelings come flooding back.

When we arrive back at my aunt's, André fixes me with his mesmerising blue eyes before leaning in and kissing me gently on both cheeks. I suppress a desire to pull him towards me and kiss him deeply as the scent of his citrus aftershave, sends me into a spin.

'Bon soir, Olivia. I've had a really wonderful evening. Until Friday. Sweet dreams.'

I watch him stroll back towards the harbourside to take a taxi home, which he told me is a few miles out of town. The night sky is clear, bringing the promise of another glorious day of sunshine tomorrow, and maybe even some hope for the future.

I climb into bed with mixed emotions coursing through me. Tonight was wonderful but it wasn't real life. I was seduced by the food, wine and company, taking me back to a time when I was young and carefree. That kiss on the cheek left me desiring more and the years melted away as André leaned in close to me. I find myself dreaming about the next time we can be together and kiss each other passionately. I wonder if André is feeling the same? Wrestling with my emotions, I know I shouldn't get carried away, as I must consider Jake. I should have had the courage to tell André about him tonight and regret not doing so. It was selfish to enjoy my evening reconnecting with him. On Friday, without fail, I must tell him.

Chapter Twenty-Two

It's a little after nine the following morning when Gen makes an appearance in the shop.

'Good morning. How are we getting on?' She looks refreshed and appears to be walking a little easier each day using her crutches.

'Really good. Busy as usual. I haven't made any bee stings this week. I'm afraid mine can't quite match up to yours,' I say.

'Ah well, that's just years of practise. Tomorrow I'll come down early and make some. And before you start fussing, I will be sat down over there,' she says, pointing to the huge wooden island. 'So I won't be taxing myself too much.'

'OK, if you insist.'

'I do.'

She takes a farmhouse loaf and some profiteroles upstairs for lunch. 'A little treat for your father. He's had several days of fruit and yoghurt for dessert at your mother's insistence, so I think he deserves it.'

'Did you enjoy your evening last night?' I ask Olivier when Gen has left.

He had been out with Faye on another date.

'Yes, I took her to the opening of a friend's bar in Juan-les-Pins. Is she still sleeping?' he asks.

'She is. I think she's enjoying not having to set an alarm clock in the morning.'

Olivier asks me how I spent my evening and I tell him I met up with an old friend, not wanting to reveal too much just yet. 'He looked me up when his sister spotted me in the bakery.'

'Lucky guy. You must both come along and have a drink one evening.'

'Maybe we will. Thanks, Olivier.'

I head out to the market for some raspberries, as the buns I made last time were a big hit with customers. I'm also going to make some lemon drizzle cake. I'm wandering along when I sport Lilian Beaumont strolling towards me with a dark-haired man who looks at least a decade younger than her. She looks effortlessly chic in navy linen trousers and a white blouse that ties at the side. Her designer sunglasses are placed on the top of her head. I take a deep breath as I prepare for my next French lesson.

'Bonjour, Olivia. How are you?'

'Très bien.'

She introduces me to her friend, Juan, and asks me, in French, what I'm buying today.

'Framboise et limones.'

'Pour les gateaux?'

'Naturellement.'

'Excellente. You are getting better.'

She air kisses me and I can smell her signature Chanel scent. 'Remember, practice makes perfect.'

I buy some raspberries and lemons from the fruit and veg guy and I also select some fat bulbs of garlic and a bunch of fragrant green parsley. He compliments me on the cupcakes –saying that he and his wife really enjoyed them.

'I will come in and buy some next time you have them in the shop,' he says as he places my fruit into a carrier bag.

'Of course. I will let you know when I make them again.'

I think about my lunch date with André and realise how much I'm looking forward to it. It was as if we had never been apart when we met up last night. Almost as if we picked up where we left off. I believe that everything happens at the right time and can't help wondering if it's fate that we are both single at this time in our life.

Back at my aunt's, I have a long catch-up on the phone with Sam, who tells me that everything is going well and Jake is continuing to show a flair for baking.

'Maybe one day he'll start up on his own. "Jake's Cakes" has rather a ring to it, doesn't it?' Sam laughs.

I'm not sure whether she's serious or not. 'Go into competition with his own mother? The sheer effrontery. Actually, is Jake about? I tried his phone earlier.'

'He's out on a delivery. He's taking a ruby anniversary cake for a couple who are having a party tomorrow. They're probably inviting him along as we speak. He's a huge hit with the customers, even the kids. A smitten ten-year-old invited him to her trampoline party yesterday.' She laughs. 'I think he's actually considering it.'

We wind up the conversation as a timer goes off in the background, signalling a cake is ready to come out of the oven.

'Gotta dash. Speak soon, Liv. Great to have a catch-up.'

Chapter Twenty-Three

Friday has arrived before I know it and I'm a bundle of nerves as I think about my date today with André. I've tried to phone Jake a couple more times but I seem to keep missing him. Perhaps it's just as well that I don't get his hopes up yet about André; I don't know how he is going to take my news today.

The morning passes quickly as the usual customers pop in for their early morning bread. I'm finding my French conversations with Lilian Beaumont are getting easier each day so it seems she is right about speaking a little of the language each day to develop fluency.

During my lunch hour I nip upstairs with a crusty baguette and prepare a bourguignon with instructions to Mum to switch it on at three for a few hours' slow cooking.

'I don't think I'll be wanting any though. I'm having a late lunch. With André.'

'Are you sure you are doing the right thing?' asks Mum, a look of concern on her face.

'Of course I'm not. I just know I've never really loved anyone since André.'

'That's the potency of first love. You're lucky if it's an everlasting love, though.'

'Yours and Dad's is, isn't it?' Mum and Dad still look at each other like a couple of teenagers and still hold hands when they're sitting together in the evening on the sofa.

'I suppose we've been very lucky, yes. A lot of people of our generation stayed together because they had little choice. But even if I had the choice, I wouldn't change a thing. Eddie Dunne always was and still is the love of my life.'

Their enduring love warms my heart and I swallow down a lump in my throat.

'Do what makes you happy,' says Mum. 'You've done a wonderful job with Jake, so no matter how things turn out, you'll always have him.'

'Thanks, Mum. Although I'd like to say *we've* done a great job. I couldn't have raised Jake without your support over the years.'

'We adore him. Now then, go and get yourself ready. I like you in that blue cotton dress. I don't think you've worn it yet, have you?'

'No, I haven't. Thanks, Mum, good choice. Right, I'm off for a shower.' I kiss Mum lightly on the cheek before I head off.

When I'm ready, I survey my reflection in the full-length mirror in the bedroom and decide that I'll do. The dress is a peacock-blue shift and I slip a silver necklace with a turquoise stone around my neck and I'm ready to go. I spritz some Rive Gauche on to my wrists, smiling at the bottle matching my dress. I remember buying my very first bottle of it from duty free when I was here with Faye all those years ago and feeling ever so grown up. It was our first holiday abroad without our parents, even though we did stay with my aunt.

I've arranged to meet André outside the Chateau Grimaldi museum, so we can take a look at the works of Picasso. I recall he was Spanish, if my memory serves me right from my school days, so I'm wondering why there's a museum dedicated to his works here in Antibes. I guess I'll shortly find out. My mind seems to be filling itself with all kinds of random things other than the big issue at hand. Maybe I'm scared to face up to it.

'Go and have a good day,' says Mum as I leave. 'You look beautiful, by the way.'

'Thanks, Mum.' Dad's down in the shop with Aunt Gen, who has decided she is strong enough to spend an hour downstairs, and in a way I'm rather glad. He hasn't said much about my meeting with André but I think he's just worried I may get hurt.

Stepping out into the bright sunshine, I head down towards the harbour before the slight uphill walk towards the chateau, perched on the walls of an ancient stone fortress. Passing two good-looking men walking out of a bar, I can feel their eyes on me as I walk past and can't resist a little glance over my shoulder. Sure enough, they are watching me. One of them smiles. It feels nice to be admired, and I think that maybe I should make the effort to dress up a little more often. Perhaps it's why Lilian Beaumont gets so many dates.

As the blonde stone walls of the chateau loom into view, I spot André leaning on a wall and gazing out to sea. I wonder what he's thinking about. He has no idea what I am going to tell him today. For all I know, he may be looking forward to a pleasant afternoon with someone he once knew and nothing more. A relaxing few hours away from the bustle of the restaurant. When I'm a few yards away he turns to face me with a broad grin on his face. He's wearing sunglasses and is dressed casually in navy shorts, a white polo shirt and leather loafers.

'Bonjour, Olivia. Tu es jolie.'

'Merci. Tu as l'air chaud.'

André's handsome face breaks into a huge grin.

'What are you smiling at?'

'Well, you have just told me that I look hot. But that's fine by me.'

'Really? I meant to say you look smart.' I laugh as we stroll along to the entrance of the museum. As we pay our entrance fee and enter the beautifully restored building, I think that Picasso himself could not have chosen a better location to display some of his works.

We wander the cool marble corridors, stopping to admire various pictures, before heading to the top floor to view the Picasso exhibits. We are greeted by a sculpture that is a jumble of guitars and I cock my head to one side as I try to figure out its meaning – the artwork is as jumbled as the thoughts swirling around in my head. I view the rest of the paintings silently, my stomach in knots as I think about the conversation to come.

'I don't recognise many of the paintings,' I remark, as we make our way around.

'That's because most of his famous paintings are in Barcelona.'

'Ah well, I knew Picasso was Spanish. So why is there a museum here in Antibes?'

I'm trying to show an interest and make light conversation, but my mind is completely distracted.

'He lived here for six months, apparently. He had a studio in the castle at the time.'

'Wow. Imagine being important enough to rent a studio in an actual castle: "Excuse me, Elizabeth, do you have a room I could rent in the west wing of Buckingham Palace? And will there be en suite facilities?"'

'I know,' André laughs. 'It was a different world.'

A pencil drawing of a goat intrigues me, although André insists his four-year-old niece could do better, which makes me laugh.

'Picasso's work always sparks debate in people. But as an artist, I imagine that kind of conversation can only be a good thing,' I reason.

An hour later we step outside into the bright sunshine once more, and André suggests a late lunch.

'At your restaurant?'

'Where else? I have reserved the best table for us, overlooking the yachts in the harbour.'

'Sounds perfect.'

Walking along, I can hardly believe we are treading the same path we did all those years ago. Back then we would be holding hands and stopping every few yards for a passionate kiss, not caring who was watching. I cast a sideways glance at him and even now his looks still take my breath away. André catches me looking at him.

'Are you checking me out?' he teases.

'I'm just thinking that you haven't really changed. Apart from the ponytail. I loved it at the time, but these days I can't think of anything more dreadful.'

André stops walking and faces me with a serious expression on his face. 'And just when I was starting to grow my hair a little, especially for you.'

'Ah, would you really do that if I asked you to?'

'No,' he laughs.

We're chatting away easily, and I briefly wonder whether we would ever be able to recapture the heartfelt passion we experienced in the days of our youth.

After a ten-minute walk we reach the end of the harbour and are soon facing the white-fronted Langousta restaurant. It has French colonial-style tables and chairs outside and green shrubs in pots at the entrance. White cotton tablecloths and expensive-looking glasses complete the elegant, stylish look. Expensively dressed diners, possibly from the yachts, mingle with more casual tourists, so it would appear that the restaurant caters for everyone.

'How gorgeous,' I say, as a passing waiter deposits a fragrant lobster dish at a nearby table.

'Thank you. It's taken a while to get things exactly right, but I'm happy with the image of the place now. We're almost constantly full. I have reserved us a table inside. That is unless you prefer to eat out here.'

'Inside would be great – it's a little hot out here. It looks amazing, though. You must have worked really hard to achieve this.' I glance around, taking in the inviting outdoor space.

André shrugs modestly. 'It was nice enough when it was my father's place. I've just put my own stamp on things I suppose. Everyone's vision is a little different.'

His vision was certainly different to mine all those years ago, I can't help thinking.

André leads me inside to a table that has been beautifully decorated with a vase of sunflowers, crystal glasses and expensive-looking cutlery. There's a jug of water and a bottle of champagne in an ice bucket. It is next to full-height windows which, as promised, have a view of the yachts in the harbour. It's perfect.

'You organised this?'

'I had my head waiter get everything ready while we were at the museum. I was just making sure you didn't prefer to eat outdoors.'

'No, this is wonderful. Thank you, André.'

The place is heaving with diners and their meals are being prepared in an open kitchen in the centre of the large dining room. Flames are shooting into the air as frying pans sizzle with butter. The chefs sauté fish and potatoes and the rich scent of parsley and garlic fills the air, making my stomach growl. The ice-blue walls are adorned with black and white photographs of the harbour. Netting is draped over a long wall and threaded with wooden starfish and tumbling white fairy lights. It's strikingly simple and beautiful.

'I thought we might have a bouillabaisse, if that's OK with you. It combines plenty of the local fish. The bouillabaisse here has a reputation for being the best in town.'

'No codding.'

'It really is the best plaice. You'll have a whale of a time.'

'I'm not sure I like you choosing my food. It's a bit shellfish.'

'Oh, for God's hake, not another fish joke.'

'Are you all done?'

'I think so,' laughs André.

'I didn't think you would flounder. I think I win.'

Our easy banter reminds me of how much fun we had when we were younger. I don't suppose people really change, deep down. At least I'm hoping this could be true of us.

I catch André staring at me as I glance around the gorgeous restaurant, thinking what a good job he has done and wondering what it was like when his father had it.

'What are you looking at?' I eventually ask.

'Sorry, I don't mean to stare. I'm just thinking how unbelievable it is, that we are sitting here opposite each other. You know, I always hoped that I would see you again one day but I didn't know if it would ever be possible.'

'Really?' My heart is hammering in my chest. I dreamt of meeting him again so many times, but never thought André would be feeling the same way. 'But you never wrote to me again after that first letter.'

'I know and I felt so guilty about that but I had such a desire to travel when I was young. There was distraction everywhere, and soon the weeks had turned into months and I suppose I was too embarrassed to contact you by then.'

I would have been heavily pregnant by then and can't help wondering whether he would have stuck around anyway.

'My life had moved on but I thought about you often,' he continues. 'Some people come into your life that you never really forget. Plus it's hard not to stare at you today. You look so beautiful.' He reaches across the table and takes his hand in mine and a shiver runs down my spine.

I glance at André's handsome, smiling face. It's hard to believe we have both lived such different lives these past twenty years. And he's been married. I can't help wondering why he never had any children. Perhaps it was a decision he made with his wife. Or maybe it was André's decision not to have children. Maybe he never wanted them. I feel sick once again at the thought of telling him about Jake.

A waiter places a basket of grilled bread topped with mayonnaise and cayenne pepper in the middle of the table and shortly after a large bowl of bouillabaisse arrives in a beautifully painted blue and white tureen. The smell is amazing. Maybe a little food will ease my nerves and make my stomach feel a little less jittery. André points out the pieces of monkfish, sea bream and octopus.

'Let me serve,' he says, taking a ladle and plunging it deep into the dish. He pours it into my soup bowl, the aroma making my mouth water.

'So do you spend a lot of time here at the restaurant?' I take a spoonful of the soup and am completely blown away by the fragrant, rich, tasty broth.

'Quite a bit. When I first took over after my father died, I was here night and day. I wanted to get the place looking just right and there was a lot of work involved. When it was all ready and I'd hired the right staff, I was able to have a little more free time. But I'm pretty much always here. When it's your own business you tend to want to keep an eye on things.'

'I know what you mean. I always check in with Sam, my assistant, even though I know she's more than capable of looking after things.'

We finish our delicious meal and André asks me if I would like a dessert. Suddenly, it all feels a bit false sitting here, eating this delicious food when I'm shortly to deliver such momentous, lifechanging news. I feel so guilty.

I try to act as normal as possible and André persuades me to try the chef's special rhubarb crème brûlée. It's absolutely perfect, the tang of rhubarb perfectly balanced with the sweet custard and hard caramel coating that gives a satisfying crack when I dig my spoon into it. I decide it wouldn't be fair to tell him about Jake in such a place. *His* place.

I'm about to suggest leaving when André excuses himself for a few minutes and disappears into the kitchen before returning with a cocktail in a vintage glass.

'You must try a French martini before you leave.'

'You're spoiling me. Either that or you're trying to get me drunk.' I take a sip of the plum-coloured drink.

'Wow, that's delicious. What's in it?'

'Vodka, Chambord Liqueur and pineapple juice. Really, the French martini was created in New York but it happens to be our barman's speciality.'

'Why is it called a French martini then?'

'Because it contains Chambord Liqueur which *is* French.'

'Well, it's my new favourite cocktail. Thank you.' I pick a fresh raspberry from the rim of the glass and eat it.

'You're welcome. And now –' André takes a glance at his watch – 'unfortunately I will have to get back to work shortly. There's a new dish on the evening menu so I would like to check the chef is still happy with it.'

André walks me along the harbour and I ask him to take a seat on a low wall overlooking the crystal-blue water. I feel a little guilty telling him about Jake when he has just told me he needs to attend to some business at the restaurant. But I can't put it off for another day. It wouldn't be fair. I turn to face him with a knot in my stomach.

'What's the matter? Are you breaking up with me already?' he jokes. 'Or maybe it was the bouillabaisse. Or the terrible fish jokes.' He's trying to keep his tone light but there's a nervousness in his voice and a slight frown across his brow.

He edges closer to me and runs his hand lightly up and down my back. I would like nothing more than to sink into him and kiss him passionately on the lips but for now, I push those thoughts to the back of my mind.

My heart is beating so loudly in my chest that I'm certain he must be able to hear it.

'There's something I need to tell you, André, but I'm just not sure how to say it.'

'I usually find the best way to say something that bothers you is to just come out and say it,' he says, unaware of the body blow I'm about to deliver.

I take a deep breath.

'When I returned to England after spending the summer here all those years ago, I discovered I was pregnant.' I practically whisper the news as I stare straight into his eyes, desperate to gauge his reaction.

It seems like forever before André finally speaks.

'Pregnant?' There's a look of confusion on his face.

'Yes. I had a baby. Your baby. We have a son.' I'm staring out across the water, as I can't bear to meet his gaze for a second time.

André is on his feet.

'You're telling me you have a child? And it is mine?'

'Yes,' I say, my eyes finally meeting his again. 'Although he's not a child any more. He's twenty years old and his name is Jake. He's kind and thoughtful, and lately he seems to be showing himself to be a talented chef.'

'A son.' André sits back down on the wall and runs his hands through his hair, the colour having drained from his face. 'All these years and I never knew. Why did you never tell me?' He puts his head in his hands and is silent for a few seconds.

'I'm sorry, André. But how could I have told you? You were on the other side of the world, remember. Travelling around as I recall. There was no way of contacting you and I never did hear from you again after that first letter.'

'I know. I'm sorry. I'm just so shocked. My God! I have a son. I can't believe it. I think I need another drink.' He exhales deeply as he gets back to his feet. 'All these years though?' He turns to face me. 'Were you ever going to try and find me?'

'Why do you think I'm here now? Jake knows I'm searching for you.'

'I'm sorry, Liv, I need to go. I will be in touch with you soon. I need to time to get my head around this.'

'Of course you do. I'll speak to you soon.' I lean in to hug him but his body is stiff. He turns to face me, the shock of what he has just been told written all over his face.

'I'll call you.'

He heads off towards the restaurant and a range of emotions course through my body. I've done it. I've finally told him. I don't know what I was expecting but I feel a surge of irrational anger that André wasn't immediately excited by the news. Anyone would be blessed to have a son like Jake, and if he doesn't like it then it is his loss. I wonder wildly whether all of this was a mistake, and I should just go home now, protect Jake from knowing that his father isn't interested. Then I tell myself to take a few steps in his shoes – I don't like leaving him like this, and might want a dream outcome, but he deserves some time alone to process the news. But I still can't help feeling deflated.

Chapter Twenty-Four

I'm heading back through the harbour, thinking about my conversation with André, when I pass Olivier's father's boat, where a pre-dinner party seems to be in full swing. Olivier waves as soon as he spots me.

'Liv! Come aboard.' Olivier heads down the gangplank towards me and wraps me in a hug. 'Are you alright? You look a little upset.' A look of concern crosses his face.

'I'm OK. I just had to tell someone some news that was a lot for them to take in,' I say, not wanting to reveal too much just yet. 'And do you know what? I think I will have that drink after all. Do you have any gin?' If anything is going to give me a temporary distraction this evening, it's a few drinks on Olivier's boat.

'Of course. And I've invited Faye over. She should be joining us soon.' Olivier is joined by a striking redhead, who drapes her arms around him, giving me a half-smile.

As I step aboard the luxurious yacht, I peer through smoked-glass windows to a lounge area inside. Several couples are seated on huge beige leather sofas, sipping drinks. A bow-tied waiter is shaking a cocktail at a bar area in the corner of the room. Outside on the rear deck, strung with fairy lights, a party seems to be in full swing. Glamourous model types are drinking champagne with impossibly good-looking young men whilst dance music blares out from speakers.

'How the other half live, hey? I feel like I'm on the set of a James Bond movie,' I say as a waiter brings me a large gin and tonic with ice and lemon. 'You're so lucky to have this place.'

'It's my father's boat. He's away on business at the moment in southern Spain.'

Which may explain the spate of partying these last few days, I think to myself.

'Come and have a seat,' says Olivier, leading me down some steps to a secluded seating area. 'Do you feel like talking about it?'

'Actually, Olivier, no I don't. One day I will give you the full story. Right now, though, I feel like getting drunk.' I take a large swig of the gin and tonic – it really hits the spot.

'Am I actually seeing Olivia the party girl?' says Olivier as he summons a passing waiter to get me another drink. One of my favourite dance tunes comes on and I find myself moving my shoulders.

I'm up on my feet as Faye appears on deck. She's wearing a skin-tight black shift dress and a silver cross around her neck. Olivier pulls her towards him and kisses her lightly on the lips. After chatting to him for a few minutes, Faye pulls me to one side. 'So how did the meeting with André go? I take it you're out celebrating? So where is he?' She glances around the yacht.

'Maybe I'm drowning my sorrows.'

I tell her a little about what happened and she hugs me tightly and says she's certain he will be in touch soon.

Olivier makes sure I have a drink before he gets Faye up to dance.

I find myself following them up on deck, where the music is belting out and couples are dancing wildly as the sun begins to slowly descend. I think the gin has gone straight to my head, as I throw my arms in the air and begin to sing along and dance with complete abandon. Sod it.

'Vous passez de bon temps, Liv!' laughs Olivier, which I think means I am having fun.

'Yes, I am.' I knock back another long drink before the next record strikes up – it's another favourite of mine.

'Woo hoo! I love this one.' It's as if no one else is there on the boat as I dance around singing 'Don't Stop Me Now' at the top of my lungs. I haven't felt so free and wild in a long time and it feels good.

'This is thirsty work,' I say, taking another long glug of my drink.

'Oi! Slow down. You can't take your alcohol as well as I can.' Faye winks as she retrieves another drink from a passing waiter.

Faye and I dance together as Olivier watches us, although he is constantly approached by a succession of women who try to gain his attention. He looks so attractive standing there on deck, it's hardly surprising he has women falling at his feet.

After a couple more dances, the strains of a certain nineties song that includes the names of different women strikes up.

'This is a blast from the past. Do you think they're playing a "best ever cheesy dance tunes" album?'

'They must be,' I laugh.

We start tapping our feet to the catchy tune despite ourselves.

Olivier is in his element, swapping partners throughout the song as it runs through a list of women's names.

He crooks his finger at a woman who jumps up and joins him on the dance floor, laughing.

I'm giggling at Olivier doing a blatant impression of a macho man, when he leads me to the dance floor as Faye nips to the toilet. We dance along for a few moments then, without warning, he puts his hands around my waist and lifts me in the air before dropping me down and shooting me through his legs. I slide through and whoosh along the polished deck with an 'AARGH!', before I crash into a passing waiter carrying a jug of mojito that he neatly deposits all over me.

'Oh my gosh, are you OK?' Faye has returned from the ladies' and is bending down beside me and trying not to laugh as she fishes a mint leaf from my hair.

'I'm OK. I think I need another drink.'

The mortified waiter disappears before quickly returning with a towel.

꙰

A little later and a little drier, a slow number strikes up, and some of the couples snuggle up together and sway along to the music. All of a sudden, my stomach lurches. I glance at Olivier, who really is the most gorgeous-looking bloke, as he wraps his hands around Faye's waist, a mischievous glint in his eyes as they sway gently to the music.

'Have we hit a bit of rough sea?' I ask Olivier as I stagger towards him. He has a perplexed look on his face.

'We are still in the harbour. What was in those drinks?' He laughs.

I steady my breathing as I suddenly feel a little light-headed. 'It just feels like the floor is moving beneath me.'

'Here, come and sit down.' Faye and Olivier guide me by the arm to a seat.

'Are you OK?' Faye asks.

I nod unconvincingly. 'Maybe I shouldn't have mixed my drinks,' I say, thinking of the wine and martini I drank at the restaurant.

'Maybe it was all that dancing. Would you like some water?' asks Olivier.

'Yes, I think so. Actually, no, I think it might make me—'

I've raced to the side of the boat and puked into the water before I can finish my sentence.

'Oh my god, I'm so sorry!' I want the ground to swallow me up.

Olivier guides Faye and me to a swanky white-marble bathroom with gold-coloured fixtures and fittings. I splash cold water all over my face and gaze at my reflection in the mirror. I look a complete mess. What the hell was I thinking? Although those gin and tonics were far more generous than pub measures.

'Jeez – the state of you,' laughs Faye as I pat my face dry. She fishes a small make-up pouch from her bag and sets about making me look half human again. Her kindness makes me feel less embarrassed, and I am overwhelmed with love for my friend.

When I finally emerge from the bathroom, Olivier is standing outside with a smile on his face.

'Stop laughing,' I scold.

'I'm sorry. I don't mean to. But that was quite a performance you put on up there. You are quite a mover.' He raises an eyebrow and Faye throws him a look.

It's only a little after nine, but I need to get to my bed.

'Sorry, but I need to go,' I apologise to Olivier and Faye.

'Let me walk you home. It's the least I can do,' offers Olivier.

'What? For plying me with large gins then laughing when I totally embarrass myself?'

'Maybe we should stop for a coffee on the way,' he suggests.

'No really, you stay and enjoy the party.' Faye winds her arms around Olivier's neck and kisses him. 'I'll see you tomorrow.'

Still feeling a little unsteady on my feet, I'm grateful that Faye's escorting me home, although I feel guilty for cutting her evening short. As we stroll along, me linking my arm through hers for support, the meeting with André comes racing back into my mind. I can't believe I've told him about Jake. I'm hoping he will contact me soon, so that we can talk some more.

I sip a black coffee and a glass of water at a small café whilst Faye has a large brandy as a nightcap.

'Don't judge me.' She grins, before taking a sip of her drink.

'I would never do that. I might show a bit of concern now and then, but that's what friends do.'

'I know, and I do need to cut down, I realise that. Alcohol doesn't really have much effect on me which means I've built up quite a tolerance to it. That can't be good.' She sighs.

'Just decrease the amount gradually. That's what they say, right? If you've been drinking steadily for a long time it's more achievable than suddenly quitting.'

'You seem to know a lot about it.'

'I saw something on TV. Some doctor was doing a phone-in. It seems half our generation will have liver problems before they hit forty. But there is support out there, you know.'

'I don't think I've reached that point yet, Liv. At least I hope not.'

'I think being aware of it helps though. A lot of people are in denial about the amount they drink. Although, who am I to preach this evening? Getting legless and making a total show of myself.'

I feel a little better after vomiting although my eyelids start to feel heavy and I long to climb into bed.

'It doesn't happen very often with you though. Come on, let's get you back home.'

'I'm sorry for spoiling your night. You and Olivier looked like you were getting pretty close,' I say as I stroll beside Faye, yawning.

'Don't worry about it. There's always tomorrow. It's more important to get you home in one piece. Besides, I've told you before, me and Olivier are nothing serious.'

When we arrive outside the bakery, I can already feel the beginnings of a thudding headache when Lilian Beaumont walks past arm in arm with her latest man-friend.

'Ah, Olivia. Have you had a pleasant day?'

She begins a conversation in French.

'Not now, Lilian,' I say, already fishing my key to the flat out of my handbag. 'I'm sorry but I need to get to bed. Bonne nuit.'

Lilian opens her mouth to speak but decides better of it, and Faye whispers something to her as she departs.

I wearily climb the stairs then pop my head into the lounge to quickly say goodnight to everyone. 'Everything OK?' asks Mum, and I tell her everything is fine and that I will fill her in tomorrow. Maybe I'll leave out the bit about puking over the side of the yacht.

Chapter Twenty-Five

Gen has decided she wants to get back to work, so this is Olivier's last morning at the bakery, whilst me and Faye have a few more days left. As usual he turned up today looking as fresh as a daisy, whilst I've swallowed two paracetamol with several glasses of water but still manage to look like a strangled poodle. I've never been so pleased to see my aunt when she appears in the shop a little after ten thirty.

'Off you go,' she says matter-of-factly as I skulk behind a huge pair of sunglasses and try not to gag at the sight of the fresh cream cakes that Valerie is just placing under the display counter.

'Off where?'

'To bed. For a couple of hours at least.'

'I'm sorry, Gen. Would you mind?'

'Of course I don't mind – I'm the one who's just suggested it. And sorry for what? You've put more than enough hours in here. Besides, I'm bored silly upstairs.'

'Well, if you're really sure.'

'Are you still here?' She shoos me away with a tea towel, a smile on her face.

Upstairs, I gulp some more water down then slip gratefully under the cool sheets of my bed. I can't believe the way I behaved last night, although I suppose I just wanted to forget about everything for a few hours. I can't recall the last time I got really drunk. Back home there's always cake deliveries to be made, so I can't risk driving around town the next day with a hangover. Or baking cakes with a hangover, for that matter. I keep going over how confused and wretched André looked when I told him he had a son. I thought I might have felt relieved once things were out in the open but my heart feels heavy. Despite all the thoughts whirling around my head, I can barely keep my eyes open and before too long I have drifted off into a deep sleep.

Three hours later I'm barely awake, just stretching my arms, when there's a tap at the bedroom door. It's Mum, carrying a tray with coffee, orange juice and croissants.

'Hello, love, how are you feeling?' she asks, placing the tray on my bedside table and sitting down gently behind me. 'You looked a bit the worse for wear last night. Did everything go OK?'

I take a long glug of the orange juice and a bite of the croissant, realising it's the first thing I've eaten since yesterday afternoon.

'I stupidly had a bit too much to drink. I ended up partying on Olivier's boat.'

'Oh, darling, well I'm sure you won't be the first one to do that. And you've been working so hard in the shop, it's about time you had a little blow out. How did everything go with André?'

It feels good to confide in my mum, and I tell her all about my meeting with André.

'I just felt so rubbish. He was so quiet when I told him. He looked distraught, which he was bound to be I suppose. I mean, what the hell did I expect?'

'Well, it's a lot to take in. He'll need to time to think. I'm sure he'll be in touch when he's ready. Have you told Jake yet?'

'No,' I sigh. 'Maybe I just wanted to see André's reaction first. The last thing I would ever want is to hurt Jake. You can never tell how these things will turn out, can you? Those long-lost programmes you watch don't always have the happily ever after ending.'

'You've done the right thing,' says Mum reassuringly. 'Jake still has many years to get to know his father, if that's what they both want. In many ways, a young man needs his father more when he grows up. I know your dad had a better relationship with his father as he grew older.' She smiles.

'Thanks, Mum.'

'Are you joining us for dinner tonight? We're having dinner later at Bistro Lemaire. It seems someone promised Gen a night out and champagne when she was in hospital.'

'Oh I did, didn't I! That sounds great, Mum, thanks.'

After Mum leaves, I check my phone for the umpteenth time to see if I have a message from André, but there's nothing apart from a text from Jo with an emoji happy face, saying that she's been on another date with Guy and is looking forward to a catch-up when I get home.

I wonder how André slept last night. I'm sure I would have tossed and turned all night long if it were not for my alcohol-induced slumber. I don't think it's something I'll be repeating too often, though.

It feels rather comforting knowing that Gen is feeling well enough to be back behind the counter of the bakery. Olivier has been a perfectly good stand-in, not to mention a lot of fun and very easy on the eye, and Valerie's a pro, but it's not quite the same as having Gen.

I take a long shower and emerge feeling a little more clear-headed. I grab a bottle of water from the fridge and head outside to the balcony to let my curly hair dry naturally. As I watch the boats in the harbour, I inwardly cringe when I think about my evening of wild abandon. And the puking! Olivier had been kind enough not to mention it this morning, for which I am very grateful, although I'm sure he'll tease me about it sometime in the future. I can't believe I'll be heading home in a few days' time. I'll really miss this view. Much as I love my home town, my place doesn't have an outlook like this as it's a short drive to the sea.

I'm about to nip downstairs and say goodbye to Olivier, when a message flashes up on my phone. It's from André.

Can we meet tomorrow? I think we need to talk.

My heart is beating fast as I tap out a reply and tell him I will meet him at the port at midday.

The reply comes through.

It's OK. I will collect you from the bakery. We can go for a drive.

A feel a huge sense of relief that André has been in touch and I feel a heavy weight lift from my shoulders. I know I can't predict the outcome of our meeting, but it's a start. He's been in touch. I feel lighter as I get dressed.

❧

Olivier crushes me in a lingering embrace and tells me he will take me and Faye out in his boat before we fly home.

'It's very tempting. We may well do that – I imagine it's a beautiful way to see the coast. Although definitely no alcohol before I step on board.'

'Not even a little champagne in a secluded bay? I know many such places.'

'I bet you do.' I laughingly say goodbye with a promise to meet for at least a coffee before we leave.

It's an hour before closing time with little of the stock left when Lilian Beaumont enters the shop. I can't help noticing a smirk on her face.

'Hi, Lilian. I think I may owe you an apology,' I say as I think of my brusqueness when I encountered her last night.

'No need for an apology. I just hope the evening was worth the hangover.' The playfulness in her voice reassures me that she isn't offended.

'How do you know I was hungover?'

'I was here this morning for my bread and there was no sign of you,' she says, lowering her sunglasses and smiling. 'It wasn't hard to figure out. Anyway, I was just calling in on the off chance you may have something for dessert,' she says, eyeing the counter. Her eyes fall on some fresh fruit tarts. 'I'll take those, please.'

'Do you actually eat dessert, Lilian?' I ask as I place the tarts into a box and tie it up with string. Her slender figure has changed little over the years.

'Just a little, yes. But I usually buy it to entertain guests. I believe in never depriving yourself of anything or you will only crave it. Being restrained is the key. A little of what you fancy really does do you good. Talking of which, I think I may have actually found someone I really like. Tonight will be our third date together. I'm going to cook my duck a l'orange, and if that doesn't make him fall in love with me then nothing will.' She smiles as she hands over some money.

'J'espère que tu as du bon temps. Bonne nuit.'

I hold my breath to see if I have correctly told Lilian that I hope she has a pleasant evening.

'Merci, Olivia. Très bien.' She leaves the shop with a broad grin. 'Oh, and next time you have a hangover, try a Bloody Mary.'

Chapter Twenty-Six

We arrive at Bistro Lemaire at seven and sit outside to peruse the menu. I know the food here is delicious, but my appetite seems to have vanished since I met up with André, as anxiety about the future runs through my body.

We share the promised bottle of champagne, before dining on the most divine food, Mum and Dad opting for juicy steak au poivre, whilst the rest of us choose a delicious blanquette de veau, which is this evening's speciality. It's a glorious veal and chicken stew flavoured with herbs, onions and garlic and no lingering hangover or anxiety could stop me eating something so delicious. We eat at an outside table, enjoying the sultry summer evening. I finish my meal with a light-as-a-feather lemon syllabub; the others share a board of local cheeses.

As I sit around the table chatting with my family, I suddenly miss Jake and wish that he was here with us. I've spoken to him most evenings since I've been here, sometimes with a video call, but I long to see his face and hear his voice. I know he is pondering his future and thinking about university and the possibility of not returning; I want to help him to make the right decision.

At around ten, Faye appears with Olivier and they join us for a drink. I can't help noticing that they barely speak to each other

– Olivier chats to Dad and Faye to me, Mum and Gen. As the evening wraps up just after eleven, we stroll back to the apartment after saying goodnight to Olivier. I'm surprised to find that Faye is heading home with us.

'Is everything alright?' I ask her as we amble along.

Faye shrugs and seems a little upset. 'Oh, I know it's silly but we had a bit of an argument earlier. Loads of women kept calling over to say hello to him and I got a bit jealous. I told him he basks in the attention but he just laughed and told me to lighten up. I knew right there and then that I'm nothing special to him.'

I stop and face her. 'Oh no. You haven't fallen for him, have you?'

'I don't think so. What would be the point?' She threads her arm through mine and paints a smile on her face. 'Anyway, forget about it. I want to enjoy the rest of my holiday.'

'Does anyone want a coffee?' asks Mum as we arrive back at the apartment.

'No thanks, Mum. I'll be heading off to bed in a minute. Gen, will you be down in the bakery tomorrow afternoon?' I ask my aunt.

'More than likely, yes.'

'Do you need me to be there?'

I tell everyone all about André asking me to meet up and talk things through.

'Of course you must go. I hope something good will come of it,' my aunt says gently.

'I told you he needed time to get his head around things,' says Mum. 'But at the end of the day he has a son he has never met. It's a lot to take in, but you never know, he might be really looking forward to meeting him.'

I say goodnight and head to my bedroom where I check in with Sam as Faye pours herself a drink and takes it outside onto the balcony. Sam tells me things are going well and she has really enjoyed working full-time. She tells me she spent the afternoon in her mother's vintage clothes shop yesterday, but found herself dreaming up new cake ideas.

As I climb into bed, I wish I could share Mum's confidence. André hasn't made any promises; he has simply said that he thinks we should talk. I pray it won't be the last conversation we ever have.

Chapter Twenty-Seven

The next day André texts me to say that he is waiting outside. I step into the sunshine and take a seat beside him in his black Audi, grateful that he didn't come inside the bakery. There's so much we need to say to each other before I even think about introducing him to my family. Besides, Jake hasn't even met him yet. Faye and Olivier are heading out for the day to Monaco, having seemingly smoothed things over. Faye's slight frostiness yesterday seemed to have worried Olivier a little, and he was round early this morning, keen to make peace and take her out for the day.

'Good morning, Olivia. How are you?'

'I'm good thanks. Relieved that you wanted to see me again. I didn't know what to think after I'd told you about Jake,' I confess.

'Sorry, I didn't mean to worry you, I was always going to see you again,' he says, firing up the engine. 'I thought we could take a drive into St Tropez.'

We turn right at the end of the street and head off towards the coast road. I'm not sure if it's my imagination but he seems a little tense.

'I've never been to St Tropez,' I say suddenly, feeling awkward.

'All those years you spent here as a child and you've never been to St Tropez?'

'I know. Is it as glamourous as I imagine it to be?' My stomach is churning as I attempt to make small talk.

'Well, I suppose it's still a playground for the rich and famous, although now Antibes is considered to be more fashionable. I visited often when I was a young boy. It holds some nice memories for me.'

We crawl through the traffic in Antibes until we are out on the open roads and the wind coming through the sunroof gently blows through my hair. We drive through the Boulevard de la Croisette in Cannes, a curving road running beside the sandy beaches. I marvel at the palatial hotels with smartly dressed doormen standing outside. The designer boutiques jostling for space on the seafront remind me that I never did buy a dress from the Gucci store. Maybe one day. The promenade is lined with the familiar palm trees, standing tall and offering shade in the searing heat. I'm trying to think of something to say but find that any words are stuck in my throat. André is the first to speak.

'When will you be going back to England?'

'In a few days' time.'

I realise going home has somewhat snuck up on me, but now that Gen is getting back on her feet I need to return to my business. At least I'm lucky to have such a trustworthy deputy in Sam, and the help from Nic and Jake.

'I am just beginning to get reacquainted with you and soon you will be disappearing again.' André turns to me briefly and smiles wistfully.

'That seems to be the story of our life.' I dare to hope that this time, things will be different. 'One of us leaving at the wrong moment.'

Driving past a long stretch of sand, André tells me it is the famous Pampellone Beach. 'You see many celebrities on this beach. A friend of mine spotted Sharon and Ozzy Osbourne here a couple of weeks ago.'

I spot beautiful women in tiny bikinis and huge sunglasses striding along the beach past a group of young men playing volleyball. In the distance, speedboats are bouncing along on the glistening sea. Trendy beach bars with cool outside seating areas line the beach road, with club music pumping out even on a Sunday lunchtime.

'This place still looks like the epitome of cool,' I say, despite André me telling me that other places have become just as popular over the years.

'All that glitters is not gold. The local authorities are rather eco-friendly, and think there are too many bars and restaurants along this natural beach, destroying it somewhat.'

'But people must spend a fortune here. Surely it's good for the economy?'

'That's the dilemma, I suppose, but they want to preserve the coastline. The government is frowning on any more establishments being built and have even set about pulling some of the old buildings down. I think the plan is to reduce the number further. I prefer the smaller beaches anyway. The secluded coves that you have to go looking for.'

I realise that we still haven't discussed Jake, but I don't want to pressure him. Perhaps once we have finished the drive.

Before long, we are pulling into the cobble-stoned La Ponche area near the old port of St Tropez. Small, brightly painted fishing boats are a reminder of the town's history as a fishing village but it isn't long before we come across the huge glossy yachts jostling for space on the waterfront. It's hard to imagine the days when fishermen would trawl their nets in the sea to provide food for their families rather than the swanky restaurants overlooking the water.

André finds a parking space and we stroll along for a short while before he suggests a place to stop and have a drink. I order a glass of cool white wine and a jug of water and André orders a bottle of beer. When our drinks arrive, André takes a sip of his beer and looks at me thoughtfully.

'I hope I didn't upset you the other day,' he says eventually. 'I suppose you were wondering what was going through my head; I hardly knew myself.'

'I wasn't upset. I just felt a little sad, really. Guilty perhaps. I know our lives were different back then and you had gone off travelling, but…'

André gently takes my hand in his as I trail off.

'As you say, we were young then. Our lives were different. And I'm the one that should feel guilty for not being there to support you with a young child.' He takes my other hand and grips it tightly. He looks soulfully at me with those blue eyes. 'Although maybe I am saying this as an older man. In truth, it may have scared the living daylights out of me becoming a father at that age,' he tells me honestly.

He keeps hold of one of my hands as we talk.

'So, tell me, Liv. Did Jake have a happy childhood? That is the most important thing.'

I take a long glug of my wine before I tell him all about our life in England and how Jake had the most doting grandparents and friends. I talk of Jake's school days and how he was always a happy, popular little boy. André's eyes squeeze shut tightly and he swallows hard.

'I'm sorry. This can't be easy for you,' I say gently.

'It's OK. I'm glad he was happy. I want to know everything about him. Do you have a photograph of him?'

I flick through my photos until I find a clear head and shoulders shot of Jake, taken last year at a wedding.

'Are you ready?' I ask as I pass him the phone.

'Ready.'

André takes a sharp intake of breath as he looks at the picture and his eyes mist over as he slowly exhales. After staring at it for what seems like forever, a slow smile spreads across his face.

'My son,' he says eventually. 'I can hardly believe it. He's so handsome. He looks a lot like you.' He raises his eyes to meet my gaze.

'Do you think so? I think he looks like both of us. He's definitely got your eyes. Swipe left and have a look through. There's plenty of photos on there.'

'I have a son,' he says again. 'I wish I would have known about him.'

He continues to scroll through the pictures, smiling at every single one.

'But how could you have known? You were about to set off on your travels when I last saw you. There was no social media back then to track you down. And I never knew your family address to write to, as you never took me there.' I realise I am sounding very defensive.

'I know, I'm not saying it's your fault.'

'Besides, you could have called in the bakery if you wanted to ask my aunt about me. If you felt as deeply for me as you claim,' I continue, trying to keep any accusation out of my voice.

'I did think about it,' he says quietly. 'But I was away for seven years. It didn't seem right to try and rekindle something with you all those years later. You might have met someone new, even had a husband and family of your own by then. Life had moved on.'

If only he'd known. I'd had relationships in the intervening years but I don't think I truly fell in love again. Not really. I'd never felt for anyone the way I felt for André, and can't help regretting all those wasted years.

'I would love to meet Jake,' he says after a short while. 'Do you think he would like to see me?'

'I'm pretty sure he would like that,' I say gently, hoping that I'm right.

It's hard to explain how I feel about the possibility of Jake's father being in his life. Since the day he was born it's been just the two of us. It feels like stepping into the unknown and my maternal instinct is to protect my son and make sure he doesn't get hurt.

We sip our drinks quietly for a while longer, mulling over the words we have exchanged. I don't think either of us meant to hurl accusations, however veiled, but emotions were bound to run high. André is the first to speak.

'I never thought I'd have children,' he says, once again staring at the photographs of Jake. 'I was married for six years and during that time we lost two babies.'

'Oh, André, I'm so sorry.'

'Very early stage pregnancies, but heartbreaking nevertheless. My wife refused to try again. She told me she must not have been meant to have children. I suggested we see a doctor, maybe try to get a little help, but she decided our life would be without children and that was that. It put a lot of strain on our marriage. I always imagined that one day I would be a father, and now...'

André covers his face with his hands and I realise he is crying. I cross the table to sit next to him.

'Oh, André, don't be upset.' I wrap my arms around him and he sinks into my embrace. 'Jake is still a young man. You have the rest of your life to get to know him. My mum told me that a boy needs his father even more when he is grown up.'

André turns to face me, dabbing at his eyes with a paper napkin.

'Thank you,' he says quietly. 'It would be nice to get to know Jake. I can't wait to meet him. I hope he doesn't think I would have abandoned him.'

'How could he think that? He knows you weren't even aware of the pregnancy. I've been completely honest with him about everything.'

I pay the bill to a passing waiter and soon enough we are back in the car and heading out of the village beyond the port. André points out local places of interest, before we pull in to one of the secluded beaches he spoke about. There is a single restaurant on the small, immaculate stretch of beach, with maybe a dozen families there, in complete contrast to the throngs lining the beach at Pampellone.

'The burgers here are the best you will ever taste,' says André. 'All hand-made too. That is, if you are a little hungry now?'

I realise I'm actually ravenous, as I was unable to eat a thing for breakfast this morning. My stomach growls gently as we take a seat on some plastic white chairs at a table covered with a red tablecloth.

'It's really pretty here.' I glance across the beach at the foamy waves and a family with young children who are jumping over them and squealing. Children are building sandcastles nearby, paper French flags at the turrets, blowing in the wind. It seems to be mainly families with children here – not a glamourous body-conscious person in sight. I hope all these people playing happy families doesn't stir up feelings of regret in André.

Our food looks mouth-watering. A fat juicy burger is topped with bacon and brie and encased in a brioche bun. It's accompanied by a generous portion of crispy French fries and a green salad.

'This looks good. I didn't realise how hungry I was.' I sink my teeth into the burger. André wasn't joking when he told me how good they are.

'Mmm, how can a beach shack come up with food as good as this?' I say, wiping my chin to catch a dribble of mustard.

'Passion for what they do, I suppose. That gets a bit lost in a chain of restaurants.'

We chat about André's restaurant and he tells me it's going really well.

'It's almost constantly full, which is a great position to be in. Even after the summer season is over, it has a good reputation amongst the locals. I'm very lucky. I may have to ask around for another staff member in a week or two. Henri in the kitchen is going travelling. He reminds me of myself when I was young, heading off into the world, looking for adventure. Although maybe the grass is greener back home,' he says thoughtfully.

We finish our food and stroll along to a secluded part of the beach and André takes my hand in his then turns to face me.

'I think I've told you before that I never forgot you, Liv. Our lives went in a different direction, yet somehow we are back here together, standing on this beach, all these years later. The girl I loved as a young man is right here in front of me.'

'I'm not sure you ever told me you loved me back then,' I say, slightly taken aback.

'Are you sure? Maybe I was a little shy to say it. But I felt it with all my heart. I was torn about going away travelling, but was worried I would regret it for the rest of my life if I didn't at least give it a try. I'm sorry.'

'How can you be sorry? You were a young man. You were following your dream.'

'Perhaps I should have followed my heart.' He takes my hand in his. 'Mon amour perdu.'

I could listen to him speak French to me all day long.

'What does that mean?' I ask, even though I know 'amour' means love.

'My lost love.' He turns to face me, his blue eyes searching mine.

And all these years I've thought that André jetted off without a backward glance, seeing me as nothing more than a holiday romance, when in reality he was wrestling with his emotions.

'I won't lie, I was inconsolable when you left. And finding out I was pregnant at eighteen years of age was terrifying. But I had to pull myself together for the sake of the baby. I couldn't have done it without my mum and dad.'

'Oh, Liv, if only I could turn the clock back.'

'Then things would probably still be the same. As you say, we were just kids.'

'I still can't believe you are here.' André caresses my cheek lightly and draws me close to him.

I inhale his scent and run my hands up and down his back and he nuzzles my neck. 'You smell delicious.' He gently nibbles my ear and I am barely able to think straight.

'So do you. I…'

André moves closer and silences me with a heart-stopping kiss. I feel light-headed and weak at the knees. Suddenly I'm eighteen years old again, standing under that pier without a care in the world, a thousand fireworks exploding through my body. If only I could stand here forever, pretending everything was alright.

'Do you think we should head back?' André asks huskily when we finally come up for air. 'Or I may have to drag you behind one of those sand dunes and ravish you right here and now.'

'Maybe we should, then. Not that it isn't a tempting proposition.'

Although look what happened last time we indulged our passion, I think to myself.

André kisses me again before we stroll back towards the car hand in hand. I feel a contentment I haven't felt in a long time, yet it's mixed with a feeling of uncertainty about the future. It's been exhilarating spending time at this wonderful little beach. I hope I get the chance to return to here sometime soon. But for now, I'm taking things one day at a time.

Chapter Twenty-Eight

We hardly speak as we drive back towards Antibes, but the silence is comfortable. André has asked me to send some photos of Jake to his phone, as he can't get enough of looking at them. It's made me think that I should really get some printed out. We live in a world where our photographs are stored on computers and phones, but what would happen if those devices were stolen? I remember spending hours as a child looking through photos in leather albums at my grandparents' houses before they died, pestering them to get them out so I could gaze at my parents when they were younger. My mother was a real head-turner and Dad a tall, handsome man with dark hair and a strong-looking physique. They are so many pictures of us all as a family when I was a young child too. Photographs taken at beaches, zoos, or sitting in pub gardens on fine days enjoying lunch, me feeling all grown up with a soft drink and a straw. The albums are crammed full of memories. I feel a stab in my heart when I think that André hasn't featured in any of our photographs with Jake when he was a young boy. But I must try not to dwell on things. Not if we have any hope of moving forward.

When André drops me back at aunt Gen's he leans over and kisses me softly on the lips.

'We must make the most of your last few days here. Can I meet you tomorrow evening? Maybe you could come down to the restaurant.'

'That sounds good.'

'We do have a very busy lunch service tomorrow,' he says with a smile. 'But in the evening there will be more staff around, so we will be able to sit down together and eat. Or drink. Whatever you prefer. I'll be in touch.'

As his car disappears around the corner, I take a deep breath. I expect to be bombarded with questions from my parents, when all I would really like is to gather my thoughts alone before getting in touch with Jake. This can't wait any longer.

I head towards the apartment and Dad opens the front door before I have pressed the buzzer.

'Hi, Dad. Did you see me arrive home out of the window?'

'I did. And I just wanted to let you know that there's a surprise for you out on the balcony.'

'A surprise?' I say, shrugging off my cardigan. It really does get very warm up here.

As Dad leads the way through the lounge onto the balcony, I could never have imagined what would await me. My hand flies to my mouth when I see who is enjoying a drink outside.

'Jake! Oh my goodness! What are you doing here?'

'Hi, Mum.' Jake gets to his feet and hugs me tightly. I hug him back, never wanting to let him go.

'Did you know about this?' I ask my parents.

'Not a thing, I swear,' says Dad, raising his hands.

'It's true,' says Jake. 'I came over here on a whim. I managed to get a last-minute flight. I'm only here for a couple of days. Nic is helping Sam out with deliveries.'

I touch his face with my hands.

'It's so good to see you.' My mum and dad join us in the centre of the room for a group hug.

'Gran tells me you've been out for the day, Mum. Anywhere nice?' As he looks at me with his large blue eyes the resemblance to his father almost winds me. A heavy feeling takes over my entire body. How can I tell him that I've just spent the day with his father?

'St Tropez. It was really nice. If I'm honest, though, I think I prefer Antibes,' I say, recalling that André had said the very same thing.

Jake doesn't ask who I've been out with, so maybe Mum told him I had gone out with a friend.

'Have you had something to eat?' I ask Jake.

'Are you kidding? I've been plied with food since the minute I arrived. I'm trying to watch what I eat. I've been baking quite a bit since you've been away. And eating most of it.'

He circles his stomach, which still looks flat and toned to me.

'You and me both,' chuckles Dad as he circles his rather rounder stomach. 'Although how I'm supposed to lose weight staying above a bakery I don't know. Your gran's decided to starve me now. Fish and salad and berries and yoghurt is all I'm allowed.'

'Starve you? As if I could ever do that, Eddie Dunne. You could hardly expect to indulge yourself with cream cakes for weeks on end. It's for your own good.'

'I know. Although I'm really developing a taste for that French cheese. Please don't tell me that's unhealthy.'

'Just don't overindulge. Make sure you have more grapes and wheatgerm biscuits than cheese.'

'Of course, love.' Dad winks at me.

'Right. Talking of food, Jake, you can choose a restaurant for this evening. I'm just going to jump in the shower.'

'OK, cool. I'm going to go for a long walk later – I'll check somewhere out then.'

As the hot water cascades over my body, tears that have been building up inside me overflow and I sob silently. I think of André and the babies he lost. He told me he had always wanted to be a father. Jake may have missed out on having a wonderful father in André and my heart breaks at the injustice of it all. I thought André was young and selfish when he hugged me goodbye to set off on his travels, yet if he had known I was pregnant perhaps he would have stood by me and things could have turned out very differently. Or maybe he wouldn't have been ready for the commitment back then. But they do say everything happens for a reason, so I will just have to trust in fate. And he has come back into my life now, which is something I never expected.

Dad once told me that we can't change the past, but we can 'bloody well have a say in what happens to us in the future'.

I need to try and figure out some sort of future where we all to get to know each other. Thinking about it, maybe this time around the future is something I am not prepared to leave up to fate.

❧

Faye taps on the bedroom door as I am sitting on the bed in a robe about to dry my hair.

'Hi, Liv, how did it go?'

'Oh, Faye, it was such an emotional day. I showed André photographs of Jake and he was overcome. He wants to meet him. I'm just not sure how to tell Jake. He's only over here for a flying visit and I'm asking him to meet his father for the first time. I didn't expect to locate him quite so quickly.'

'No one says he has to meet him this time round. It's only a short flight over to Nice. He could come over whenever he's ready. Give him some time to think about it.'

'I suppose you're right. I just know Jake – he's quite impulsive. If I tell him about his father there's a chance he'll want to see him right away. Of course, there's always the possibility that now that I've found him, he won't want to see him at all.'

'Of course he will. He's been talking of looking him up, hasn't he?'

'I know, but he'll kind of have it thrust upon him suddenly. He might not be prepared for it.'

'Things will work out for the best, don't worry. Remember, whatever happens Jake has you. And us lot. That will never change. Anyway. I'll see you later. By the way, should I tell your mum that your dad's just nipped in to the shop? Gen's been slipping him little sweet treats.'

'I wouldn't get involved in that,' I say with a laugh.

Drying my hair, I reflect on the day spent with André. And that kiss! It was as electrifying as the first kiss we had under the pier at Antibes. I wasn't sure there would still be an attraction between us, but now I know for sure. Maybe an attraction to someone remains forever, given the right circumstances. It is chemistry after all. I suppose walking along a beach and eating at romantic restaurants certainly helps to stir any dormant desire. It makes me wonder how many relationships lose their sparkle simply because they are bogged down with everyday life and the problems it brings, fun and romance never having the chance to surface. I used to laugh at the idea of 'date nights', but maybe they do serve as a reminder to take a little time out for each other.

Chapter Twenty-Nine

We're walking down towards the harbour just after seven when Gen asks Jake if he has decided on somewhere to stop for dinner. I think her knee might have had enough now.

'I did, actually. I went for a long walk this afternoon and found a nice-looking place. It's a bit of a way though. Right at the very end of Port Vauban. I'd say it's maybe a fifteen-minute walk but the menu looks amazing. It's a fish restaurant. Aunt Gen, we can get a taxi down there if you want.'

A fish restaurant right at the very end of the port. Suddenly the colour drains from my face.

'What was it called?' I ask, my heart beating like crazy in my chest.

'Langousta Seafood, I think.'

'Right. Actually, Jake, I think that maybe we should look for somewhere else. I've heard the food there is terrible.'

'Really? I've heard it's difficult to get a table there. Jake did well to get us a reservation,' Gen pipes up.

I glare at my aunt; Mum has clearly not told her about André's restaurant.

Mum clears her throat. 'That must have been a while ago, then. Lilian Beaumont told me that someone got food poisoning there last week. I wouldn't chance it.'

'Oh, right. Well it looked pretty decent when I was down there earlier but I don't suppose you can tell until you actually try the food.' He shrugs.

'Did you make a reservation?' I'm wondering who he spoke to. What if he has already spoken with his father? I feel sick.

'Yeah, a young woman at the front desk booked us in. I'll ring and cancel if no one fancies it though.'

'I'm a little off fish at the moment,' Dad chimes in. 'I didn't feel too good after I had some mackerel a few days ago.'

'So, shall I cancel then?'

'I'll do it. You choose another restaurant around this end of the harbour if you like. Besides, it's too far for Gen and we don't really want to be getting taxis. There's plenty down this end to choose from.'

'OK.' He shrugs.

I ring the restaurant, praying that André doesn't answer the phone. On the third ring a cheery young woman picks up.

'Bonjour, Langousta restaurant, puis-je vous aider?'

I ask her if she speaks English and when she says yes I cancel the dinner reservation. Despite my little exchanges with Lilian, my French is a long way off being fluent.

My goodness, that was close. I need to speak to Jake as soon as possible, as I can't risk something like this happening again. What a mess.

After a five-minute stroll we arrive at our second choice of restaurant, which is a small bistro called Sacha's. Thankfully, when our food arrives, it's delicious and everyone relaxes and settles in for the evening.

'So, how does this compare to Southport, Jake?' Gen asks as we glance around our stunning location.

'Oh yeah, pretty similar.' He laughs.

'When I was a young woman, Southport was a very popular choice for a summer holiday in the north of England,' says Mum. 'People flocked to Blackpool too, of course, before foreign travel really took off, but Southport was always, how can I put it, a little more restrained.'

'You mean a bit more upmarket,' says Dad. 'Although these days, truth be told, it's not the same as it once was. I don't know how half of those hotels and guest houses survive,' he muses.

'Stag and hen parties.'

I often see groups of young men and women in fancy dress walking along the promenade when I'm out with the girls.

'What are people's plans for tomorrow then?' asks Jake over coffee as we wind up our meal. 'I've been reading up on local stuff and I fancy going to the diving boards at the beach in Juan-les-Pins.'

'Isn't that a bit dangerous? Jumping into the sea from rocks? Sounds like a risky business to me,' I say.

'That's just you being my mum. Tons of people do it. The diving boards would have been taken down if they were that dangerous.'

'Technically it's illegal,' says Gen. 'But the police seem to turn a blind eye. The boards have been there for so long, they've become a bit of a tourist attraction. You can book a tour with a local guide though.'

'I wouldn't mind going to the beach in the late afternoon, but I'm afraid you won't be getting me near any diving boards.' Dad laughs as he drains his coffee.

'Well, I could do us all a nice picnic,' Mum offers. 'Let the young ones do whatever they like. I wouldn't mind a spot of sunbathing and a few chapters of my book.'

'Sounds like a plan,' says Jake.

We stroll along in the moonlight, me linking arms with Jake and savouring the last moments of a wonderful evening, when a young man smiles at me as he walks past.

'Bonjour. How are you?'

I wonder if he's mistaken me for someone else, but suddenly recognition dawns. He's the head waiter from André's restaurant; André made a point of introducing us.

'Oh hi, I'm fine, thank you.' I'm walking away as I speak, desperate to get away as fast as I can.

'OK. I hope to see you again soon at Langousta . Bonne nuit.'

'Langousta?' says, Jake turning to face me. 'You told us to avoid it like the plague. What on earth is going on, Mum?'

This is it, then. Jake and I walk on as I tell my parents we need some time alone to talk. Once again I seem to find myself in a situation that has been thrust upon me and all because of a dinner reservation. I'd planned to take Jake for breakfast in the morning and speak to him then. My stomach is in knots as I gesture to a bench up ahead on a secluded area of beach.

'So, what was that all about?' he asks as he takes a seat on the bench. 'You started acting really strange when I spoke about that restaurant.' He looks perplexed.

'I'm not sure where to begin. Something has happened that I wasn't quite prepared for.'

'Go on.'

'You know you talked about wanting to try to find your father, and that I was going to make some enquiries while I was over here as to where he might be. Well…'

'Don't tell me you've managed to find out where he is?' asks Jake, his eyes wide with surprise.

'As a matter of fact, I have. In fact –' I pause for a moment, wondering how he is going to take the news – 'he's living right back here in Antibes.'

Jake is silent for a few moments. He pushes up from the bench and strides across the beach before stopping and gazing out towards the sea. It seems forever before he turns to face me.

'Did you know he was back in France?'

'No, I didn't. And to be honest I never imagined seeing him again. As I said to you, I really thought it was a long shot. It just seemed an opportunity for me to do some asking around. You seemed keen to track him down.'

'Only recently though, if I'm honest. Maybe seeing some of my university friends having bonding experiences with their fathers made me think about my own dad. So have you actually been in touch with him? Have you spoken?'

I think of André's touch, his scent, his kiss, and suddenly and inexplicably feel riddled with guilt.

'I have.'

'How is he?' Jake asks in almost a whisper.

'He's really well. He runs the restaurant that you tried to book us into this evening. That's why I panicked. I wanted you to meet him properly – for you both to have a chance to prepare yourselves. I've told him all about you. He would love to meet you.'

'He'd love to meet me? Really?'

'There's nothing he'd like more.'

'How come he ended up back here? I thought he was desperate to see the world.'

'I suppose a lot of people head home eventually. Although he was away for over ten years.'

I tell Jake all about André and how he had spent his time travelling, and had been married and divorced in Canada before returning to France almost ten years ago.

'Couldn't he have tried to have contact you?'

'But why would he? There was no reason to. He knew nothing about you. I was probably just a holiday romance. At least I thought I was.'

'How do you mean?'

'Well, it seems he thought about me a lot over the years, but assumed my life had moved on.'

I'm watching Jake's expression, which is hard to read. I usually know exactly what he's feeling.

'I'm sorry, Jake. It took me completely by surprise. His sister called in at the bakery and somehow she recognised me from André's description.'

'Well, you still look really young.' There's a half smile on Jake's face.

'I had no idea they lived in the area. Your father still lives a few miles away, in a small village.'

'My father. That sounds really strange. I've never been able to call anyone that.'

'Oh, Jake, I'm sorry.' I can feel tears welling up in my eyes but I must keep it together. 'Maybe it's not too late to get to know him. How would you feel about meeting him?'

'To be honest, Mum, I'm not sure.' He sits back down on the bench again. 'I thought it was what I wanted but it's all so sudden. I never expected to come over here for a few days and be told this. If I'm honest, it feels a little scary.'

Maybe Jake isn't ready for this just yet. I think of André and how excited he was by the prospect of meeting Jake. But it can't be all about his feelings. I have a son to protect.

'I'm curious, naturally. But I've spent all these years without a father and managed so far. And it's not like he's just up the road, is he? He lives in the South of France. How the hell is that going to work?'

I realise I have absolutely no idea.

'I don't know, love. I was just kind of thinking one day at a time, really. There's no pressure. I know we're both going home soon. Maybe you could think about it and come over another time?'

André doesn't know Jake is over here so he can wait a little longer before he meets him. After all, he knew nothing of him for twenty years. It has to be when Jake is ready.

'Do you want to head back?' I ask Jake.

'Actually, Mum, I fancy a beer. Want one?' He points to a quiet bar across the road.

'Sure, maybe just a coffee for me though.'

We cross the road and find a seat at an outside table.

'Did you tell André that I would meet him?'

'I said you probably would, but it's your call. I know you weren't prepared for this, at least not yet. And he doesn't know you're in France. It's up to you if you want to meet with your father. Even if it is out of curiosity, as you say.'

Even though I've already reconnected with André and have spent almost every minute reliving that breath-taking kiss on the little beach in St Tropez, Jake's comments questioning the practicality of a long-distance relationship have really made me think. Is this another holiday romance, twenty years after the last one?

We finish our drinks and stroll slowly along the side streets of the old town – its ancient buildings a feast for the eyes illuminated in soft lights. The Chateau Grimaldi is lit in a soft yellow, a guiding light towards the harbour for returning boats.

'Goodnight, Mum.' Jake squeezes me in a hug before he heads off to the camper van – Mum and Dad are currently enjoying sleeping in the third bedroom. 'I'll sleep on what you said. I'll see you in the morning. Goodnight.'

'Goodnight, Jake. Are you sure you're alright?'

'I'm sure. Night.'

In my bedroom, I have a look at my emails in an attempt to distract myself from my thoughts. There's one from Jo.

Hi Liv,

Really looking forward to seeing you and Faye soon. We definitely need a girls' night out at Le Boulevard. Or maybe you're sick of French food? Perhaps we should try that Indian restaurant I discovered with Guy.

Me and Guy went to the cinema last night to watch the latest Mark Wahlberg film. I can't honestly say it was really my thing, but Mark got his shirt off a few times so it wasn't all bad! Harold the Great Dane tried to hump a six-foot teddy bear in the open-air market today and sent all the stock crashing to the floor (soft toys mainly). The stall holder was fuming. Maybe I ought to stick to walking small dogs. Harold is becoming a bit of a liability even when he's on a lead!

Anyway, see you soon.

Love as ever

Jo xx

Three dates in as many weeks? That's really good going. Things must be moving along nicely for Jo and Guy. I flick through a magazine on my bedside table before trying to settle. I'm exhausted but I find sleep won't come. Was it a mistake to mention André to Jake knowing he was only here for a few days? Should I have waited until we got back home? I have a sudden desire to speak to André but know he will be busy at the restaurant during the evening service. I would love Jake to get to know his father, but as a grown man I suppose only he can make that decision in his own time. As I lie here in bed one thing has become clear to me though: *I* want to get to know André again. To be in his life, however impractical that may be.

Chapter Thirty

We've just finished a breakfast of orange juice, scrambled eggs and bagels on the balcony and Mum is bustling about in the kitchen making up a picnic. She fills a bag with apples, peaches and baguettes with various fillings and two large bottles of elderflower cordial. She pops them all into a cooler box.

'Ooh, I almost forgot my book.' She tucks a paperback into a striped beach bag.

Jake was up early this morning for a run before the heat of the day got too much, and has just emerged from the shower. He grabs a bagel and takes a long swig of fresh orange juice. Gen has decided to stay behind with Valerie in the bakery, insisting just the four of us go and enjoy a day out before we return home. Faye is going to have a day sunbathing, no doubt popping to the harbour from time to time to chat to Olivier.

I've decided I'll definitely go back to England with Jake. My heart tells me it would be good to spend more time with André, but my head is telling me to return to my life in Southport. Much as I've trusted Sam in my absence, I need to go home and see how things are with my business. My real life is back home.

We take the short drive to the beach at Juan-les-Pins and I view the diving boards jutting out from the rocks. There's a small expanse of beach and quite a few people seem to be there already so we're lucky to get a place to settle down. Dad flips open a couple of camping chairs and Mum sets out the large blanket.

'Come on, Mum.' Jake peels off his T-shirt and heads for the boards. 'Didn't you used to be a pretty decent swimmer?'

'I used to be a lot of things. I haven't been swimming for a long time. And there's no way you'd get me on even the lowest diving board.'

I look around for a lifeguard station but there doesn't seem to be one. Perhaps that's why the local police are not keen on people still diving here unsupervised.

There's a trio of boards of varying heights and the tall one seems to soar high into the clouds. Jake is a very accomplished diver but even he stops at the middle one. He bounces gently before springing into the crystal-clear water below and I watch the ripples spread outwards in the sparkling water. He quickly resurfaces and shakes his hair out of his eyes before climbing the steps for a repeat performance.

Several dives later, Jake comes and joins us on the picnic blanket. Crowds have poured in to the tiny beach area in the last half hour and there's barely room to move.

'That was amazing. Are you sure you won't have a go, Mum?' Jake hungrily tucks into a baguette.

'No thanks.'

'How about you then, Grandad?'

'I used to dive off the top board at Southport Municipal Baths when I was a lad. I'm sure I could have a go off the first one.' He stands up and winks at me and Jake.

'No you bloody well will not!' says Mum, tugging at his T-shirt. She looks as though she's about to faint.

'Oh, OK then. I forgot to bring my swimming shorts anyway,' says Dad, sitting back down.

'You stupid bugger.' Mum sits down on the blanket next to Dad and puts her hands around his throat and jokingly throttles him. 'One of these days, Eddie Dunne.'

Dad pours us each an elderflower cordial and we chat easily.

'It's lovely here,' says Jake. 'I think I could get used to living in a place like this. It's getting a bit crowded though. I'll have a couple more dives, then we could find a quieter stretch of beach if you like.'

'I know a place a couple of miles up the road,' I say, recalling the Café Flore where I met Françoise, where she gave me the photographs of Marineland. The café overlooked a quiet stretch of beach with a short pier.

Jake climbs above the middle board and heads to the top one and my heart is in my mouth. I shout up to him but he can't hear me. Instead he gives us all a wave. What the hell is he doing? Hardly anyone has dived off the top platform and suddenly a group of people are gazing up at him. Jake jokingly flexes his muscles, playing to the crowd, and a few seconds later, he leaps off. His dive is as smooth as a swallow. I know I shouldn't be too concerned, but my insides are jittering. I seem to be staring at the turquoise water forever, along with the other onlookers, and a feeling of panic engulfs me. Where is he? I'm about to scream for help, fearing the worst, when Jake resurfaces and punches the air. He lets out a loud whoop and the crowd erupt into loud applause. I breathe a huge sigh of relief.

'Don't you ever put me through that again,' I tell him when he jogs back over. We're heading towards the quiet beach, and I think I need a large brandy from the café when we get there.

'I've told you, Mum. You worry too much.' Jake laughs.

Driving along, I realise I need to speak to André. I'm supposed to be meeting him this evening at the restaurant but I'm going to have to put him off. I guess things never turn out as neatly as we would like them to.

The beach is long, with soft golden sand, and as expected is a lot less busy. Half a dozen people are swimming in the sea and a couple riding a pedalo quietly drift by. We grab a table outside on the terrace of the café and order some drinks.

'It's gorgeous here,' says Jake as he sips a bottle of beer. 'I think I might hire a speedboat tomorrow and have a whizz around the coast if you fancy it, Mum.'

'Speedboats make me feel a little nauseous, if I'm honest. All that bobbing up and down on the water.'

'Would you prefer to be on one of those fancy yachts then?'

The mention of yachts makes me think of vomiting over the side of Olivier's father's yacht.

'Not especially. I don't really have sea legs at all, come to think of it.'

Jake has always had a love for water. He learned to swim at a very young age and I could never get him out of the swimming baths. Even now, when he heads to the gym, he always finishes off with a long swim. Perhaps he takes after his father. André loves the sea and he told me his father had a fishing boat all his life. Maybe these things really are in the genes.

Whilst everyone is enjoying a cold drink, I excuse myself and nip inside to ring André.

'Bonjour, Liv. How are you today?'

I barely know what to say to André. How can I tell him that his son has turned up unannounced? And that he isn't sure whether or not he wants to meet him? Maybe I should just cancel this evening's date, and reassess everything when we get home. But that means not seeing him again before I leave. I must have left the silence too long, as André asks me if everything is alright and despite myself I find myself telling him all about Jake's arrival.

'Oh, André, I can't believe what I'm about to tell you. I had a visitor arrive here yesterday.'

'A visitor? To see you?'

I let out a long sigh. 'I was thrilled to see him because I'd missed him quite a bit since I've been over here, but I just wasn't expecting it. It's Jake. Here's here in Antibes.'

'Jake is here?' André sounds completely shocked. It seems to be an age before he carries on talking. 'How long is he staying?'

'Well, that's the thing, he's only here for a couple of days. I was going to wait until we were both home before I told him about us being reacquainted, but somehow it all came tumbling out.'

'You have told him I live here?'

I tell André all about Jake booking the restaurant last night and how I had to cancel it.

'I didn't want you meeting him like that. Oh, André, it's such a mess. I wish I'd never said anything now. I'm not sure if he's ready to meet you just yet,' I tell him honestly.

'Well, I can't blame him for that. It took me a while to figure things out in my head when you told me about Jake. Give him some time.'

We chat for a short while longer before André tells me he will be in contact shortly and we wrap up the call.

Outside, I take a stroll to the water's edge and Jake jumps up and follows me.

'Fancy a paddle then, Mum?'

I slip my sandals off and dip my toe into the frothy waves. The water is warm so I let my feet sink into the soft wet sand, which seems to gently massage my toes. It feels wonderful.

Jake peels his T-shirt off and gently pushes off into the water before flipping over onto his back. He's gazing up towards the blue sky with a contented grin on his face. Maybe it was exactly what he needed, coming over here. Everyone needs a change of scenery from time to time and I can't really remember the last time Jake took a proper holiday, aside from the odd weekend with his uni friends.

'I'm really enjoying being here,' he calls to me. 'The weather's brilliant. I can't imagine swimming in the sea back home like this. It was raining when I left.' Jake grins as we stroll back towards the seating area to join Mum and Dad.

'So where do you fancy for dinner tonight then?' Jake turns to face me and I get a glimpse of his father. I've noticed it a lot more since I've met up with André. I never realised quite how similar they are.

'Is that all you ever think about?'

Jake ate breakfast and most of Mum's picnic but, looking at his slender physique, I really don't know where he puts it.

'I'm in France. I want to sample all there is to offer.'

'What do you fancy then? Classic French? Modern European? I think there's even a couple of Italian restaurants in the old town.'

'I was thinking fish. I fancy a nice sea bass. Maybe we should try the restaurant that you cancelled last night.'

'Langousta?'

'Why not?' He shrugs. 'That is, assuming they've sorted out the hygiene problem. Or did they poison someone? I can't quite remember.' He narrows his eyes and grins.

I can't believe Jake is being so jokey about André's restaurant but perhaps he's playing it cool. I assumed he would want to meet him alone, but maybe that's exactly what he doesn't want.

'Are you sure? You do know André will be there? Is this the way you want to meet him?'

'I think so, yeah. Gran and Grandad can come too. They've been like my parents, as well as you.'

'Well, in that case I'll phone André. See if that works – he can reserve the best table.'

Chapter Thirty-One

My thoughts are in a spin as I rifle through my wardrobe and select something for this evening's meal. My arms are a warm brown and the whole of my body is beginning to take on a golden glow despite me spending long hours in the bakery. I choose a black linen shift dress that has a neckline studded with colourful gems.

I phoned André as soon as we arrived home and he was delighted to reserve a table for us all this evening. He said that he hoped he would be able to spend some time with Jake tomorrow, just the two of them, if all goes well.

I'm surprised Jake didn't want to meet his father alone, or at least with me. But it's nice to see the closeness between Jake and his grandparents and his desire to have their support tonight as well. I feel so proud of him.

I glance out of the window that overlooks the street and am stunned to see Lilian Beaumont dismount the pillion of a motor-bike, her handsome bearded friend in the driver's seat. She tucks a helmet under her arm and heads into the shop. It would appear she has nurtured her friend back into good health.

I decide to avoid going downstairs and engaging in my almost daily French lesson with Lilian, as I don't want to be drawn into discussion about Jake. Not just yet. Aunt Gen has told me she won't discuss things with anyone until I am ready to do so.

I'm just stepping out of the shower when there's a tap at my bedroom door. It's Mum.

'We're going to meet on the balcony outside shortly for a pre-dinner cocktail,' she tells me. 'I've bought the ingredients for a French martini. Gen has a cocktail shaker and I found some lovely vintage cocktail glasses in that huge cabinet in the lounge.'

'Sounds great, thanks, Mum. I had a French martini when I went to André's restaurant the other day, it was delicious.'

Mum comes and sits down on the edge of the bed.

'Are you sure you're alright, love? Your head must be spinning with everything that's been going on this past week.'

'It's been a bit of a roller coaster of emotions I suppose, but everything happens for a reason. Isn't that what you always say? What were the chances of André's sister walking into the bakery when I was here behind the counter? I would never have known where André was living otherwise.'

'That's true, although I suppose if you were really serious about tracking André down you could have looked into it properly. You know, got some professional help or looked on the Internet. Maybe even contacted that show I watch about reuniting families.'

'You're right, maybe I could have. But I always thought it was Jake's decision if he wanted to meet his father, not mine.'

She nods and stands to leave. 'Faye's joining us for a cocktail before meeting Olivier. Oh, and Aunt Gen won't be coming with us tonight. She has a date with Lilian Beaumont later, who will no doubt fill her in on all the details of her latest romance. Would you believe she rocked up at the bakery earlier on the back of a motorbike?' Mum laughs.

'I know, I saw her from the bedroom window. And yes, I would believe it anyway. Nothing she does ever surprises me.'

At seven we are all sitting on the patio furniture on the balcony, sipping our delicious cocktails.

'What a view,' says Jake, taking in the view of the harbour. 'How could you ever get tired of looking at it?'

'I suppose wherever you live you eventually take it for granted,' says Dad. 'You become a bit immune. Until you move away, that is. I grew up in a village house with a huge back garden full of apple and pear trees. I looked out of my bedroom window every morning to the sight of my tyre swing threaded through an old oak tree. I missed that garden for years when we upped sticks and moved to Southport, as Mum had always dreamt of living near the sea. I'm glad we moved though. Or I never would have met your grandmother.' He casts an affectionate glance at Mum and she places her hand over his and smiles.

'Right then,' says Dad, looking at his watch. 'I think it's time we made a move. We don't want to make a bad first impression by being late. Are you ready for this, Jake?'

'Ready as I'll ever be,' he replies, finishing his drink. 'Let's go.'

Chapter Thirty-Two

We make small talk, me a bag of nerves as we amble along the cobbled streets, Mum occasionally commenting on something in a boutique window or Dad admiring a parked car. Jake stops and eyes a shirt in a shop window with a price tag of €100. He's probably as nervous as I am, and enjoying the distraction of the designer clothes on display.

'I don't think that's quite your colour,' I say, trying to quell the rising nerves in my body.

'I don't think it's my price range either. I'm a poor student, remember.'

For how long? I think to myself, but don't say anything.

As we approach the far end of the harbour and the white frontage of Langousta comes into view my stomach begins to churn. How will Jake react when he sees his father for the first time? And then what? I like to think that I'm someone who takes life one day at a time but I can't help worrying about it all. Maybe Jake was right when he implied he couldn't see how our lives could mesh together, given the distance between us.

'Do you want to wait out here, Jake?' I gesture to an empty table outside. Jake nods and I wrap him in a hug and wish him good luck.

André had texted me and suggested he meet Jake alone for a few minutes before they head inside and join the rest of us for dinner.

André strides towards us with a smile on his face when we head inside and I introduce him to my parents; he shakes hands with them warmly. Mum's hand goes to her mouth when she meets him.

'Oh my goodness, you look just like him,' she says, her eyes misting over.

'I hope it goes well,' I whisper.

'Merci. See you soon.'

André shows us to our reserved table and gestures to a waiter to take our drinks order. I see him take a deep before he heads outside. He's clearly nervous.

We sip our drinks and it seems like Jake and André have been outside forever. I stand up for the umpteenth time, debating going outside, before sitting back down again.

'Sit down,' orders Mum. 'You're like a jack-in-the-box. You're making *me* nervous.'

In an attempt to distract me, she comments on the décor in the restaurant and Dad says that the delightful smells coming from the open kitchen are making him hungry.

'What a glorious place to have a restaurant. Look at those windows.' Mum glances out at the boats in the water.

'It's beautiful, isn't it? André said it took a lot of time and effort to get things just the way he wanted.'

'It's very smart,' says Dad as he sips a bottle of beer. 'And very popular too, by the look of things.'

Every table is full, even on a Monday, and waiting staff zip back and forth carrying plates of fragrant seafood to the tables.

I still can't sit still and I'm about to nip to the ladies' when the door opens and in walks André, closely followed by Jake. As they stride towards us I can see that they both have red-rimmed eyes, but broad smiles, and I exhale deeply. I think it's going to be alright.

'Shall we?'

'There are so many things we have to say to each other,' says André after he has ordered himself and Jake a beer. Mum and I share a bottle of crisp, cold Sauvignon Blanc. 'It's a shame you have to leave so soon.'

Jake nods, a little forlornly.

'We will have to get to know each other a little more in the time we have,' André adds. 'Although I warn you, given your love of cooking I may rope you into helping in the kitchen.'

André has probably just delivered the best news Jake could wish to hear.

'And now,' says André. 'May I recommend the speciality of the house? Sea bass in a special saffron cream sauce.'

'Sounds good to me,' says Jake.

André speaks to a waiter, who disappears before reappearing swiftly with a basket of bread accompanied by balsamic vinegar and olive oil.

'We have so much to talk about. You must tell me all about what you do back home. I want to know everything about your hopes and dreams for the future.'

We talk amiably, but are all silenced when our food arrives and we tuck into the most delicious sea bass. It's served with sautéed potatoes and roasted vegetables.

'This is heavenly.' I savour the taste of the delicious food, which is perfectly balanced —none of the flavours overpower the gentle taste of the sea bass. 'Compliments to the chef.'

'I'm very lucky Marco has stayed here. He was hired by my father as a young chef. He tells me there is nowhere else he would rather work.'

'Quite right. This is a pretty idyllic place to spend the day working. Not to mention taking a coffee break out there.' I point to the stunning view through the window.

If anyone would have told me that I would come to France this summer and find myself sitting at a dinner table, glancing across at Jake and his father, I would have said they were crazy. I can still barely believe it.

As we step outside into the moonlight a little after ten, we say our goodnights.

'I was wondering,' says André, turning to Jake, 'would you like to come out on a speedboat tomorrow? Have a ride around the coast. Just the two of us.'

Jake's face breaks into a broad smile.

'Sure, why not?'

As André hugs me goodnight I whisper a thank you in his ear. I can't think of a better way for them to spend the day together than going out on a boat. Even though I long to wrap my arms around André and end the evening with a passionate kiss, for now that can wait. I'm just happy he is making an effort to get to know Jake.

'How are you feeling?' I ask Jake as we walk home in the moonlight, passing the busy bars and restaurants, the sound of laughter ringing out.

'I'm not sure,' he replies, and my heart sinks a little. 'Don't get me wrong, André seems like a great guy but it all seems a bit surreal if I'm honest. I wasn't really prepared.'

Jake is quiet as we walk along and I'm wondering if I might have made the wrong decision in telling him about André. Perhaps I should have waited and chosen the right moment. Maybe it is all a bit too much for him to take in.

Turning left to take a shortcut through the old town, we pass a bar with two women seated outside sipping cocktails. It's Aunt Gen and Lilian Beaumont. They beckon us over to join them.

'Bon soir! Have you had a good evening?' asks Lilian.

'Great thanks, Lilian. And thank goodness you are not speaking to me in French. I don't think my brain could come up with the right responses at the moment,' I say with a laugh.

'You have had too much to drink?' she queries.

'No, not at all. It's a long story.'

'Then you can tell me all about it over a cocktail.' She snaps her fingers at a young waiter, who is clearing a nearby table, and he takes our order.

'Jake, will you have a cocktail too? Or would you prefer a beer?'

'No, go on, a cocktail's fine.'

'Which one?'

'Surprise me,' says Jake, as he excuses himself to nip inside to the toilet.

'I saw you getting off a motorbike earlier,' I tell Lilian. 'How are things going with the man-friend?'

'It's been wonderful,' she says with a faraway look in her eyes, and not one that I've seen before on her face. 'Juan is such fun. So spontaneous. We headed off into the hills today with absolutely no idea where we were going. We are going to go skiing at Val d'Isère when his leg has completely healed.'

'I must admit I never had you down as a biker, Lilian.'

'I'm not a biker. I'm just open to different experiences. It's the only way to live life. Ooh, here we are. Santé.' Lilian takes a sip of the drink that the waiter has just placed in front of her as Jake reappears at the table.

'What's this then, Lilian? Are you trying to make sure I'm getting my five a day?'

Jake's drink is served in a pineapple-shaped glass with a profusion of tropical fruit poking out from the top.

'It's a piña colada. Is that alright?'

'It's fine. I told you to surprise me.' He takes a sip of the drink with a smile on his face.

'Did you find a nice restaurant for dinner?' Lilian enquires as she sips a brandy Alexander.

'Really good,' says Jake. 'We went to Langousta fish restaurant at the very end of the harbour.'

'Ah yes, Langousta is excellent. It has quite a reputation.'

'For what? Giving people food poisoning?' He glances at me with a raised eyebrow.

'I don't understand,' says Lilian, looking perplexed.

'Never mind,' I say. 'It's a long story. I'll fill you in tomorrow, that's if it's OK with you, Jake?'

'Yeah, sure. Anyway, santé!'

Mum and Dad are in bed when we arrive back at the apartment, so we say our goodnights to Gen. Faye is still out with Olivier, no doubt having a lot of fun. Jake looks shattered, the raw emotions of the meeting with his father etched across his face. But he's actually met him! I can hardly believe it. I just hope they enjoy spending the day together tomorrow. As I climb into bed exhausted, I pray that everything will be alright and soon enough I slip into a deep, dreamless sleep.

Chapter Thirty-Three

André has arranged to meet Jake at a little jetty opposite Bistro Lemaire at one o'clock and I can't help wondering how he's feeling about it.

I ask Jake if he's OK when I load the dishes from our utterly delicious eggs Florentine, which Jake made for breakfast, into the dishwasher.

'I'm fine, Mum, really.'

'It's just you seemed a little uncertain about meeting André again today.'

'I think I was just tired last night. Maybe a bit overwhelmed. But I would like to get to know André better – he seems like a really good bloke. And that restaurant – wow. It's just amazing.'

'I know. It was quite a humble place to start with I believe. André has spent a lot of time, and probably money, getting the place exactly how he wants it.'

'Right, well, I'm off for a mooch around the market. See you later.'

I make a coffee and take it into my bedroom to have a quick catch-up with Faye, and Jo on speakerphone. I fill them in on the details about André and Jake. Jo is thrilled that things are going well, although thinks I should take things slowly with André. 'I don't want you getting hurt for a second time.'

'I can hardly believe what's happened lately. How do you feel about going home? It would be difficult having a long-distance relationship,' Faye reminds me.

'I honestly don't know. Me and André haven't really talked too much about the future. There's definitely still a spark between us, but really it's all about Jake's relationship with him at the moment. He's got a lot of catching up to do.'

'So have you,' Jo says. 'You deserve to be happy too, remember.'

I sigh as I think about the impracticalities of the situation. Perhaps I shouldn't be looking back to a time when I was here with my first love, but looking forward. My business is back home in England. My life is there. I've been so grateful to Sam for taking charge these last couple of weeks, but she can't do that forever. And of course there's my parents. Even though they're in good health at the moment, they're marching on in years. Things could change. But then I think of André. That kiss at the beach stirred up feelings of longing I haven't felt in such a long time. Having that kind of attraction to someone is rare and some people only experience it once in a lifetime, if at all. I've never felt for anyone the way I felt for André all those years ago. I'm not going to lose him a second time. I feel so torn about everything.

'Right, I'll see you later. I'm meeting Olivier for a drink at the harbour later but I want to do a last bit of sunbathing first,' Faye says, glancing at her watch.

I try to busy myself throughout the next couple of hours, popping down to the shop to help out, but Gen and Valerie are back into their old routine and I'm mostly in the way. In any case, my thoughts keep flitting to Jake and André, and I wonder how they're getting along. André couldn't have come up with a better suggestion than hiring a speedboat and setting off into the sea, given Jake's love of water. I imagine them pulling into little coves, grabbing a beer from a bar then chatting about this and that, putting the world to rights. But what if they have nothing to say to each other? At around two thirty, I decide to take a walk down to the harbour and maybe have a drink.

I buy a glass of wine from a small bar and gaze out to sea. It's so peaceful here, even with the crowds of people strolling along the waterfront. It has such charm. I'm daydreaming about that kiss with André, getting goose bumps, when I spot Olivier in sunglasses tying up a speedboat. I raise an arm and, when he realises it's me, he heads over.

'Olivia! How are you? Fancy a spin?' He's looking as smooth as ever in a black T-shirt and white shorts. Surprisingly, he doesn't have a stunning girl in tow.

'You know I'm not really one for the water,' I say.

'You prefer the larger yachts as I recall.' He has a wicked grin on his face.

'Don't remind me, please.' I grimace at the thought.

'OK, if you don't want to hop aboard, I'll finish mooring up and come and have a drink with you. I'm meeting Faye here shortly.' He takes a glance at his watch.

As he strides back towards me a few minutes later, I think I must be the envy of every female within a thousand paces. Women seem to appear from nowhere, saying 'Bonjour, Olivier' and peering over their sunglasses to eye me up and down.

'It's good to see you, Liv.' He crushes me in a hug and I get a whiff of the most alluring musky aftershave. 'I'm missing our mornings in the kitchen.' After ordering a beer, Olivier chinks his bottle against my glass of wine, which has begun to relax me a little.

I find myself telling Olivier all about Jake and André as, despite his playboy persona, he's a really good listener. I found him really easy to talk to when we worked together in the bakery.

'I just passed two men near a cove swimming and snorkelling. I don't know if it was them, but they looked about like they could be father and son.'

'Did they look as though they were enjoying themselves?' I ask, keen to know if things are going well.

'I didn't pay too much attention, but I think I remember them laughing, so yes. It looks as though they were enjoying themselves. Maybe you are worrying a little too much.'

'Jake always tells me I worry too much. I can't help it. I suppose I just want everything to be perfect.'

'Then you are always going to be disappointed. Nothing in life is perfect. But you are very lucky if life is good.'

'You're right. I must learn to count my blessings. Thanks, Olivier.'

'No problem.' Olivier sinks back into the bamboo chair and smiles at me.

'Do you have nothing better to do than sit around chatting to attractive women?' comes a voice from behind me. It's Faye.

'Faye! You are here! And looking delightful.' Olivier is up on his feet and kissing her on both cheeks.

'I wish I had your life,' sighs Faye as she takes a seat.

'Which bit? Messing about on the water or talking to beautiful women?'

'I meant baking bread. Just kidding. No, I mean the freedom to seemingly do as you please. I bet it doesn't feel like you're on a treadmill like the rest of us.'

'Sure, I suppose I am lucky. But as Liv and I were just saying, we should learn to count our blessings.' Olivier asks Faye if she would like a drink.

'Just a tonic water please. I'm taking it easy. Have you finished taking tourists out for the day then, Olivier?' Faye asks.

'I have. So now it's time for a little fun. I was thinking of maybe heading across to Cannes for something to eat?'

'Sounds amazing.'

We finish our drinks and Olivier and Faye stand up to leave.

'It's been a joy running into you, Olivia. You have my number. Call me anytime you like if you want a chat.'

It's nice to have a man to talk to and Olivier could easily become a really good friend, much to my surprise.

He kisses me on both cheeks before climbing back into the speedboat with Faye and roaring off into the sea, the boat leaving white foamy waves in its wake.

I think about Olivier's comments. *Nothing in life is perfect.* Maybe that's why I'm such a perfectionist with my cakes, as they're something I can have a little control over, but even when I do a good job I can't guarantee the customer won't be disappointed. Human beings aren't like that. We're inherently flawed. We mess up. I suppose all any of us can do is try to be the best person we can possibly be.

Chapter Thirty-Four

Back at the apartment, I make a half-hearted effort to start packing. It's a strange feeling. I almost feel I have left my own life behind in England, although maybe that's because I'm here with my parents and more recently Jake. And, of course, Aunt Gen, so it all feels a little like home from home. I don't have any siblings, so all of my family is right here in Antibes at the moment.

But I have a different life back home. And friends who are as good as family. Not to mention a business to think about, so no matter what I must return and carry on with life. I wonder where Mum and Dad's next adventure will be. Maybe they'll head back to Spain when they leave here. Mum always fancied going to Andalucía and stopping at Toledo. Or maybe she would like to go home, where she can sleep in her own bed. The travel thing is probably something that will come to an abrupt end when Dad has got it out of his system anyway. Mum may get the garden of her dreams when they eventually settle down into old age, spending their days quietly dining out and visiting garden centres. It's hard to imagine, as they're so fit and active at the moment, but old age creeps up on us all.

It's almost four thirty when there's a gentle tap on my bedroom door. It's Jake.

'Hi! How was your afternoon?'

I'm relieved to see that Jake has a broad smile on his face.

'It was good, thanks. Want a drink? We can take it outside if you like, and I can tell you more.'

'Sounds perfect.'

'So what did you get up to?' We're seated on the balcony and I take a sip of the crisp, cold Chardonnay.

'We went snorkelling and swimming in some of the smaller bays, then we went to the far end of Juan-les-Pins and had something to eat. Some of the yachts we saw were something else. There's some serious money around here.'

'Money isn't everything,' I say.

'Suppose so. It gives you freedom to do exactly what you want though,' he muses.

'I agree. But we do have to have some sort of plan for our future though, or we end up aimlessly drifting along.'

Maybe being over here will give Jake some time to really think about his own future and what he wants from his life.

'It doesn't seem to have done André any harm.' He takes a sip of his coffee.

'What do you mean?'

'Well, he went travelling the world and ended up coming back here and landing on his feet.'

'That's because he inherited his father's restaurant. Most people don't find themselves in such a situation. He could have come back to France with nothing, having to scrape a living in his thirties.'

There's an unease rising in me and I'm not sure what Jake is trying to tell me. Has he been seduced by the sunshine and glamour of the Côte d'Azur? He's only been here a couple of days!

'It might have been cool to have spent this summer travelling around, but I don't really have the cash,' says Jake.

'That's because you never save any money.'

Jake has a student loan and does bar work, but money slips through his fingers. He's nothing like me. I like to save at least a small amount of money each month.

'I know. When I'm back home I like going out with my mates, though, and that costs money. I wouldn't mind staying here for the summer actually.'

'*Here?*' I'm not sure I've heard right. 'Do you mean with your aunt?'

'Yeah. I thought I might work here over the summer. One of André's kitchen staff is going off travelling next week.'

'Yes, I remember him telling me that.'

'So, he's offered me a job.' He looks at me with those blue eyes, that I can never say no to. 'I told him all about my love of cooking and baking. I'd be at the very bottom of the brigade to begin with, of course, chopping and preparing things and probably washing pots, but who knows where it could lead?'

He's grinning broadly and there's a real excitement in his voice. I don't want to burst his bubble, but for a moment I'm too stunned to speak. I have thoughts of Jake spending the summer working here and eventually abandoning all thoughts of going home and finishing his degree and I feel such conflicting emotions. I tell myself it's just a summer job. Don't most students take such jobs? And at least he would be bonding with his father, which can only be a good thing.

'Well, I didn't expect that.' I'm hoping the mixed feelings I have about this aren't etched across my face. It feels strange to think that I'll soon be heading back to England and could be leaving my son here with his father.

'What do you think Sam will say about you spending the summer holidays over here?'

'Sam? What's she got to do with it?' he asks, with a slightly puzzled expression.

'I just thought you two had grown close, that's all. Maybe I got that wrong.'

'I really like Sam, a lot, she's cool. But not in that way. She's more like a big sister to me. She's such a talented baker. I think she's really enjoyed taking the helm at the business while you've been over here. You're lucky to have her, considering her grand plans for the future.'

'Grand plans?'

'Well, you know, she wants to open her own cake shop or café eventually, she's made no secret of that.'

'True, and she's obviously proved to herself that she can run a business these past couple of weeks.'

Maybe change could be afoot for us all.

We're finishing our drinks when a text comes through on my phone. It's from André.

Hi, beautiful. Just to let you know I had a great afternoon with Jake, and you will be relieved to know that we got along really well. Do you fancy going out for dinner? Jake can come too of course, although I won't lie, I'm desperate to see you alone. X

Mum and Dad appear on the balcony and ask us if we fancy a drive to Nice this evening. 'It's meant to be lovely there in the evening. Lots of little squares with fountains and restaurants with ivy-covered walls.'

'It sounds very romantic. Are you sure you two don't want to go alone?' I tease them.

'I'll drive if you like, Grandad,' Jake offers. 'I quite fancy cruising along the coast road in my Ray-Bans with the music pumping.'

'Pity it isn't in a more glamourous car. I don't think a campervan quite cuts it,' Dad smiles.

'Actually, André has just invited me for dinner tonight. You too, Jake, if you like.'

'No, you're alright, Mum. You two go and spend some time together. I really do fancy driving along the coast road.'

I feel a tingle of excitement at the thought of meeting up with André alone.

'Well, if you're sure. Although I am pretty tempted to come along with you all. I remember Nice is lovely, though it must have changed since I was last there.'

I feel excited at spending the evening alone with André and tap out a reply accepting his invite. He tells me he'll collect me at seven.

An hour later, after the shop has closed, everyone heads off for their evening in Nice and I slip into a jasmine-scented bubble bath. I get butterflies in my stomach when I think of André's strong arms around me, kissing me slowly underneath the stars. If I close my eyes, I can smell his masculine scent as I nuzzle up to him.

Once I'm out of the bath, it takes forever selecting something to wear for this evening, but I eventually settle on a slightly low-cut, green skater-style dress. I add a silver necklace and jewellery before slipping into some cork wedges. The dress colour brings out the green in my eyes perfectly, and contrasts with my curly hair. Looking at my wedges, at once I remember carefully making my way up on to the wet stage at Marineland over twenty years ago, wearing similar shoes. I can hardly believe how much things have changed these last few days. Here I am, deliberating over what to wear for a date with André, and Jake has actually met him!

Soon enough it's time for me to slip downstairs and wait for André. I'm surprised to find that he's already waiting for me outside.

'How long have you been here?' I ask in surprise. 'You should have rung the bell and come up.'

'I was about to.'

'You could come in and have a drink first, if you like. There's no one home.'

'Really?' says André with a cheeky grin. 'Then lead the way.'

'OK. Maybe just the one drink. I've booked a table for seven thirty but it's not far.' I take a glance at my watch that shows it's exactly seven o'clock.

I pour us each a gin and tonic and André carries his to the balcony to take in the view.

'What a great place. Right in the heart of the old town and a view of the harbour. This place would be snapped up if it ever went up for sale.'

I can imagine it would. It even has its own car park. It's a little gem.

'Your aunt has really good taste,' André remarks as we finish our drinks and he takes in the stylish interior of the large lounge.

'She always did. I remember coming here as a child and being fascinated by all the gorgeous things here. I thought everything was so glamourous, including my aunt. She was a real beauty.'

I point to one of the black and white photographs on the wall, where she is standing on a boat with Uncle Enzo.

'Obviously good looks run in the family. By the way, you look beautiful tonight. I'm thinking maybe I should cancel the dinner reservation.' André circles his hand around my waist and pulls me towards him.

'No chance, I'm ravenous.' I pull away from him, even though my senses are reeling. I'm determined to enjoy the anticipation of the evening, savouring every minute of the time we have together before I have to head home.

We walk for around five minutes before we stop at an old stone building with red shutters at the windows. A small illuminated sign shows the name: Al Fassia.

'Moroccan?' I say in surprise.

'I thought it would make a nice change. You do like this type of food, don't you?'

'Oui. There's such a strong Moroccan influence here – some great restaurants.'

André pushes the door of the restaurant open to reveal a richly decorated room with a gentle waft of cinnamon in the air. Dark wooden tables sit on a striking blue mosaic floor, and ornately carved wooden lamps with coloured stained-glass shades hang from the ceiling. A smiling waiter guides us to a table set with glass tumblers richly decorated in gold. He puts down a jug of water with ice and lemon.

'This place is really gorgeous.' I take a seat and André pours us each a glass of water from the jug.

We peruse the menu and in no time at all, our waiter is delivering the most fragrant of lamb dishes to the table. It's served with couscous and pitta breads, along with a side salad decorated with pomegranate seeds that look like little jewels.

'Has Jake spoken to you about staying here over the summer?' André asks me matter-of-factly. 'It would be great for him to have a bit of experience in a real kitchen. He told me all about his love of cooking.'

'He did mention it, yes. I'm happy that you two seem to have got along so well together today. I spent the whole afternoon worrying about it.'

'He is a grown man, Liv. Maybe you need to cut the apron strings a little.' There's a smile on André's face as he says this and I know he's teasing, but his words sting. I've had to be both mother and father to Jake all these years, so maybe it's not surprising that I am a little overprotective of him.

'Well, you can't blame me for feeling anxious about Jake meeting you for the first time. It could have been a disaster,' I say in my defence.

'I know. It sounds like you've been a wonderful mother to Jake. He wouldn't be the fine young man he is otherwise.'

I feel a sudden surge of pride and swallow down a lump in my throat as André leans across and covers my hand with his. 'I regret I wasn't around to see him growing up, but I'm grateful for the chance to be a part of his life now.'

The lamb is deliciously tender, infused with the gentle flavours of rosemary and cinnamon and I hungrily eat every single bit. We have a light dessert of rose-flavoured ice cream dotted with sultanas, which is creamy and delicious. I've enjoyed every moment of my time in this surprising oasis of calm down a busy side street, but I'm looking forward to a cocktail now.

We stroll along the cobbled side streets until we eventually arrive at the bar with the blue metal chairs, the same place we met a few days ago. I order a French martini and André asks for the same.

'I can't believe this time tomorrow night I'll be ready to head home,' I sigh, sipping the delightful cocktail.

'I will drive you to the airport. Then I'll be counting down the days until you can return. You will be returning again, won't you?' He looks searchingly into my eyes.

'Of course I will but I'm just not sure when that will be. I can't expect Sam to look after the cake business forever.'

'What happens next, then?' André takes a sip of his drink.

'I go home, and I will also be counting the days until we meet again. And then we need to have a serious discussion about our future.'

'That's all I need to hear. That you are willing to discuss our future together.' André smiles and his sexy blue eyes crinkle at the corners. He really is heart-stoppingly good looking.

It feels strange to think that when we get home, Jake will be packing up to return to France a day or two later to spend the rest of the summer working at the restaurant.

'At least you'll have Jake here. You can get to know each other properly.'

'I think it will be nice for Jake to have a summer job,' André says. 'It will give him a chance to consider what he wants. He seems pretty sure that he won't be returning to university, though, and judging by his passion for cooking, I think it's a great idea for him to spend time at the restaurant. He could learn a lot.'

'You don't think his decision has been influenced by you offering him a job here, do you?'

'I think his mind was made up long before then.'

'Really?'

André takes a long sip of his drink and exhales.

'He wasn't really inspired by the course he chose, I think he told you that. But there was a little more to it. He couldn't face seeing an ex-girlfriend each day. Someone called Amelia. She broke his heart, apparently.'

My heart sinks down to my shoes, as a feeling of sadness engulfs me. Poor Jake was going through heartache and all I ever banged on about was the need for him to finish his education. I feel so hurt and excluded. I thought Jake told me everything.

'Did he tell you what happened?'

'She dropped him for someone called Ben. A man he thought had become a good friend.'

I recall him talking about someone called Ben, part of his extended friend group at uni.

'He went out with her for five months and thought she was the one. He was going to bring her home to meet you, when he discovered she was cheating. It was a double blow when he realised it was with one of his friends.'

'Oh no, poor Jake.' My heart breaks when I think of him suffering quietly. No wonder he was evasive when I questioned him about his life at uni.

'I think if he would have been more passionate about his studies, he would have stayed. His lack of enthusiasm for his studies, along with having to face Amelia each day, was probably a bit much for him to bear. And don't worry. I was simply a listening ear. I am not about to offer him any advice, I have no right to do that, at least not yet. It's you who has been a mother and a father to Jake all these years. I respect that.'

What kind of a mother am I? I think to myself with a sinking feeling. Has Jake perceived my concern for him as being controlling? Have I been the kind of overbearing mother whose children tell them nothing? He wasn't able to tell me about his heartache yet felt able to tell André, who is a virtual stranger to him. Although maybe that's the whole point.

I glug down the rest of my drink, feeling like the worst parent in the world. Maybe my worrying nature has prevented Jake telling me about things he fears will upset me. I know that we're close, but he shouldn't have to keep things secret in case I make a fuss. I'm supposed to be the parent after all. Someone he can turn to, to shoulder his problems, not fret over them.

'Are you alright?' André looks at me with a little concern.

'Yeah, I'm OK. I just feel so sorry for Jake. He was going through all that and I never knew.'

'Don't think about it. Sometimes men find it easier to talk to other men about such things – and even more often to someone other than their mother! I bet he's met up with his friends and drowned his sorrows back home a few times.'

I think of the nights he had spent with his old pals in Southport as soon as he got home.

'I suppose you're right.'

'I know I am.'

He has a sympathetic yet self-assured smile on his face. 'You can't fix everything for Jake, much as I'm sure you'd like to. He has to figure some things out for himself.'

'You would have made a good father,' I find myself saying.

'We'll never know. But I'm hoping there's still time for me to offer him my guidance in the future. If he wants it, that is.'

He's resting his chin on one hand and staring at me with his gorgeous eyes and my heart does a little flip. We drink the rest of our cocktails and André suggests a brandy as a nightcap.

Sipping the brandy under the stars, I experience alternate feelings of contentment and heartache. It's hard to imagine me peering through the glass doors of my oven at home waiting for a cake to be ready, yet in a couple of days' time that's exactly what I will be doing.

As we stroll on, the effects of the cocktail and the brandy relax me. We pass a bar that has wine barrels outside used as tables and fairy lights around the doorway. A grey-haired man somewhere in his sixties is standing in the arched doorway and beckons us inside for a drink.

'Shall we?' asks André, and I find myself agreeing and stepping inside. It's a small, cosy bar with wooden floors and yellow walls lined with black and white photographs. There's a young man in the corner playing the guitar and singing. He has a beautiful voice but I don't understand the words.

'He's singing about a lost love,' says André, as he places a Napoleon brandy in front of me. The small room is a little stuffy, so after the singer has finished his song and the applause finished, we step outside once more into the fresh air. When we finish our drinks, we walk on. Suddenly, André pulls me down a dark side street.

'I've been desperate to do this all evening.' His lips are on mine and my head feels fuzzy as he kisses me deeply, his tongue probing my mouth. We break apart when a couple of revellers walk past chatting and laughing.

'Hey, monsieur. Prenez une chambre.' They laugh as they walk on. I realise they have just shouted the equivalent of 'get a room', and it makes me smile.

André guides me further down the road until we are facing a row of white taxis near the harbour.

'I have a room. In my house,' he breathes. 'We could be there in five minutes.'

It would be so easy to get in that taxi and go to his home – every fibre of my body is filled with longing. But I'm not that eighteen-year-old girl I was all those years ago. I can't let my emotions run away with me.

It takes all my resolve but I ask André to drop me off at the bakery. I can't spend the night with him. I'm confident this is the right thing to do. This time tomorrow I'll be back home and my heart already feels heavy when I think about it. If we sleep together, much as I want to, it will make everything so much more difficult.

'Of course. Whatever you want,' he says softly. 'I'm sorry if I'm rushing things; you get me so fired up I can't help myself.'

Dropping me off outside the bakery, he kisses me again before jumping back in the taxi.

'I will take you to the airport tomorrow evening, but you must see my home before you leave. I will take you there for lunch, if that's alright. I'll ring you in the morning.'

'I'd like that. Thank you.'

I head upstairs and flop down on the bed, a million thoughts racing through my head. Where is this going? There's still so much attraction between us and, even after so much time, I still know we are meant to be together. But we have a lot of talking to do about our future. There is one thing I am clear about now, though – I need to be with him.

Chapter Thirty-Five

Jake has packed his things and is downstairs chatting to Gen when I remind him that André will be collecting us at one to have lunch at his house outside town.

Faye has already packed, and is shortly off to spend her last day at the beach with Olivier, to top up her tan before we leave.

'Are you sure you don't want to go alone, Mum? I wouldn't mind hanging around the beach today before I go home. I'll be back here again in a few days anyway. I've got all the time in the world to see his home.'

'OK then,' I say, even though a part of me doesn't want to risk being alone again with André, as I'm finding it so hard to resist him. 'If that's what you want.'

I step outside into the sunshine and inhale the scent of my surroundings. As a customer exits the bakery, a yeasty smell of bread and vanilla hits my nostrils. On the street, the scent is a strange mixture of car fumes and salty sea air. As I see André approaching in his car, I nip inside the bakery to grab us a treat for after our lunch.

'What will your staff at the restaurant say about you sneaking off all the time?' I ask as I take a seat in the car.

'I'm the boss. I can do what I like,' he jokes. 'It's the chefs who do all the hard work, and there's enough staff to cope with front of house in my absence. They'll probably all be relieved to have a break from me.' André smiles at me as we turn right at the harbour and head towards the edge of town. 'I really enjoyed myself last night.'

'So did I. I wish I wasn't going home tonight.'

I gaze out of the window as beach roads give way to hills and farmland. In the distance, a cluster of medieval buildings looms into view and André tells me it is a village called Biot, where he grew up.

'It's gorgeous. How lucky were you, growing up in a place like this.'

'It has quite a turbulent history with pirates. Thankfully before I was born, but it still gave us a lot to imagine when we were playing as children.'

Less than ten minutes later, we are pulling into the driveway of a traditional French farmhouse with cream-painted walls and brown shutters at the windows. As we step inside I can see at once that it's beautifully furnished. There's a neat kitchen with cream wooden cupboards and brightly coloured wall tiles. A jug of sunflowers sits on a windowsill overlooking a long, narrow garden. The kitchen leads through to a lounge with stone-coloured sofas and a log burner.

André leads me outside through French doors to a covered patio area with wrought-iron furniture.

'Please, take a seat, I'll grab our lunch from the fridge. I hope pâté and salad is OK for you.'

'Sounds perfect.'

I gaze around the garden and could easily imagine myself staying here. It's bursting with wild flowers – daisies, clover and a cheerful white plant that looks like cow parsley.

André returns from the kitchen with a jug of lemonade and some crusty bread, pâté and cheeses. There's also a bowl of mixed olives.

'This is such a gorgeous house.' I imagine being a child in a house like this, exploring the wild garden and the small meadow beyond.

'I'm lucky my brother and sister didn't force a sale once my parents died. But they're both doing well financially, so they're happy for me to live here. I could buy out their shares, but I may move nearer the coast anyway, if the restaurant continues to do well.'

'Really? I'm not sure I'd ever want to leave a place like this.'

We finish our lunch and André goes over to a drawer in the lounge and takes out a photo album. He shows me a picture of his parents and I gasp as I look at a photo of his father – the resemblance to Jake is remarkable. I look at photos of his family together, and there's one of André when he was a young man.

'That wasn't long before I started working at Marineland,' he says, turning the picture over to look at the date on the back. It shows February 1998 – just a few months before he started his job.

'I'd taken a gap year from studying. Maybe that's why I understand Jake's desire to try new things.'

André flicks on the coffee machine and I retrieve the paper bag I placed on the kitchen table when we first arrived.

'Something to go with the coffee.'

He opens the bag and a huge smile spreads across his face.

'Bee stings. I haven't had one of these in years!'

He reaches into a cupboard and places the buns onto small plates.

'I can hardly wait.' He sinks his teeth into the honey-glazed brioche bun, which is dotted with crystallised violets and filled with crème pâtissière.

'Fantastique. As good as I remember. Maybe better.'

I take a bite of the bun and think that my aunt has lost none of her skill in baking, as it tastes exactly as I remember it from my childhood.

Soon enough it's almost four, and time for us to be heading back. As we head for the door, André stops me and pushes a strand of hair from my eyes. I shiver at his touch. He runs his thumb gently down my cheek.

'I'm going to miss you. It's as though all the years have melted away and we've never been apart.'

He traces the outline of my lips with his fingers before bending to kiss me.

'I'll miss you too,' I say as we pull apart. 'I promise it won't be long before I come and see you again.' But as I utter the words, I can't help wondering when it's really going to be possible.

We speak little as we drive down towards the harbour. André drops me at the bakery and heads to the restaurant for a few hours, telling me he will collect Jake, Faye and me for the airport at seven. Mum and Dad are staying on for another week. I dearly wish I could do the same.

Chapter Thirty-Six

When we say goodbye at the airport it's all I can do to stop the tears from streaming down my face as I hug André tightly, not wanting to let him go. I said goodbye to everyone else at the bakery, and even Lilian came over to give me a hug.

'You must speak a little French when you get home,' she advised. 'Or all your hard work will have been for nothing.' She kissed me lightly on both cheeks, with a promise to take my aunt out for lunch dates to keep her spirits up. I'm not sure there's much opportunity to speak French in a northern seaside town, although I suppose I could try it out at Le Boulevard.

The flight is uneventful and we arrive at John Lennon Airport just after midnight. I have mixed feelings as I head to my home in Southport, not even sure that it feels like my home any more.

'See you soon for a drink at the pier.' Faye hugs me tightly when we drop her off. I'm going to miss seeing her every day.

'I hope Sam's left some cake in the tin. I'm starving,' says Jake as we walk through the front door. There's milk and bread, eggs and bacon in the fridge, with a little note.

Thought you might have missed having an English breakfast.

Welcome back!

Sam. xx

There are also two generous slices of a Victoria sponge in the cake tin, and Jake punches the air in delight.

After some tea and toast, I take a quick shower and head off to bed. I've messaged André and told him we've arrived home safely and he tells me he will ring me in the morning. I find I can't settle. Everything has changed. To my surprise I find myself gently weeping into my pillow before I finally drift off to sleep.

I'm awoken the next morning just after nine thirty by my phone ringing on the bedside table. It's André.

'Are you still in bed?' he asks, picking up on the sleepy tone in my voice.

'Yes,' I say, stretching my free arm above my head. 'It took me a while to get to sleep last night.'

'Me too. I couldn't stop thinking about you. How's Jake?'

'Currently making an English breakfast, I think.' The smell of bacon and fresh coffee suddenly hits my nostrils and I'm fully awake.

We chat for a while longer, skirting around discussions about the future, before I grab a robe and follow the tempting smell downstairs to the kitchen. Sam is sitting on a stool sipping a coffee and holds her arms out to greet me.

'Sam. Hi!' I lean in and cuddle her back. 'Sorry about the breath. I haven't brushed my teeth yet. I've not long woken up.'

'Full English or a bacon sandwich, Mum?' asks Jake, brandishing a spatula.

'A bacon sandwich will be fine thanks. I noticed some lovely thick granary bread. Thanks for that, Sam, you're an angel.'

'You're welcome. So how was France?'

'Pretty eventful as it happens. I'm not sure how much Jake has told you.' I pour myself a coffee.

'Well, I've only been here for half an hour but he's pretty much filled me in. Are you OK?'

'I'm fine. Just a bit tired.' Jake places a bacon sandwich in front of me before going upstairs.

'I'm going to grab a shower,' he says. 'I'll leave you two to talk.'

I tell Sam all about meeting up with André after his sister walked into the bakery.

'My goodness, what where the chances of that happening?'

'I know, it was uncanny. Maybe it was meant to be.'

'Maybe it was.'

'I can't thank you enough for keeping things ticking over here. I would never have been able to go to France otherwise. Jake's going back over soon for the summer holidays. I'm not sure when I can go back again, what with the business.'

'You could always give it up, I suppose. I mean, if you ever decided to settle in France you could always work at your aunt's bakery.'

'Are you trying to get rid of me?' I laugh.

'No of course not, but the thing is –' she pauses for a second before continuing – 'I'm thinking of starting up my own business. Spending the past few weeks here alone, running things, has made me realise I can do it.'

'Really? Well, that's brilliant,' I say. I'm overjoyed for Sam, though I can't help wondering where on earth I am going to get somebody as good to replace her.

'I'm hoping to open a tea and cake shop on the pier, so we won't be direct rivals! There's an empty unit next door to one of the gift shops. Mum and Dad have offered to help me out with the rent on the place. I'm so excited about it all, but I don't want to let you down. Now that you're back home, it's something I really want to press on with.'

'Of course, you must, as soon as possible. I knew it would happen one day.' I cross the room and wrap her in a hug. 'Do you know, I once dreamt of running a tea shop on the pier myself. You're fulfilling my dream for me. Promise me I can be your first customer.'

'It's a deal. Thanks, Liv.'

Chapter Thirty-Seven

It's a blustery afternoon, even though it's supposedly high summer, and I turn the collar up on my jacket as I walk along the pier to meet my friends. The blue train chugs past and the bell dings as children wave out of the window, their little faces pressed up against the glass. It's a sight that would normally make me grin from ear to ear, but everything just seems a little flat.

My friends are already there when I arrive and Jo jumps up to hug me, quickly followed by Faye, who had her nose in a menu.

'My goodness, look at you,' says Jo as I shrug my jacket off. 'You've got a fabulous tan. I thought you were slaving away in your aunt's bakery all day?'

'I was. Well, in the mornings mainly. I had the afternoons to wander the markets or stroll down to the sea. It's so gorgeous there.'

'And you –' she nods at Faye's glorious tan – 'can move over there.' She points to an adjacent table. 'You're making me look ill.'

We order some drinks and paninis and I fill Jo in on everything that has happened in France. Faye tells me that Olivier has invited her back over to Antibes, and that she'll be going to visit him towards the end of the school holidays. 'After I've sorted my lesson plans for the new term. One final little jolly.' She laughs.

'So, how are things going with Guy?' I turn to Jo, who has a big smile on her face.

'Really well. He's lovely. We're actually going on our first weekend away together next week.'

'Ooh, things must be getting serious. Anywhere nice?'

'London. I haven't been since I went on a school trip when I was fifteen. We've got tickets for *Wicked*.'

'Well, have a great time. Have you got any dog stories for me?'

I could really do with one of Jo's funny stories right now, as I try to navigate myself through a range of emotions. Jo is on the cusp of an exciting new relationship and Faye seems to be having the time of her life, yet I don't know where on earth my renewed acquaintance with André will lead.

'Um, I think I've told you most of them. Did I tell you about Harold eating my lipstick?'

'Oh no, why is it always Harold?'

'You tell me. Anyway. I tripped over something in the road as we were walking and my handbag tumbled to the ground. My bright-red lipstick fell out, along with a cereal snack bar. Before I could do anything, Harold had gobbled up the snack bar, quickly followed by the lipstick, which ended up smeared all over his mouth. Anyway, you know how he sometimes takes a fancy to certain people? Well, a minute or two later, he leaps at this bloke and starts licking him all over. It looked like a murder scene by the time I could stop him. The poor bloke was traumatised, thinking he'd been savaged, but Harold wouldn't hurt a fly.'

'The poor man!' I'm laughing loudly as I picture the look on his face.

'Never mind the poor man. That was my best Chanel lipstick.'
The three of us laugh hard.

'Oh, girls, it's so lovely to be back together. Just what I needed, in fact.' I tell them all about Sam setting up her very own café here on the pier.

'Maybe it's a good time for you to think about a change too, then,' says Faye.

'How do you mean?'

'Well, you could always wind up the cake business and move over to France for a bit. Maybe even sell it to Sam? Or at least refer your loyal customers to her. Maybe you could rent your house out over the summer, if Jake's away.'

'Who's going to want to rent a house for just a couple of months?'

'It's funny you should say that. One of the teachers at school has just split from his wife. He's been staying at a dodgy bed and breakfast on the seafront until he can find something better.'

I think long and hard about what Faye has just said. Maybe things do happen for a reason. And every so often, at the right time.

'I'll give it some thought. Cheers, everyone,' I say as we raise our lattes to each other.

Chapter Thirty-Eight

Two weeks later I'm heading over to France for a long weekend. I've spoken to André and Jake every day and Jake seems to be loving his time in the restaurant. André tells me he is showing a real talent in the kitchen and that he was born to cook. I've decided to relax and quit worrying about where Jake's future lies, as I've learned that things in life never quite go according to plan. He should do what makes him happy.

Stepping into the arrival area at Nice airport, I spot André ahead and my heart skips a beat. It still feels so special every time I see him. That longish grey-streaked hair and those hypnotic blue eyes still have the same effect on me as they did when I was a teenager. He crushes me in an embrace and a few moments later we exit the glass doors of the airport into bright sunshine.

'I won't be needing this then,' I say, slipping off my hoodie that I wore for the journey.

We travel along the glorious coast road and before long we pull up outside my aunt's bakery, where Jake is waiting outside. My aunt welcomes us warmly, and we head upstairs for coffee on the balcony.

'I've reserved a table for dinner tonight at a nice restaurant,' André tells me. 'Will you be joining us, Jake?'

'I think maybe you two should spend your first evening together. I'm meeting Olivier later for a drink anyway. He said something about a party.'

'I've heard all about Olivier's partying ways. I hope you're not late for work tomorrow.' André winks.

André tells me he will collect me for dinner this evening, and I nip inside the shop to say hello to Valerie, before going upstairs to hang my things in the wardrobe. It hasn't really been discussed where I will be staying, but I decide I'll pack an overnight bag.

I spend the rest of the afternoon having a wander around the market and the nearby shops, and before long it's time to head back and prepare for my evening out.

I take a long, leisurely shower and select a black cotton dress. André hinted that it would be a smart restaurant, so I take time applying my make-up to look my very best. A silver necklace sets off the plain black dress perfectly and I feel good when I look at myself in the mirror.

'Wow,' says Jake when I walk out of the bedroom. 'You look really lovely, Mum, Dad's a lucky man.'

A warm feeling floods through my body when I realise what Jake has just said. He called André 'Dad'.

'Thank you.' I give a little twirl as Gen walks into the lounge.

'Ooh, you look stunning,' she says, coming over and giving me a kiss on the cheek. .

'Thanks, Gen. I wasn't sure about black at first, but it shows my tan off nicely.' I stretch my arms out, admiring my smooth skin which has a healthy golden glow.

André collects me at seven thirty and I throw the overnight bag onto the back seat. André notices and smiles suggestively, but doesn't comment.

'You look incredible,' he says, kissing me lightly on the lips.

'Thanks. So do you.' He's wearing jeans and a white shirt with a navy linen jacket.

He turns to smile at me and I feel a rush of attraction.

After five minutes' drive, we pull up outside a restaurant and are shown to an outside seating area with lights threaded through the trees. It overlooks the sea and I can't help thinking that it seems a little familiar.

We dine on lobster thermidor and to my surprise André orders a bottle of champagne.

'This is gorgeous. What's the occasion?' I ask.

'You being here with me is enough of a reason to celebrate. Although maybe only one glass for me, as I'm driving.'

'How's Jake getting along at the restaurant?' I ask.

'He's doing well. He's very popular, especially with the young women. But he doesn't let anything distract him from his work.'

I think of the comments Françoise made about André when he worked at Marineland and never got romantically involved with the other staff.

'He's been helping the pastry chef with desserts this week. He shows a real flair for baking.'

André's right. Jake's lemon drizzle cake is the nicest I have tasted. I tell André all about Sam back home, and how she is setting up a little tea shop on the pier.

'I'm not quite sure how I'm going to replace her, and business seems to be booming lately. She hasn't stopped since I've been away. I feel a little guilty being here again actually, although we're up to date with things, and it is the weekend I suppose.'

'It is. And everyone should relax at the weekend.'

He raises his glass. 'To us, and whatever the future may bring.'

'To us.'

As we sip our drinks, dusk slowly begins to draw in. I don't choose a dessert, yet before long a smiling waitress places something in front of me. It's a heart-shaped chocolate mousse decorated with fresh raspberries and drizzled in white chocolate. She places a cheeseboard in the middle of the table for André.

'How gorgeous! It almost looks too pretty to eat.'

'You'd better eat it. I had that especially made for you.'

'Really?' I'm flattered that he would go to so much trouble.

I dig my spoon into the mousse and taste the rich, feather-soft chocolate. It's absolutely divine. When we finish our desserts, André leads me to the edge of the decking area and we glance out across the water, glistening with light from some distant boats. Taking in my surroundings, the water features nestled between plants and the place where we are stood now, I suddenly realise that I *have* been here before. It's La Terrace restaurant, where I came with André when I was a young woman, although these days it's called Le Jardin – The Garden.

'We've been here before, haven't we?'

'Yes.' He breathes deeply as he pulls me towards him and stares into my eyes. 'It's where you gave me this.'

He pulls the silver necklace with half of the heart from his pocket.

'You kept it for all these years?' I feel a rush of emotion.

'Of course. Are you telling me you never kept yours?'

'I think it may be nestled somewhere at the bottom of a jewellery box, tucked away somewhere at home. But truthfully, I couldn't look at it for years. It hurt too much.'

André gathers me in his arms. 'I'm so sorry. I never meant to hurt you like that. I promise I'll never hurt you again.'

We kiss under the stars and I feel complete. When we arrive back at André's house, I take my small case from the back seat of the car and André smiles.

'Maybe you should have brought a bigger case.' He puts his arms around my waist and pulls me to him. 'That is, if you want to stay here with me.'

'Of course I do. There's nowhere I'd rather be.' I glance around the little village and as we step through the front door I have sense of coming home.

I put my bag down and André scoops me up into his arms and we head straight for the bedroom. 'What time do you like your breakfast?' he asks as he gently pins me to the bed and covers me in kisses.

'Let's forget breakfast.' I pull him towards me and kiss him deeply. 'I plan on a long lie-in. Lunch will be just fine…'

Epilogue

Almost two years later

The restaurant is packed and we're struggling to keep up on a glorious summer afternoon.

'I told you we need another couple of waiters out there,' I say to André as I take some dishes through to the kitchen, before taking a long glug of water.

Langousta has steadily become one of the most popular fish restaurants in Antibes, and is constantly booked up. It has gained something of a reputation for mouth-watering desserts, as Jake produces exciting new dishes that he has devised himself. At the end of that first summer, André thought he had such a talent as a pastry chef that he offered him a full-time job, and Jake was only too eager to accept. There was no way Jake was ever going to return to university now that he had found his father and begun working in his restaurant. But as he once told me, it's his life and he seems to be managing it just fine.

As for me? Well, I divide my time between working at Aunt Gen's bakery and helping out at the restaurant. Oh, did I not mention that I live here too?

The stars seem to have aligned for us, as André, Jake and I all live in the gorgeous French village house with the cow parsley and the wild flowers in the garden. It's a good life. No, wait, it's a GREAT life. The church bells wake us on a Sunday morning and we have breakfast together before going for a walk in the countryside. The restaurant only opens at one on Sundays so we spend some precious time together. Sometimes Jake joins us for a walk, other times he goes for a bike ride with Michelle, our pretty nineteen-year-old neighbour who he has become rather friendly with.

Mum and Dad seem to have restricted their travels to England for the time being. At least in the campervan, that is. They're flying over in a couple of months and I'm looking forward to seeing them. I'm planning on heading over to Southport myself in a couple of weeks, so will pop in on them then. I want to have a cake and a pot of tea at Sam's teashop on the pier. And show André off, of course!

Jo moved into Guy's place a few months ago and they've got a dog. You'll never believe it, but it's Harold the Great Dane! Harold's owner was offered a dream job in London, and decided the big city would be too much for his ageing companion – and Jo had always had a soft spot for the 'daft mutt'. Guy pretends to find him exasperating, but it's quite clear he adores him. He brought them together after all.

Olivier is still charming the females of the Côte d'Azur, and is currently dating a model from Latvia. He and Faye had a few more meet-ups in France, but things eventually fizzled out. She's become assistant head of her primary school in Southport and is dating a musician from Liverpool, who appeared at the local pub in a rock band. Things seemed to really click into place for her when she got home from France. She tells me she needed that time to reset and stop putting pressure on herself to find a man, or go out drinking every night, and that once she let it go, good things just started happening naturally.

Gen has completely bounced back from the surgery and is now happily making use of her new and improved knee, as well as the free time I give her by working at the bakery, by gadding about town with Lilian Beaumont. The two are irrepressible!

So, as you can see, things can change a lot in no time at all. We never know what's around the corner. But whatever it is, you should grab life with both hands. Who knows what may happen in the future, but for now, 'Vive La France!'

Recipes

Here are a couple of recipes for cakes that have appeared in the book. The cupcakes and buns are from Patisserie Genevieve and the blueberry scones are Nic's recipe (the ones the café owner on the pier raved about!) I hope you enjoy making them!

Madame Beaumont's favourite St Clements cupcakes (makes 12)

Ingredients for the cakes

    175 g caster sugar

    175 g unsalted butter, lightly softened

    Finely grated zest of 1 lemon and 1 orange

    3 large free-range eggs

    175 g of self-raising flour, sifted

Method for the cakes

    Pre heat oven to 180°C/gas mark 4. Set aside 12 paper cake cases. Using a wooden spoon, cream together the sugar and butter.

    Beat the eggs and add the mixture slowly to the sugar and butter. Fold in the flour and grated fruit zest then mix together with a balloon whisk or an electric hand mixer, until the mixture is smooth. Add a little milk if necessary.

Pour into the cake cases and bake for around 12 minutes, or until the cakes are golden brown. Allow to completely cool before icing.

Ingredients for the icing
    85 g of softened butter
    2 heaped tsp finely grated orange zest
    1 tsp grated lemon zest
    4 medium cups of icing sugar
    A pinch of salt
    1 tbsp fresh orange juice
    2 tsp lemon juice

Method for the icing
Mix the butter, salt, icing sugar, lemon and orange zest together in a bowl. Add the fruit juice a little at a time until you have a thick consistency for piping onto the cakes. Using a piping bag, swirl the icing mixture on top of the cakes. (Or just spread thickly!) Decorate with edible flowers or decorations if desired.

Raspberry buns (makes 8–10)

These are quick and easy to make and are always a firm family favourite. If you have time, you could make your own raspberry jam. If not, purchase a good quality jam.

Ingredients

    200 g self-raising flour

    A pinch of salt

    100 g of salted butter

    1 large egg, beaten

    1 tbsp milk

    Good quality raspberry jam

Method

Pre heat oven to 200°C/gas mark 6.

Mix together the flour and salt, then cut in the butter and mix between fingertips until mixture resembles breadcrumbs. Add the sugar, then mix in the egg and milk until a dough forms. Divide into eight portions (or ten for smaller buns).

Shape the dough into buns and make a well with your thumb in the centre of the bun. Spoon some raspberry jam into each hole.

Place the buns onto a baking tray lined with baking parchment.

Bake for 12–15 mins or until risen and golden. Dust with icing sugar if desired. Allow to completely cool before eating, as the jam will be very hot!

Nic's blueberry scones (makes around eight)

There are many scone recipes around, but my favourite ones contain an egg, which makes them slightly softer.

Ingredients

　　260 g plain flour plus another tbsp

　　65 g of caster sugar

　　1 tbsp baking powder

　　A pinch of salt

　　85 g of chilled butter

　　150 g blueberries

　　2 large eggs

　　120 ml milk

　　1 tsp vanilla extract

Method

Pre heat oven to 200°C/gas mark 6.

In a bowl, mix together the dry ingredients (except the extra tablespoon of flour), then rub in the butter until the mixture resembles breadcrumbs.

Toss the blueberries in the tablespoon of plain flour to prevent sinking then set aside.

In a separate bowl, whisk one of the eggs, milk and vanilla extract together.

Add the liquid to the dry mixture, then gently add the blueberries, taking care not to crush them. Work gently into a dough.

Divide into eight scones. Beat the other egg and brush it over the tops of the scones, before placing on a parchment-lined baking tray.

Bake for 18–20 minutes or until the scones look risen and golden.

These are delicious served with clotted cream and a good dollop of blueberry jam!

A Letter from Sue

I want to say a huge thank you for choosing to read *A Very French Affair*. If you enjoyed the story, and want to keep up-to-date with all my latest releases, just sign up at the following link. Your email address will never be shared and you can unsubscribe at any time.

www.bookouture.com/sue-roberts

I hope you loved *A Very French Affair* and if you did I would be very grateful if you could write a review. It's been such a joy revisiting the South of France through this book and maybe I have even inspired you to visit the area! Who wouldn't love the culture, food and the setting of the Côte d'Azur?

I'd love to hear what you think, and it makes such a difference helping new readers to discover one of my books for the first time.

I love hearing from my readers – you can get in touch on my Facebook page or through Twitter.

Thanks,
Sue

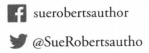

suerobertsauthor

@SueRobertsautho

Acknowledgments

I would like to thank everyone at Bookouture for all their hard work involved in publishing this book. Huge thanks to my editor Emily Gowers for her invaluable input and guidance, ensuring this book is the best it can be. A mention to Christina Demosthenous for her continued support and encouragement.

A huge thank you to all my family and friends who continue to encourage and motivate me. It feels good when people tell me they are looking forward to reading my next book! And finally, thanks to all you wonderful readers and reviewers, who shout about our books and share reviews. It really is much appreciated.

Made in the USA
Monee, IL
16 January 2022